I0603140

INTO
TEMPTATION

INTO TEMPTATION

DELIVER US FROM EVIL
BOOK II

International Bestselling Author
MONICA JAMES

Copyrighted Material

INTO TEMPTATION

This book is a work of fiction. Names, characters, places and incidents are the product of the author's imagination, or are used fictitiously. Any resemblance to actual events, locales, or persons living or dead, is coincidental. Any trademarks, service marks, product names or named features are assumed to be the property of their respective owners and are used only for reference.

Copyright © 2021 by Monica James

All rights reserved. No part of this work may be reproduced, scanned or distributed in any printed or electronic form without the express, written consent of the author.

Cover Design: Perfect Pear Creative Covers
Photographer: Michelle Lancaster
Cover Model: Lochie Carey
Editing: Editing 4 Indies
Formatting: E.M. Tippetts Book Designs

Follow me on:
authormonicajames.com

OTHER BOOKS BY
MONICA JAMES

THE I SURRENDER SERIES

I Surrender

Surrender to Me

Surrendered

White

SOMETHING LIKE NORMAL SERIES

Something like Normal

Something like Redemption

Something like Love

A HARD LOVE ROMANCE

Dirty Dix

Wicked Dix

The Hunt

MEMORIES FROM YESTERDAY DUET

Forgetting You, Forgetting Me

Forgetting You, Remembering Me

SINS OF THE HEART DUET

Absinthe of the Heart

Defiance of the Heart

ALL THE PRETTY THINGS TRILOGY

Bad Saint

Fallen Saint

Forever My Saint

The Devil's Crown-Part One (Spin-Off)

The Devil's Crown-Part Two (Spin-Off)

THE MONSTERS WITHIN DUET

Bullseye

Blowback

DELIVER US FROM EVIL TRILOGY

Thy Kingdom Come

Into Temptation

STANDALONE

Mr. Write

Chase the Butterflies

Beyond the Roses

AUTHOR'S NOTE

CONTENT WARNING: *INTO TEMPTATION* is a continuing story, therefore, not all questions will be answered in Book Two. If you don't like cliff-hangers, best you turn back now.

Although I've consulted with many locals, please be mindful, this is a work of fiction. Places, events, and incidents are either the product of my imagination or used in a fictitious manner.

INTO TEMPTATION is a DARK ROMANCE. It contains mature themes that might make some readers uncomfortable.

Godspeed…

ONE

PUNKY

Freedom.

Seven letters which, on their own, aren't anything special. But when strung together, can change a man's life forever.

"We couldn't let ya leave without a proper goodbye."

Punch to the jaw.

Kick to the ribs.

Nothing hurts anymore. My mind, as well as my body, is numb to the pain.

As the officers continue kicking the shite out of me, I lie on the cold floor of my prison cell, using their violence as fuel. Each strike simply feeds the demons inside me. They've had time to mature and grow into the ruthless, callous beast I am today.

Once they're done, they spit on my broken body, laughing happily. The door to my cell slams shut, and I'm swathed in darkness—my only friend.

My muscles burn as I drag myself along the floor to lean my back against the wall. Clutching my side, I measure my breaths because I'll be free in a few hours. However, I'll be escaping one prison, only to be sent to another with invisible bars.

"Forgive me, Cara, I needed a fall guy, and that guy is Punky…our son."

Slamming my fist against the floor, I squeeze my eyes shut, unbelieving of the words I read in Sean's journal. I wish they were a lie, but they're not. The only person I ever trusted in this world has betrayed me.

Sean fooled me in every way possible. I've spent the past ten years believing his death, as well as Connor's, was my fault. I thought the Kelly name was dead and buried because of my reckless actions. I believed I ruined my family.

But I was merely a plaything, a chess piece for Sean to win his devious game.

He used everyone to get what he wanted, not caring who he had to deceive and kill. I cannot believe I am his son. And I cannot believe he killed my ma.

The door to my prison cell opens, and when Officer Grenham sees the state of me, he sighs. "Those fucking bastards. Come now, let's get ya cleaned up. Ye've a big day ahead."

Officer Grenham was the officer who changed my life forever six months ago. He was the man who told me Hannah was waiting for me, waiting to tell me the truth. If it wasn't for him, I would never have agreed to see Hannah, and I would never have been free.

Hannah shared with me that Darcy Duffy was now some big-shot lawyer who was certain she could overturn my conviction. She was right.

I don't know how she did it, but thanks to that fucker Chief Constable Moore being a corrupt bastard, Darcy was able to convince the courts to set me free. I didn't want to know the details or see her because if this proved to be another ploy, I feared for my already fragile state of mind.

But Darcy did it.

Officer Grenham knows better than to help me. I come to a stand on my own, pushing aside my injuries because the ones inflicted on my conscience are a lot worse. He cuffs me one last time before leading me to the bathroom.

The scalding water helps wash away some of the pain, and once clean, I dry off and dress in the clothes Hannah provided for me—black jeans and a white button-up shirt. I tie my laces on my black boots, marveling at the simple task because it's been ten years since I last wore shoes with laces on them.

Looking at my reflection in the mirror, I run a hand over my face—how time has aged me.

I'm no longer the Punky I once was. That person was

merely a boy. Now, I'm a man, intent on one thing and one thing only—and that is revenge.

"D'ya want to shave?" Officer Grenham asks, watching me as I gawk at the face I barely recognize anymore.

"Naw," I reply, my voice hoarse.

My hair is similar in length to when I was first thrown into prison. But my beard is now thicker, longer. My nose and lip piercings are long gone, but looking at the cross tattoo on my wrist and my ma's name across my knuckles, that's something that has remained the same, as has the meaning behind them.

"All right then. Whenever yer ready, I'll take ya to see yer lawyer. She has some paperwork ye need to sign, and then… yer free to go."

Taking one last look at my image, I turn to Officer Grenham and reply, "I may live outside these walls, but I'll never be free."

He nods, understanding that a place such as Riverbend House never lets you go. Not only has this place robbed me of my freedom; it's robbed me of my humanity. The small shred I clung on to was destroyed the moment I set foot into this hellhole.

We don't speak further, and Officer Grenham gestures we're to go. He doesn't cuff me. I know this is against the rules, but Officer Grenham wants me to take this first step as a free man.

I need to relearn how to walk without being shackled because being bound has been my norm for ten years. Freedom is now the foreign world I need to once again learn.

We walk slowly as I take it all in. Officer Grenham opens a door, and a parful woman dressed in an expensive-looking trouser suit stands when we enter. Darcy Duffy has grown. As we all have, I suppose. I'm still finding it difficult to wrap my head around it. I'm expecting to see the people of my past as I remember them, as I left them ten years ago.

But we're not those people anymore.

"Punky. Oh my God, yer face," she says, staring at me, her shock clear.

"Bout ye?" I reply, not sure what to say because a simple thank you seems so inadequate.

My curt response clears her emotion, making way for why she's here.

"Please, sit." She gestures to the plastic chair at the table. I do as she says.

Her hands tremble as she rummages through her brown leather briefcase. Is she nervous? Or afraid?

When she finds what she's looking for, she slides a piece of paper across the table. "I just need ye to sign this document. It's the terms of yer release. We can discuss anything if ye have any questions once y've read it."

She offers me a pen, and it rests heavy in my hand as I accept it.

Once upon a time, this would have been an extension of me as I used to love to draw, but now, I can't even remember what that feels like. I can't imagine sitting in front of a blank canvas and drawing what's inside my mind because all that's in there is blackness.

"I don't need to read it," I state, signing along the dotted line.

"Oh," she says, surprised as I slide the document back to her.

I know I make Darcy uncomfortable. I don't know what she's expecting. A happy reunion, maybe? But this is my happy face.

She clears her throat before signing under my signature. "All right. We're done then. I'll file this with the appropriate parties, but now, yer a free man."

If Darcy is expecting tears or some sort of emotion, she'll be waiting a long while.

Nodding, I come to a stand, watching the way Darcy's chest shudders with the deep breath she takes. Before this happened, she was interested in me, and from the scarlet of her cheeks, I think those feelings still linger.

"Thank you, Darcy," I say, hoping she understands how thankful I am.

"No bother. I'm sorry it took so long." She wrings her hands in front of her.

"Y've nothin' to be sorry for. I owe you my freedom."

She smiles, but it's not in vain. Rather, she seems genuinely happy she could help. I don't understand why. I wasn't awful nice to her.

"Some people are waitin' for ya," Officer Grenham says, breaking the sudden silence.

Darcy discreetly wipes away a tear from the corner of her eye as she turns her back, busying herself with her briefcase. "I'll be out in a moment. You head on."

I don't know why she's crying. I don't know much anymore.

Not sure what to say, I nod and follow Officer Grenham out the door. We walk the long hallway, which suddenly feels like the longest walk of my life. The steel gate buzzes open, and Officer Grenham glares at the man who opened it, knowing he was one of the arseholes who partook in my parting gift.

Walking past him, I take great satisfaction in seeing him flinch. But his time is coming, and there won't be any witnesses when it does. Instead, I blow him a kiss.

Officer Grenham opens the door at the end of the hallway and stands by it with a smile. He is the only officer who actually gives a fuck. Hannah steps into view, tears streaming down her cheeks. But the person standing behind her has my heart clenching with the memories I hold.

"Punky!" Hannah rushes forward, not bothering with personal space as she hugs me tightly.

Instantly, her unique fragrance eases my nerves, and I hug her back loosely. I need to relearn how to walk before I run.

"I'm so happy right now," she cries against my chest.

"Bout ye, wee dote?"

"I'm grand. Everythin' is grand because yer here."

I kiss the top of her head, still shook that this is my wee sister, the wee sister who saved me. Even though she is actually my cousin, I'll always see her as my little sister. That'll never change.

She lets me go when she's ready while I wipe her tears away with my thumbs.

Looking at the person behind her, I smile—the first genuine smile in a very long time. "How's things, Cian?"

He has always been a handsome devil, but time has been quare and kind to him. He is built like a brick shithouse and matured into the big man I always knew he was going to be.

He nods, holding back his tears. He's always been a big softie—some things don't change.

I offer my hand, but he doesn't take it. Instead, like Hannah, he pulls me in for a tight hug. "Ye too good to give yer best friend a hug?" he teases as he tightens his hold.

It's suddenly too much, but I fight the impulse to push him away. This is Cian—my best friend, the lad who stood by me through thick and thin. Ten years may have passed, but that hasn't changed the strength of our friendship.

So, I embrace him as best I can.

He slaps me on the back before letting me go. "Ye look like shite."

I shrug in response.

Hannah greets Darcy as she joins the reunion. "Should we head?"

"Aye."

There is one last thing I have to do.

"Thank you." I address Officer Grenham. "Ye were the only officer who gave a shite. Yer a good man."

He nods and extends his hand, which I shake. "And so are you, Puck. Good luck out there."

With nothing further to say, I turn and embrace this new life…as a free man.

The moment I step outside, I shield my eyes from the daylight—it's something I haven't seen in a long while. Hannah is chatting happily to Darcy, but stops when she notices me lagging behind. Cian instantly wraps his arm around my shoulders, offering me his strength.

"Ye feelin' all right?"

"Aye, I just need a minute."

Cian doesn't let me go, and anyone else's touch would be unwelcome. But not Cian's. He is familiar. He reminds me of happier times. A time when I fell in love with a parful doll…

I've tried to keep her out of my thoughts, but it's hard to do that when she became a part of me. Even though I know the truth, I can't expect her to be here, welcoming her "brother" with open arms, which is why I don't allow my disappointment to show.

I asked Hannah not to tell Babydoll the truth. I wanted to be the one who did that. I owe her that. But ten years is a long time. I don't even know if she's in Northern Ireland anymore.

What reason would there be for her to stay?

Hannah mentioned she helped early on with trying to set me free, but I hurt her. I don't blame her for moving on, which I'm sure she has. These past six months, I haven't spoken to Hannah about Babydoll, and the thing which has surprised me most is that Hannah hasn't spoken about her either.

Just like always, Babydoll leaves me with more questions than answers.

When I'm ready, I take a deep breath and recommence walking. The lights on a flash red Mercedes flicker when Darcy deactivates her alarm. She tosses her briefcase into the car.

"I've a meeting to finalize everything. Can I call on ye later?"

I don't realize she's talking to me until no one replies, hinting the question was for me. "Ach, sure. If ya want."

"He's stayin' with you?" she asks Cian, who nods.

But I won't be having that. "No, take me home."

"Punky, the castle is boggin'. There's no electricity or water," Darcy says, trying to make me see reason. But I don't care.

"I'm not worried about that. I just want to go home."

Hannah works her bottom lip, but Cian understands. "All right. If that's what ya want."

"I'll come by after tea," Darcy says, thankfully respecting my wishes. I appreciate everything she's done for me, but that doesn't mean she has a say in how I live my life.

Nodding, I follow Cian as he walks to a gray Ford Fiesta.

I pause, not expecting my best friend to be driving such a… conservative car. However, I don't say anything and get into the back. Hannah offers the front, but I decline.

Darcy beeps her horn as she zips past us before Cian starts our journey home. Hannah and Cian make small talk, leaving me to take everything in.

I stare out the window, refamiliarizing myself with the sights and sounds which shaped my life. But now, they're foreign, and those memories are just out of reach. I see Northern Ireland with new eyes. So much has changed, while in the same breath, some things are frozen in time.

There is so much green. My eyes can't adjust to the color. I once took this for granted, but I won't ever again. I see a paddock filled with cows. I'd forgotten how big they were. I've forgotten a lot of things.

It's suddenly too much, too fast.

Closing my eyes, I lean my head against the headrest and stay this way until Cian's tires crunch over gravel. This sound transports me back in time.

I'm home.

Slowly opening my eyes, I adjust to the lighting, and when I see the castle, I wonder if I'm stuck in a nightmare. The once majestic building is now in shambles.

The windows are smashed in, and by the graffiti tags, it's safe to assume they were broken by the hallions who thought it was okay to vandalize a place that once was the envy of many.

The door is kicked in, and I notice the side wall is crumbling.

No matter how much I hated Connor, I never wanted to see his home end up this way. This was the last place his essence remained, and now, nothing is left. It's just an empty shell housing broken memories.

Unsnapping my seat belt, I open the door and step outside. The fresh air fills my lungs, and I inhale deeply, the smells of the past warming me. It's replaced with bitterness a second later.

"Punky, I don't want ya stayin' here," Hannah says, her eyes nervously searching the grounds.

I know why she's worried.

She told me she saw Sean here, lurking in the shadows like the monster that he is. But I'm not afraid of him. I want him to know I'm back and plan on claiming what is mine.

Cupping her cheek, I gently assure her, "I'll be all right, wee one. Go now. I'm sure y've got better things to do than be here."

"I want to be here," she presses, leaning into my hand. "I never want to leave yer side."

Cian stands off to the side, but it appears he shares the same sentiments as Hannah.

"I'm not goin' anywhere. Ye made sure of that when ya fought for me when I didn't even fight for myself."

She sniffs back her tears.

"But I need some time to adjust. This is all…a lot."

"Of course," she replies with a nod. "Promise me ya won't leave me again?"

Her plea breaks my heart because I crushed her when I left. I never realized how my actions would impact the twins. They were small, and I thought with time, they'd forget me. But I never forgot my ma, and I was a similar age to the twins when she was snatched from my life.

"I promise," I assure her, bringing her in for a hug.

She clings on tight, and it's hard not to reminisce about when she was a wain, holding me with all her might. "I'll save him. I won't fail ye again," I whisper into her ear.

She sobs into my shoulder, her tiny body shuddering with her pain.

Ethan not being here means, unlike Hannah, he's not interested in reminiscing on the past. He's happy to leave me dead and buried. He sees what I did as a betrayal, as I left them to rot. But I thought of them every single day. I thought I was doing the right thing.

But I was fooled by the man who is now fooling him, and I'll be damned if I allow that to happen to Ethan.

"I'll come by later with some food and clothes for ya. And I'll try to get the power and water connected."

There's no point in arguing with her, so I nod as I kiss her forehead. "Thanks."

Cian hands me a mobile phone. It's awful fancy compared to the one I once had. "My number is programmed in there. If ya need anythin', ya call me. Also, I'll call on ye later and lend ya my truck. I have another car, so it's just collectin' dust."

"Thank you," I say, accepting the phone and the offer to use his truck until I can buy my own. "I'll pay ya back once I get my finances sorted."

He clucks his tongue. "Don't be worryin' about that."

We have so much to catch up on, like where Rory is. And what they've both been up to these past ten years. I don't ask about Babydoll because I figure if Cian wanted me to know, he'd tell me.

"All right. Let's give Punky some time, wee cutty." Cian gestures with his hand that they're to go.

I realize the pressure I put him under when I asked him to look out for the twins for me. But looking at the strong, brave woman Hannah has grown into, I know he's done a brilliant job. I owe him everything.

Hannah's eyes are filled with tears as she gets into the car. Cian waits for her to close the door before he digs into his pocket and produces something I almost forgot existed.

"I kept it safe for ya," he says, offering me my ma's brooch. "I always knew y'd be back."

The sunlight seems to illuminate something which already shines so brightly in my eyes. I accept it, and the weight feels familiar in my hand. "Thanks, Cian. For everythin'. I know it seemed like I just didn't want to see ya, but there was a reason. Ya never gave up on me. I don't deserve ye."

"Ach, stop that," he says, shaking his head. "Yer my best mate. That's never changed. But—"

"But what?" I press when he pauses.

He tongues his cheek in thought. "But some things *have* changed."

"Is that why Rory isn't here?"

He nods slowly.

"He can't forgive me?"

When Cian lowers his eyes, I know the answer is yes.

"I'm sorry for all the pain I've caused youse. I would have done things so differently. But that's the thing about hindsight… it's fucking useless."

Cian laughs, and the sound is one I've missed. "We'll grab a pint when yer up to it. I'll be back later with Hannah."

He hugs me again as if he still can't believe I'm here.

We say our goodbyes, and I watch as his car turns down the drive and onto the road. Once the car is out of sight, I bend in half, place my hands on my thighs, and take three deep breaths. I need a moment to compose myself.

Once my heart stops racing, I stand and absorb everything before me.

Even though the castle wasn't my home, I hate to see it in the state that it's in. This rubble now belongs to me, and I intend to restore it to its former glory. It's what Connor would have wanted, as well as my ma.

With hesitant steps, I walk toward the building built with Kelly blood, sweat, and tears. Phantom shrills of the twins catch the wind—my mind playing tricks, transporting me back to simpler times.

As I step through the doorway, I'm hit with poignant nostalgia. The riches are no more. This place is merely a carcass of what it once was. Debris litters the floor—food wrappers, cigarette butts, and broken beer bottles.

This place is a haven for misfits.

I continue my tour, my mind flashing from the present to the past, comparing what is to what it once was. There is now a mingin' single mattress where Fiona's beloved dining table once stood. I hate to think of what lewd acts occurred on that boggin' surface.

There are burnt-out candles all over the floor and in the alcoves of the walls, solving the no electricity problem. The atmosphere is haunting. No wonder ghost stories thrive here. Hannah told me this is where the local kids go to hang out, get bladdered, and scare each other with tales of the boogeyman— aka me.

Peering upward, I see sunlight streaming in from the holes in the ceiling. The once polished floors are now ruined after being exposed to the harsh elements over the years. There are etchings in the stonework of people who have come and gone.

I run my fingers over the engravings, wondering if the initials of the lovers inside the hearts are still in love. They clearly wanted to make their union known to others, but nothing lasts forever.

Once I'm done with the tour inside the castle, I walk out the back door and into the vast fields. I stand still and tip my face to the heavens. So many memories crash into me. I loved it back here—it's where my mum's gardens once were.

The rose brooch tingles in my pocket, and on instinct, I dig my hand into my pocket, fingering over it. "I'll replant them for ye, Ma," I avow aloud. "I'll make this place what it once was."

I walk through the grounds, taking in the unkept state. It hurts to see it this way because this castle has been in my family for generations. It angers me that Sean, a Kelly, doesn't seem to give a fuck about that. He's allowed it to wither away and, instead, used it for his corrupt ways—like meeting Ethan here.

My jaw clenches at the thought.

I make my way to the stable yard building. The gardens are overgrown and littered with bottles and feg butts. When I come up over the hill and see it, I sigh, overwhelmed. This place was my sanctuary, the place where I could grieve for the life I never wanted to live.

I walk the same paths I did ten years ago, but so much has changed. That boy didn't know who he was destined to become. I'm surprised the door is still intact. It's unlocked, of course, so I open it and peer inside. The interior is different, but the feelings are still the same—I'm home.

Walking into my gaff, I stand in the middle of the room, taking everything in. My possessions are long gone, but the memories will never fade. I close my eyes, and all I see is Babydoll. I can hear her laughter, her breathless moans as we lost ourselves in one another over and over again.

I remember the way she tested me, refusing to back down. She was the strongest person I knew.

Her scent, her taste is amplified in here as this was our private oasis where the outside world didn't exist. It was us versus them. I miss her so fucking much.

I never allowed myself to think of her because when I did, all I felt was this—this gaping hole in my chest. I never knew what love was, but now I know that I loved Babydoll with every fiber of my being. There wasn't a specific event or time when I fell for her; it was simply inevitable.

Being apart from her is like missing a part of me, and now that I know she isn't my sister, I can't stop thinking about how she made me feel. I want that feeling back.

I want *her*.

And just like that…I get my wish…and I can finally breathe again after ten long years.

"…Hi, Punky."

TWO

PUNKY

Turning slowly, afraid my mind is playing tricks on me, I prepare to be greeted by a ghost of the past. But when I lock in on those expressive green eyes, I realize she's here. She's really here.

I need a minute to take her in because she's changed, although, in some ways, she looks exactly the same.

Her long hair is now a light brown with blonde through it. I remember when we met, it was a brighter blonde. I wonder if she dyed it to help disguise who she really was. She wears fitted blue jeans and a short knitted jumper. She has some makeup on, and I focus on her glossy pink lips.

How I want to taste them.

"I wanted"—she clears her throat—"I wanted to come pick

you up."

My body instantly responds to her voice, and I wonder how I lived without it for ten years. I realize I was only half living.

"But I didn't know if I should. I didn't know if you'd want me to."

Her chest shudders as she exhales. She's nervous.

"You look—" She scrunches up her nose when she takes in my black and blue state. "Just how I remember you. But older."

I want to speak, but I'm addicted to hearing her voice, so I remain quiet.

She brushes a strand of hair behind her ear. "I guess that's what happens when ten years pass. We get old."

I can't take my eyes off her, and when her cheeks turn scarlet, I know she still feels this pull between us. It never left. It was merely in a ten-year slumber. But the beast has awoken, and it needs to be fed.

"Are you going to say anything?" she asks, biting her bottom lip. "Do you want me to go? You're not happy to see me?"

She's clutching at straws as I haven't said a word. I'm afraid to. I'm afraid to tell her I love her because I've never told anyone that I've loved them before.

"This was a mistake."

She spins on her heel, intent on running out the door, but I lunge forward and seize her arm, stopping her. The sparks between us almost set me alight. Touching her winds me, as I'm reminded of the times when I devoured every inch of her skin.

But when a breathy whimper leaves her parted lips, I realize she's not privy to the secret that we're not blood. So I let her go because I don't want her feeling ashamed for the attraction which still lingers between us.

"I am happy to see ye." I finally speak, watching the way her body softens to my words. "I'm sorry. It's just…a lot."

She nods, lowering her eyes. "I know what you mean. I don't know where to start."

"Aye. It's fucking weird," I say, wishing I could be a little more articulate. "Ya look…good."

I wanted to say beautiful, but it's hardly appropriate.

"How are you? I mean…" She quickly covers her face with her palms, shaking her head. "I don't know what I mean. Why is this so difficult?"

I understand how she's feeling. I want to say so many things, but words escape me.

Stepping forward, I gently remove her hands so I can see her face. She allows me to touch her openly. I don't let go of her hands. I can feel her pulse racing wildly on her wrist.

"It's okay to be nervous. I'm nervous too."

"You are?" she asks with a small smile. "You don't look nervous."

"How do I look then?"

She exhales deeply, her eyes filled with tears. "You look like you," she confesses softly. "Why didn't you want to see me? I wrote you hundreds of letters. I came to see you. But you just…

forgot about me? Is that it? You couldn't forgive me? What you said to me…you meant it?"

Her insecurity hurts me because she's got it all wrong. I was forced to stay away from all of them to protect them. But it seems even though their safety was ensured, the pain I caused mentally has been far worse than I ever imagined.

Brushing over her knuckles, I reply, "I didn't want to see ye in there. Not caged up like some animal. And I never forgot ya."

A tear trickles down her cheek. "I'm sorry for everything. I thought I was doing the right t-thing."

"Shh, it's all right. We all made mistakes. How's yer ma? Yer wee sister?"

She sniffs back her tears. "My mom is good. She's been in remission for almost eight years. My sister isn't so little anymore," she says with a smile.

"Ach, I'm happy yer ma is all right."

"She's okay because of you, because of what you did. You went to prison for me. For all of us," she says, squeezing my hands.

"I'm doin' this so we're even. But I don't want to see ye again. No matter what ye did, ya lied to me, and now I have the deaths of my family on my hands. I cannot forgive ya. And ye shouldn't forgive me."

Those are the last words I spoke to her, yet she still sees me as the hero in this story.

"I've missed you…so much," she declares in a whisper,

ashamed. "A piece of me died when you left. I've been searching for it since you were gone—"

"I need to tell ya somethin'," I interrupt, unable to stomach her pain a second longer. But what she says next changes everything forever.

"I met someone," she blurts out, lowering her eyes. "I'm sorry. I just…we can't be together. And…fuck. He's a good man. I'm sorry, Punky. He makes me ha-happy."

She throws herself into my arms, sobbing into my chest guiltily.

Her words play over and over in my mind as I try to digest what she shared.

"He's a good man."

Closing my eyes, I curse every fucking breath I take because I may as well be dead.

Holding her, I inhale her scent and commit it to memory because all I've ever wanted was her happiness. If this man can offer that to her, then I have to let her go.

"Don't be sorry. Ya did what I wanted—ye lived. That's all I ever wanted for ye. For ye to be happy."

She cries, never letting me go as I console her, ignoring this pain in my chest. If I tell her what I know, what does that achieve? Babydoll is happy. I can never give her that when I don't know what true happiness is.

All I can offer her is pain. All I represent is our past mistakes—a past paved with bloodshed and lies. She will think about that every time she looks at me.

I love her more than life itself, which is why I have to set her free. I will carry this secret to my grave and never burden her with a choice because if she believes we're blood—they'll be no choice to make. She'll live a happy and safe life without me.

Connor's dying words come back to haunt me.

"Yer a leader. Lead with the compassion yer ma gave ya. And rule with the cruelty I taught ya because it's the only way to survive in our world."

Love makes you weak. It allows you to be human. Babydoll is collateral, and I refuse to allow my selfish needs to put her in harm's way ever again.

"I wish…"

"Come now, we can't change what's done," I say, not wanting to hear what I desperately want in fear I'll crack and tell her the truth. I won't be that selfish.

This is Babydoll's chance to live a life away from me and away from the shame she feels for what we did.

"I know," she whispers, still holding me. "It's good to have you home."

"Home?" I question. "Ye live here now?"

She gently pulls away, brushing her hair from her cheeks. "No, but my…fiancé does."

Fiancé?

I just accepted her seeing someone, but engaged to be married…fuck.

However, I smile even though I'm secretly dying inside. "He's a lucky lad. I'm happy for youse."

She nods but doesn't seem to buy it either.

An uncomfortable silence wedges its way between us, and I suddenly can't breathe. The thought of another man touching her…I want to break every bone in his fucking body.

Babydoll tilts her head as if attempting to decode my silence. I know for this to be convincing, I need to push her away. I can't have her near me. She represents everything I want but can't have.

"Thanks for stoppin' by. But I need to organize a few things," I say, giving her a not-so-subtle hint that our reunion is over.

She nods, quickly wiping away her tears. "Of course. I'm sorry. Once you get settled, maybe we can catch up?"

"Catch up on what?" I question, folding my arms across my chest.

A range of emotions are coursing through me right now, and at the forefront is the need to destroy everything within reach.

She blinks, appearing stunned by my bluntness.

"We just did that, did we not?"

"I…sure, whatever you w-want," she replies, fumbling over her words. "It was good seeing you."

"Aye. Say hi to yer boy for me."

She narrows her eyes, sensing my sarcasm. We're suddenly transported back ten years where Babydoll and I could go from love to hate in the same breath. Some things don't change, and some do—like Babydoll being engaged.

She nods and appears to want to say something but decides against it at the last minute. "Goodbye, Punky."

"Bye, Babydoll."

A gasp leaves her when I use that name, but she'll always be Babydoll to me. She quickly exits while I force myself not to follow. That won't achieve a thing.

I don't know how long I stand staring at the open doorway, processing what she just shared. Time doesn't seem to make a difference because my feelings for her haven't changed. I still want her with my last breath.

But she's moved on, and I need to accept that. Telling her the truth will amount to nothing. This is for the best.

So why do I feel like killing someone, preferably Babydoll's fiancé?

Unable to deal with this right now, I decide to clean the place up a bit as I need to keep busy. It's going to take months to get everything back to how it once was, but with nothing but time on my hands, I may as well start now.

Lost in my head, a dangerous place to be, I don't realize I've got company. Thankfully, it's only Cian, but I need to focus because I can't make that mistake again.

"Need help?" he says, holding up a bottle of whiskey in one hand and a broom in the other.

"Thanks."

But he instantly senses my bad mood.

"What's happened?"

"Nothin'," I reply, snatching the bottle from his grip. When I unscrew the lid and throw back a large mouthful, Cian arches a brow.

"Don't give me that shite."

"Ack, leave it alone, will ye," I snap, turning my back on him.

But Cian won't. "Stop this! I understand yer needin' time, but don't shut me out. Do ye know what we all went through? We were locked up with ya!"

"I doubt that." I snicker, spinning around to face him. "I was the one behind bars. Don't compare us because there is no fucking comparison!"

"We all tried everythin' to help ya, but ya didn't want us to. I felt fuckin' helpless!" he argues, unable to stop his emotions. "Do ya know how that made me feel? I've been livin' with this guilt for ten fuckin' years! I would have traded my freedom for yours. In a heartbeat. But ye just left us…ya fuckin' broke me."

"I had no choice," I say between clenched teeth.

"Bullshit! Ya could have seen me or written me back. But ya chose not to!"

"I never chose anythin'!" I scream, arms out wide. "Brody Doyle made me promise not to make contact with all youse! If I did, he'd kill the lot of ya, includin' the twins. I needed to be gone, forgotten, to keep ya safe! Ya think I wanted to be alone, rotting in that cell? I would have given anythin' to see ya. See all of youse!

"But I couldn't. I was tryin' to keep youse safe. I was tryin' to do the right thing for once! Besides, with me gone, youse had a chance to live a better life. A life ye *chose*, not forced onto ya!"

Cian stands before me, his mouth agape. I never wanted to tell him this, but I can't go on with him thinking I did this because I wanted to.

"He wanted Belfast as his own, and he couldn't do that with me in the background. I had to be forgotten."

"How could we forget someone like you, Punky?" Cian says, shaking his head. "I fuckin' love ya. Yer my brother. I needed ya."

My heart can't take this any longer. I tried to be strong. For ten years, I refused to think of them because it just hurt. But now that I'm out, I can't allow them to think I never cared. It was because I *did* care that I did what I had to, to keep them safe.

"I wanted a normal life for ya."

"Normal?" Cian scoffs. "There's nothin' normal about a Doyle takin' over Belfast! We were nothin' without the Kellys. My da put a fuckin' bullet in his head because of what happened to yer da! Tell me, how's that normal?"

"Oh, fuck, Cian," I say with utter regret. "I'm sorry. I didn't know." His dad is dead? This war has seen so many casualties.

"That's right, ye didn't know 'cause ya locked us all out! All I wanted was my best friend, but ya just—" A sob leaves him, and I reach out to hug him, unable to see him in pain.

"I'm so sorry. Forgive me."

He hugs me back, sobbing into my shoulder. I failed him. I failed them all. I believed I was saving them, but all I've done is hurt them terribly.

Brody Doyle and Sean Kelly are going to fucking pay.

"I need to tell ya somethin'," I confess, realizing I can't do this alone. I wanted to give Cian a chance at living a normal life, but this is our normal.

Cian pulls away slowly, wiping away his tears.

"Hannah found Sean's journals in storage," I reveal, needing to retell this at my own pace. "Brody Doyle isn't my dad."

Cian's eyes widen. "Then who is?"

With a sigh, I reveal the truth, the truth which has plagued me since I found out who I was. "I *am* a Kelly, Cian. Sean is my dad."

Cian opens but soon closes his mouth before snatching the bottle from my hand and gulping the contents down.

"He killed my ma because she was going to tell Connor that Sean was in business with the Doyles. He was the one behind all of this. Hannah saw him here. He's trying to recruit Ethan. He needs a puppet he can control.

"I didn't fit the prototype. That's why he has no issues makin' me the scapegoat."

"Yer fuckin' jokin' me?" Cian gasps when he can finally

construct a sentence.

"I have it in his own handwriting. Everything he did."

"But we buried him? Did we not?"

"I don't know who ya buried, but it wasn't Sean. He's been waitin' in the shadows, ready to strike when the time is right. He failed once before, but he's learned from his mistakes. He's got what he always wanted—Connor and me out of the picture.

"He couldn't be the top dog with Connor and me alive. His greed, his need to be number one, is what started all this. My ma made a mistake. She fell for Sean's lies. We all did. And that cost her her life. She was in that bungalow, trying to escape, to make a better life for me, but he found her and made her pay for betraying him."

"Why did Brody say he was yer dad then?"

"'Cause Brody thought it would benefit him in the long run. If I were to denounce my Kelly name, that would leave Sean in charge of it all. Therefore, Brody believed with me gone, he could steal Belfast from Sean when the time was right."

"They were going to double-cross each other?" Cian asks, cluing into their plans.

"Aye. They never trusted one another. They were using the other to get what they wanted. But Sean outsmarted us when he faked his death. Brody can't fight a dead guy. But Sean is workin' behind the scenes with Brody's men, just how he did with ours. He's earnin' their trust, showin' them he's the better leader.

"And when the time is right, when he's compiled his army, he will strike and take Brody down."

"Fuckin' hell," Cian says, shook. "I cannot believe it. It was him this entire time? Goin' behind our backs and recruitin' the weak? He promised them the world, and they fell for his lies!

"He's responsible for Connor's death. And my da's," he spits, his anger palpable. "And now he's tryin' to ruin Ethan's life. That fucking fuck cunt arsehole!"

I allow him to vent because it's a lot to take in.

This is the reason I didn't want to tell him. He's suffered enough. But I need him.

"He's goin' to pay, I promise ye. But for that to happen, I need to work with Brody Doyle."

Cian attempts to process what I just shared. "Away on!"

But when he realizes I'm very serious, he pales.

"There is only one person who can help me. I need an inside man, and that man is Brody. He is clueless about Sean's plan. He either has no idea that he's still alive, or if he does, he doesn't believe Sean can outsmart him."

"And ya think he's just gonna be believin' ye when ya tell him?"

"Aye," I affirm, as I've had nothing but time to perfect this plan. "He'll work with me 'cause we both need the other to get what we want. And when I do…I will finally finish what I started ten years ago.

"I want Belfast back. It's ours. And I can't do that with

Brody in the position he's in. He's too powerful, and the men who are loyal to him will do everythin' to protect him. The ones who aren't, they're loyal to Sean.

"It's better the devil ya know, so it is."

"I think this plan is fuckin' stupid," Cian says firmly. "Can't we just kill Brody?"

"How do you propose we do that? He knows I'm out, and it's only a matter of time before he comes knockin'. We've got no men to fight with us. And as for our aul' allies, ten years is a long time. Their loyalty is no longer with us. Besides, it was Connor they had alliances with, not us.

"We need to start from scratch. We need to find out who's pullin' the strings. Everyone here in Belfast knows Brody as the kingpin. The Kelly name is a thing of the past. I'm guessin' Cory's da is no longer involved with the business?"

Cian shakes his head. "Naw, like my da, he was lost without Connor. He didn't know what to do, so he handed everythin' over to Brody. I tried to fight them, but no one wanted to deal with us. It was the Kellys who they dealt with, and because the Kellys were no more, that fucker, Brody, could move in without any trouble.

"I tried to have him killed, many times. But with Connor gone, Sean dead, and you in prison, no one would help. We were on our own.

"When my dad died, I just gave up," he confesses sadly. "I forgot that part of my life and moved on. Last I heard, the

Doyles were runnin' Belfast with an iron fist. Our men, our suppliers are now theirs. We are a forgotten memory."

Clenching my fist, I take a deep breath. "It's time to change that. I don't know what Sean is waitin' for as our alliances would deal with him. So, I'm guessin' he's simply waitin' for the right time to strike because when he does, he'll be unstoppable.

"If I thought I could do this alone, I would. But I have no men and a name that only *once* incited fear. I need to regain both. And to do that, I need to work with the man who is now in control. I need to crawl into the belly of the beast. I know this plan is far from ideal, but if I don't side with Brody, I will be fightin' both him *and* Sean. I hate to admit it, but I don't stand a chance against Brody.

"He's the lesser of two evils."

Cian sighs, but if he has any better ideas, then I'm all ears.

"I don't expect ya to—" But he doesn't let me finish.

"I'm doin' this with ya," he affirms with conviction. "There's no way those two fuckers are goin' to get away with this. I owe that to my da."

I understand what he means. Therefore, I know there is no changing his mind.

"Time to claim Northern Ireland as ours. Our fathers would want us to do that."

"That's the truth, so it is," I agree. Even though Connor wasn't my father, he would want me to fight for what is mine. Which has me thinking about Babydoll.

"Babydoll is engaged," I reveal, while Cian doesn't seem surprised as he obviously already knew. "She came to see me."

"Aye, she is. Yer mad at the fact?" he asks, confused. "I mean, she's yer sis—" But he soon stops, realizing what he just said.

"Naw, she's not."

Cian runs a hand through his snarled hair, blowing out a deep breath. "Ach, this is minus craic. What are ye goin' to do?"

What I want to do versus what I should do are two completely different things.

"She said she's happy. That he's a good man."

Cian nods.

"Sure look, what can I do? She couldn't be waitin' around for me, obviously. She still thinks we're brother and sister, and I want to leave it like that."

"What?" He gasps in surprise. "Yer not goin' to tell her? I don't think that's a good idea."

"No, I'm not. If she's happy, then so am I. What can I offer her, Cian? A life where she's constantly lookin' over her shoulder? My ma lived that life, and that's what got her killed. I won't be havin' that for Babydoll."

"And what about yer happiness? Yer to live with this secret while watchin' the woman ye love with another man?"

With a shrug, I reply, "Aye. It's better this way."

"Better for who?" he questions.

"For everyone. This is the only way I can keep her safe."

Cian shakes his head, clearly not on board with this plan. "She's tougher than she looks. When ye were in prison, she did everythin' to try to help ya. Nothin' scared her. She worked until it made her…sick."

"Sick?" I question Cian, who instantly appears to regret his words.

"All of us suffered in our own personal ways with ya gone, Punky. Babydoll never stopped lovin' ya, even when she knew she shouldn't. She was disgusted in herself, thinkin' ya were her brother and that. I think she needs to know."

"I tell her, and ya know what happens?" When he doesn't reply, I continue, "We go back to hurtin' one another. It seems to be our pattern. We both want to save the other, but it just turns to shite. It's better this way.

"I need to focus on Sean and Brody. And I can't do that while worryin' about Babydoll."

"And yer okay knowin' she's about to marry another man?"

"Aye," I reply, but it's a lie. I am not fucking okay. "If he makes her happy, then that's enough for me. Ye can't be tellin' anyone 'bout this, ye hear?"

Cian isn't fooled, but he doesn't press. Nor does he share who her fiancé is. "Yer a bigger man than me. If Amber—"

But when he suddenly stops, I realize he's got a secret of his own. I realize they've all moved on while I've simply been stuck in time.

"Away on! You and Amber?"

Amber was the twins' nanny. Cian has always been interested in her. I'm happy he finally got the girl.

"Aye. It's not…weird?"

"Naw, course not. Why would it be weird?"

Cian shrugs. "Dunno. Thought it might be."

I know what he means. Amber showed some interest in me, but I never felt that way about her. There was only one doll for me.

"I'm happy for youse." And I mean it.

"And what about you? When do you get yer happiness?"

Considering his question, I smile. "The day I kill Sean and Brody, which has me thinkin'…"

Cian nods, indicating he's listening.

"I need to know whose body they buried. They may have the answers I'm lookin' for."

"And?" Cian coaxes, knowing so much more is to come.

"And I need to find Brody Doyle before he finds me."

This is dangerous, and if Cian is having second thoughts, I wouldn't hold it against him. But when he smirks, it's like we're picking up where I left things.

"Keep 'er lit. It's time we took back what's ours."

"Ach, sure, we're suckin' diesel now."

THREE

PUNKY

"This would be a lot easier if Rory was here," I whisper discreetly to Cian, so the aul' doll behind the glass screen doesn't hear me.

It's been two days. I've had no luck finding out who really was buried in place of Sean, and Brody Doyle has gone into hiding. I know he's simply playing it cautious as he doesn't know what my plans are, but he can't hide forever.

I still haven't seen Rory. I understand he needs time to adjust to things, but I fucking miss him. And I could really use his computer expertise to help us out.

"I'm sorry, lad, but I can't help ya," says the woman behind the counter as her fingers tap away at the keyboard.

We're at the cemetery where "Sean" is buried. The

information online is useless. It's all above board to any unsuspecting person, but I know better. I need to know whose body is in that grave.

"Best ask the family for this personal information," she adds, looking down the top of her silver-framed glasses at me.

I would, but Fiona won't talk to me, and Hannah can't get the information from her either. I need to know who the coroner was because they signed off on "Sean's" death. I also want to know who the funeral directors were.

But I can't get any fucking answers because this aul' doll won't talk.

Rory would be able to hack into this system, giving me the answers I need. But he's a big girl's blouse at the moment.

I could let on that I'm family, but this will rouse suspicion. I'd have to tell the aul' doll that the reason I don't know this information is because I was in jail, and I was put in there because I played a part in the man's death I'm asking about.

This is a fucking dog's dinner.

"All right. Thanks."

Cian and I step outside, back to square one.

"Fuck," I curse under my breath as we walk away, in case of any earwiggin'. "This is useless. If I can't find any information on Sean, then I'm going to Dublin. Least I know where I can find some Doyles."

Cian clucks his tongue. "Fer feck's sake! Cool yer jets. Remember what happened the last time we did that?"

"Fair play," I reply with a sigh.

"I'll chat to Rory."

"Don't bother."

I don't want to annoy him, seeing as he's still mad at me. I never expected him to welcome me back with open arms. He needs to do it at his own pace. But his own pace is killing me slowly.

Cian's phone rings, and when he answers it, I guess Amber is on the other end. He speaks to her for a few seconds before nodding and disconnecting the call. "I've got to go. That was Amber. She—"

But I cut him off. I don't need an explanation. "I'll see ye later."

I know he wishes things could return to how they once were. But they can't. Amber, Rory, and the others will see me when they're ready. I'm not expecting miracles.

"How will ye get back?" Cian drove, but I'm not ready to leave yet. I have to do something first.

"I'll walk."

It's a long way, but the fresh air will do me good. Cian lent me his truck, but I'm not ready to drive yet.

"All right then. Call me if ya hear anythin'." He gives me a loose hug goodbye before walking toward his car.

Once he's gone, I make my way toward a place I've wanted to visit for as long as I can remember. I just didn't know where to look—until now. I pass a florist along the way and buy a bunch of red roses.

It's so quiet, but I suppose the dead don't talk.

Passing the rows of gravestones, I wonder what each person whose name is etched into their respective stone was like. Were they loved? I can't help but think about my own gravestone. What would mine say? And who would grieve for me?

With a sigh, I follow the signage and walk down the plush green rows until I come to a modest gravestone that has been weathered with time. I stand before it, unbelieving I'm here. I read over the name three times to ensure I'm really standing before my ma's grave.

It's simple. But I expected that because when my ma was laid to rest no one was here to mourn her. She was buried a liar and an adulterer.

There is no epigraph, just her name and the dates of her birth and death. Why didn't my grandparents ensure she got more?

Dropping to a crouch, I brush the fallen leaves and twigs aside and take a moment to process everything. Now that I'm here, I don't know what to say.

"I'm so sorry, Ma," I start with regret. "Ya didn't deserve this. We were so close to gettin' out of here. I often wonder how my life would have turned out if we had left. If that arsehole, Sean, hadn't found us. I think we would have been happy."

Sighing, I tug at the blades of grass, trying to picture a life away from here. A life away from the Kelly name.

"I promise ye, he'll pay for what he did. To you, and to Connor. I know Connor hurt ya, but in the end, he saved me as best he could. Even though he knew I wasn't his son, he still left everythin' to me. That says somethin' about his character. That shows me that he still loves ya as he did this for you.

"I hope yer happy. I love ya and will make it right."

I remove a single rose from the bunch before placing the bouquet at Mum's gravestone.

"Goodbye, Ma."

Coming to a stand, I promise myself I won't return until Sean and Brody are dead.

With the single rose in hand, I walk toward Connor's grave at the opposite end of the cemetery. No doubt that was done by Fiona, as she wouldn't want Connor near my ma; alive or dead.

His marbled gravestone is elaborate. Fiona ensured his was the biggest here.

Beloved husband to Fiona.
Cherished father of Hannah and Ethan.
Forever in our hearts.

It doesn't surprise me I didn't make the family tree. I'm the reason he's buried in this grave. Besides, he isn't my father. However, it still stings that Fiona made sure I was nowhere to be seen.

Placing the red rose on his grave, I say the only thing I can.

"Thank you."

Even knowing what he did, he tried his best to save me. He believed he would go to prison, not me. But Sean made sure we both suffered.

Just as I'm about to leave, the air turns thick, and instinctively, I dive behind Connor's gravestone, taking cover as a bullet zips past me. I'm under attack in a fucking cemetery—no respect for the dead, it seems.

Peeking around the gravestone, I see a man in a black balaclava running toward me. I'm waiting on a gun from Cian, as I can't obtain one legally, so I'm unarmed. Desperately searching for a weapon, I reach for a porcelain vase filled with flowers on a stranger's grave—it's the best I can do.

With his gun trained on me, the man gets closer and closer, and I know if I don't do something, he'll shoot me as there is nowhere to hide. My aim has always been good, so I kiss the vase for luck before jumping up and throwing it at my attacker.

The two bullets that slice through the air miss me, but my throw is on target and hits the fucker straight between the eyes. He stumbles, and his gun slips from his hand. Without delay, I charge at him as he attempts to regain his footing.

Diving on top of him, we both fall to the ground, where I raise my fist and connect with his face. "Who sent ya?" I scream, yanking him up by the collar of his shirt and pressing us nose to nose.

He doesn't reply, which infuriates me further.

I headbutt him, the crack singing to my depravity, rattling the bars of his cage, demanding more. Just as I'm about to break his nose, he raises a shaky hand in surrender, his blue eyes pleading I show mercy.

And I do, because those eyes…I've looked into them before. "Ethan?"

I quickly jump to my feet, looking down at the trembling man who is merely a boy. I don't want to believe this is my baby brother, but I know that it is.

"Answer me, lad!" I demand, offering him a lifeline because if this were anyone else, they'd be dead.

He shakes his head, his chest heaving. He's afraid.

"Sean has sent ya to do his dirty work, is it? I taught ya better than that, cub. If yer gonna shoot, best not miss."

Bending down, I pick up Ethan's gun.

A winded hiss leaves him as he raises both hands in surrender.

"Ya think I'd hurt ya?" I question, saddened. "I never would."

I could hurt him to teach him and Sean a lesson, but I can't do that to Ethan. He's just as much a victim as I am.

"It's only a matter of time. You think on that, Ethan, because if yer not with me, yer against me. Away now."

His confusion is clear, but when he realizes I'm giving him one chance and one chance only, he scrambles to his feet.

"Tell him ya couldn't get a clear shot," I instruct, looking

Ethan dead in the eye. "If ya don't, he'll look on this as weakness. Don't ever think yer valuable to him—yer not. Once he's done with ya, he'll dispose of ye like nothin' but shite on his shoe.

"Like he did to me, to my ma, and to yer father, Connor. Don't you ever forget that yer a Kelly—Connor Kelly's son."

If Ethan tells Sean what happened, Sean will punish him for his mistake, and Ethan realizes what that means for him. He doesn't understand why I'm letting him go, but he doesn't stick around to find out. He takes off, looking over his shoulder once to ensure I'm not following. I'm not.

Once he's out of sight, I let out the breath I was holding, unbelieving that my baby brother pulled the trigger on me. If his aim was straight, he would have wounded me, and it seemed as though he didn't give a fuck about that.

He's in deeper than I thought.

Placing the gun at the small of my back, I look at Connor's grave. "I'll save him. I promise ya that."

I decide not to tell Cian what happened at the cemetery but send him a text asking if he can bring over some guns and other weaponry as soon as he can. He said he'd bring them over tomorrow as he's busy tonight.

I spend the rest of the day buying a bunch of cleaning

supplies as I want to commence work on the castle as soon as possible. As I'm picking up the endless rubbish from what was once the dining room floor, I hear Darcy call out from the front door.

She was supposed to call on me last night, but I sent her a text, asking if we could postpone. I didn't give a time when, but it doesn't seem to matter. Darcy wants something, and I wonder what that is.

"I'm in here."

Her high heels announce her arrival.

I don't stop cleaning, which is no deterrent for Darcy. "How are you?"

"Ach, I'm all right. Sorry I didn't have a chance to tidy up before ya came over," I tease while she smiles.

She takes the place in, not hiding her horror at the castle's state. "This place is a right mess," she says, placing her hand over her brow as she looks at the ceiling, which is caved in.

"It's looked worse," I counter, sweeping the broken bits of glass from the floor. "I mean, did ya see the fucking awful décor Fiona fitted this castle with?"

Darcy looks at me before bursting into laughter. "I suppose yer right. Yer gonna need some help restoring it."

"A'll be fine," I say, not wanting anyone's help. "Why are ya here, Darcy?"

She tucks a piece of hair behind her ear. "I need ya to sign some paperwork. As Hannah told ya, this is yours. Connor left it to ya. He also left money for ya. Fiona was given the majority, but she spent that awful quick."

Hannah told me this. But Fiona no doubt blames me for having "nothing" when Connor died.

Darcy opens her briefcase and offers me a pen and papers as I lean the broom against the wall. "Sign here, here, and here," she instructs, her sweet perfume lingering as she gets in close to show me where I need to sign.

I quickly scribble my signature, but I pause when I notice the date the will was drawn up. "This is the right date?" I ask her, pointing the pen to the date.

She nods. "Aye. That's when this last will and testament was drawn up. Is there a problem?"

Looking at the date, I see that Connor finalized this *after* he found out I wasn't his son. Yet he still left everything to me. No wonder Sean wanted us both dead. He gains nothing with me being alive.

Did Connor know Sean was corrupt all along? Did he have his suspicions that his own brother was the one stabbing him in the back? I'll never know, but what I do know is that Connor left all of this to me, knowing I wasn't his son.

I don't know how to feel.

My entire life, I hated the aul' lad, but I can't now. Not after everything I know.

"No problem," I reply, signing on the dotted line.

"Congratulations then," she says, shaking my hand. "The

castle is officially yers. So is Kellys' Aluminum."

"Getawaytafuk," I say as Hannah failed to mention anything about that.

Our front was this business—a company that manufactures aluminum casting products for the automotive industry. This was how we could import and export our product—which has nothing to do with cars—without detection.

"Aye, no word of a lie. It's yours. It's not operational, but the piece of land it's sittin' on is very valuable. Ya can sell it and make yerself a grand profit."

But I shake my head. "Naw, I'm not sellin' it." And the reason for that is because I plan on picking up where Connor left things.

That's where I'll base myself—in honor of the man who left it behind. This will be a secret for now, as I can't have Brody knowing of this plan, but like a smart predator, I'll wait and strike when my prey is unaware.

Darcy doesn't ask questions and points to where I need to sign the deed. Once signed, she puts everything back into her briefcase. "I'll organize getting the keys to ya then. The money should be in yer bank account within a week."

I didn't even ask how much. But it matters not. I don't want his money. I will make my own.

Darcy hints she has something else she came here to see me about when she doesn't leave. "I'm happy yer home. I missed ya."

Her comment confuses me. "Ya did? Why?"

She smiles, appearing amazed I asked her this. "I couldn't stop thinking about ye. I know it's silly, but I really liked ya."

"Oh," I reply, unsure what to say because she's caught me by surprise.

"You probably think I'm stupid."

"Naw, Darcy, I don't think that. How could I?" And I mean it. "If it weren't for you, I'd still be locked up. I owe ya everythin'. As soon as I get the money Connor left me, I'll pay ya—"

"I don't want yer money," she quickly interrupts.

"Then what do ya want?" I don't like owing anyone anything, but the truth is, I don't know how to pay Darcy back.

When she steps forward, I can guess what she wants. "Will ya come with me tonight? To a party?"

Folding my arms across my chest, I arch a brow. "I don't really do parties. Or people."

"I don't either. We can be miserable together then."

"I don't have anythin' to wear."

She smiles, taking another step toward me. "I'll organize that. All ya have to do is turn up as my date."

There is no such thing as no strings attached in this world, which is why I nod. "All right. I can do that."

Darcy's face lights up as I know this means more to her than she's letting on. I don't bother asking whose party it is. "I'll have someone drop off yer suit this afternoon."

So, it's a black-tie affair. The last time I wore a suit, things turned to shite. I hope tonight is different.

"I'll come pick ya up around half seven?"

"Aye. I'll be ready."

Darcy smiles, and with an apprehensive touch, she cups my cheek.

I try my hardest not to recoil because I know she means no harm. But physical touch is something I need to pace myself with.

"Y've always stolen my breath away, Puck Kelly."

My mouth parts as she stands on her toes to kiss my cheek, before leaving me alone, wondering what the fuck I just agreed to.

Whistling, I bend low to look out the windscreen as Darcy drives toward a grand mansion. This private country estate has a Gothic vibe, adding to the mystery this night holds. The gardens are vast, and there is no denying this estate's beauty.

A valet gestures he will park the car. No expense is spared, it seems.

As I exit the car, I button up my black tuxedo jacket, peering at the huge mansion. Darcy slips into her gold high heels—she couldn't drive with them on—which complement her ball gown. She smiles shyly.

I offer her my arm, which she accepts, and we make our way inside.

Music sounds from a string quartet, playing softly in the corner of the room. The entrance is filled with people who talk animatedly among themselves. There's no indication of what we're celebrating, but it's a grand affair judging from the fancy dresses.

A waiter offers us champagne. I take two glasses.

"I'm glad I polished my shoes," I tease, offering a glass to her. I'm also thankful I'm now clean-shaven as I would have looked like a savage with the beard I was sporting.

She accepts with a laugh. "Let me show ya around."

I don't argue and follow her through the mansion since she's clearly been here before. The staircase is marbled, and branches off into two directions. Darcy leads me to the left, which seems to be less populated than the right.

"I don't think we're supposed to be up here," I say when it's evident that this upstairs area is off-limits to guests.

"Since when do you follow the rules, Punky?" Darcy says over her shoulder.

"Aye," I reply with a shrug, curiosity getting the better of me.

Numerous doors branch off the long hallway, which has me guessing these are guest rooms. The expensive paintings hanging off the walls and the low-hanging crystal chandelier adds to the wealth this place exudes.

Darcy grins before softly opening a door to the left. She pokes her head inside and gestures I'm to follow. This can't be good. When I step inside and see the pressed white linens and the four-poster bed, I realize I was right.

"Whose party is this?" I ask, watching as Darcy walks over to the large window overlooking the grounds.

But she doesn't reply.

"This estate is part of my father's portfolio," she says instead. "When I was a little girl, I used to pretend this was my castle, and I was awaiting my prince's return. That prince was you."

I adjust my bow tie as it's suddenly suffocating me.

She turns over her shoulder slowly and smiles. "Yer finally back."

"I'm no prince, Darcy."

"Yer right." She saunters toward me, stopping a few inches away. "Yer far too good for that. Yer a king. So now, the question is, are ye looking for a queen?"

She waits for me to reply, a brazen smirk tugging at her red lips.

However, I never get the chance to reply.

"Punky?" Hannah gasps, pausing in the doorway when she sees Darcy and me together.

I, too, am surprised to see her here, but don't have time to question it because Cian and Rory almost crash into her as they attempt to see what she's gawking at. When they do, I know I shouldn't be here.

"Don't be mad," Darcy whispers into my ear as she stands on her toes. "I brought you here because no one wants to tell you the truth, and you deserve to know."

"Whose party is this?" I repeat, dangerously low.

She nervously licks her lips. "It's Rory's engagement party. His and…Camilla's. They're getting married."

Even though I heard her, my brain doesn't want to process her words as truth. But when Babydoll enters the room, laughing with Amber, oblivious to what's going on, there's no denying that her "good man," the man who can do what I cannot—make her happy—is my best friend.

My best friend is marrying the woman I love.

But Darcy isn't done.

"I also wanted you to come because Brody is here. It's time people stopped treating you like a fool."

When Babydoll and I lock eyes, I realize that Darcy is right—it's time to quit actin' the maggot. It's time for war.

All eyes are on me—eyes which look at me with a mixture of guilt, sorrow, and shame. So this is what Cian was talking to Amber about today. He had ample opportunity to tell me why Rory didn't want to see me. Just how Babydoll could have shared who her fiancé is.

No wonder Hannah was so incredibly sheepish when speaking of Babydoll. She didn't want to be the one who broke my heart. But you can't break what is already broken beyond repair.

Before me stand the people I held closest to my heart, but now, all I see are strangers. So much has changed in ten years. Even though I was stuck in time, my friends moved on; just how I wanted them to. But seeing them together, realizing they had a life without me, fucking stings.

Worst of all—seeing Rory wrap his arm around a stunned Babydoll cements that she moved on with my fucking friend. And he on to the woman he knew I sacrificed everything for. But no one knows the truth, that Babydoll isn't my sister. I can't hate them for living their life.

So why can't I shift this urge to throttle Rory with my bare hands?

Hannah's eyes fill with tears, tears for me. But I don't want her pity.

"Congratulations," I say, breaking the ice as I raise my glass of champagne in the air.

"Punky—" Rory tries to make amends for betraying me in the worst possible way, but I cut him off, not interested in his excuses.

"To the happy couple."

Darcy smirks, clinking her glass against mine before we both throw back our drinks.

Babydoll looks like she's about to pass out, but that's not my problem anymore. None of this is.

Cheers to new beginnings.

FOUR

Cami

Why is he here?

We didn't invite him because I wanted to avoid this—this uncomfortable silence. Rory's arm around me suddenly feels so wrong. I subtly shrug from his hold. He sighs, while Punky looks like he's about to rip out Rory's throat.

I can't do anything right.

When a grin tugs at Darcy's lips, I realize Punky is here because of her. She knew the scene it would cause. She knew how uncomfortable this would make me feel. She also wanted to reassert her claim over him, but there's no need.

She's won.

I'm so thankful she helped him because if it wasn't for

her, Punky would still be behind bars. But there is still some unspoken competition between us which makes no sense. When I "worked" for her family, she always made sure the line was drawn—I was beneath her.

Not that I could ever forget.

And now, ten years later, she still insists on hurting me.

She and Rory were once a thing, and I know he still harbors some sort of affection for her. It doesn't bother me. I know it should, but it doesn't, and that's because I feel the same way about Punky.

Years of therapy have helped me "deal" with my love for him, but seeing him now, I realize I still love him and not how a sister should love her brother.

I'm sick, I know I am, but I can't help it. I've tried so hard to stop feeling this way, but I just can't. My love for him hasn't changed, and that's why I agreed to marry Rory. I thought if I attempted to live a "normal" life, these feelings would eventually fade.

But they haven't. They've only grown.

Looking at him now, I feel complete. Something is always missing when he's not around, but now, the noise…it's silenced, and I feel whole again.

My therapist assures me this is normal, but nothing is normal about wanting your half-brother the way I want Punky. Something is very wrong with me.

Ashamed, my walls are erected, and I go on the defensive.

"What are you doing here?"

Even I flinch at the harshness of my tone, but he can't be here. I can't do this. I can't pretend Rory is the man I want to marry because Punky is the only person who can see through my lies. He will see how disgusting I am.

Rory makes me happy, and I do love him so much. But with him, I settled. I learned to love him. But he doesn't give me the butterflies I get with Punky. Even now, just being in his presence robs me of air.

Falling in love with Punky was innate, and I don't think I'll ever feel that again.

"He's my plus-one," Darcy says smugly.

Punky is deadly quiet. I wonder what he's thinking.

"Ach, I'm glad I could celebrate this happy occasion with youse," he says, his gaze never wavering from mine.

He feels betrayed, I'm sure of it.

Before him stand the people he once called his family. But family don't exclude one another, which is what we did to him.

"Can I speak with ye?" Rory asks, clearing his throat.

He's avoided Punky, saying he needs time, but I know the real reason is that he wanted to avoid this confrontation. There's no easy way to approach this. Even though Punky and I can never be, that doesn't lessen the guilt we feel.

We bonded over our love for Punky, and that bond grew into something more.

Rory makes me happy, and I'm so glad he wants to spend

the rest of his life with me. However, there's always a but lingering, and I don't know why.

Cian and Punky exchange a strange look. It's gone a second later.

"Sure," Punky says.

I step aside to let him pass, unable to face him as he leaves the room with Cian and my fiancé. Once he's gone, I exhale softly, needing a minute to compose myself.

"I better see to our guests." I try to conceal my thoughts, but the girls know it's just an excuse.

As I turn on my heel and leave the room, I hear Hannah call after me. I want to keep walking, but I don't.

"Are ya all right?" she asks, gently touching my arm.

"I'm fine," I lie, and she sees straight through me.

"Don't be pretendin' that wasn't weird."

I shrug in response. "We all knew this wasn't going to be easy. But I didn't want him finding out this way," I confess with a quiver. "I wanted to tell him when the time was right."

"Was there ever a right time to tell him?" Hannah questions. She's not having a go at me, but she did suggest we tell Punky before something like this happened.

"I suppose not. Fuck, this is a mess." I refuse to cry and mess up the hours Amber spent on my makeup. "He won't forgive me for this."

Hannah rubs my arm. "Don't be quick to judge him. He understands ten years is a long time. Ye were right to move on."

"But with his best friend?"

"Aye, that will come as a shock, but ya can't help how ye feel."

If only she knew how I really felt.

"Thanks, Hannah. I should be the one giving you advice, seeing as I'm supposed to be the adult."

She laughs. "I just want everyone to be happy. And I know Punky is happy if you are. It'll take some gettin' used to, but he'll want the best for youse, and if that's together, then he will accept it.

"Besides, it looks like Darcy is still keen on him. He could do worse."

Just the mere mention of her name has me clenching my jaw. "Yes, you're right. She has been a great support to him."

I don't elaborate because Hannah won't like what I have to say.

"I better get downstairs before people start to talk."

She reads the blow-off for what it is but doesn't press.

I conceal my emotions, as I've become a master of hiding how I really feel, and put on a smile as I descend the staircase. All the faces are friends I've made via Rory because my friends and family are back home.

They promised to attend the wedding, but I don't expect them to come. Besides, Rory and I haven't discussed that far ahead. When he proposed six months ago, it came as a huge surprise. We have been seeing one another for about three years—on and off.

Our relationship has been strained because I've been coming and going between Belfast and America for ten years. The moment I ran out of money, I'd go back home and work eighteen-plus hours a day at any job that paid so I could save enough money to come back to Belfast.

But when I came back to Northern Ireland this last visit to see my friends and to hopefully see Punky, Rory said he wanted to marry me. I accepted, tired of being alone. Even though my feelings of loneliness never dissipate, they lessen with Rory.

But I had no idea things would happen so fast.

A few days later, Hannah told me she had seen Punky. I couldn't believe he agreed to see her. I also couldn't believe it when Hannah said Darcy believed she could help free him. I instantly felt guilty for accepting Rory's proposal. I felt like I had let Punky down.

I knew I couldn't be with Punky, but that didn't lessen the guilt.

It still doesn't.

Looking down at the beautiful diamond ring on my finger, it doesn't change the fact that I wish I was wearing Punky's ring.

Swallowing down my disgust, I paint my face with a broad smile, playing the part of the happy fiancée because Rory deserves that. He has been nothing but wonderful and supportive, understanding why I need space, and he still wants to marry me regardless.

One of Rory's colleagues and his wife make small talk while I attempt to look interested, but I can't stop thinking about Punky and how seeing him with Darcy angered me more than it should. I should never have come back here. Northern Ireland is filled with nothing but ghosts that continue to haunt me every single day.

My mom and my sister, Eva, are back home in Chicago. It's hard to believe Eva is almost the same age as me when I first came here. How naïve I was ten years ago. I never thought I'd not only fall in love but that I'd meet my soulmate—in every sense of the word.

When Punky was sent to prison, I received a life sentence too. Of course, our imprisonment was different, but with each day, week, month, and year that he refused to speak to me, the walls of my cell caged me in further. I lost myself because Punky was my true north.

Even knowing what I did with us being related didn't make a difference. I still loved him. And even though he refused to see me, I never gave up on him. We tried everything to help him, but after exhausting every possible avenue, we accepted that we had failed.

I went to visit him every week. I wrote to him every day for ten years. Some letters I sent. Others were my form of therapy. But not a day went by that I didn't try. However, he made it clear he wasn't interested in seeing me when my constant visits were denied.

I don't know if he got the letters I sent as he never replied.

After months of trying, I had to go back to America to check on my mom and Eva. Brody stuck to his word, and the money he sent saved my mom's life. The experimental drugs worked. With the extra money, I was able to send Eva to a good school where she got the education she deserved.

Life was the best it had ever been, but it meant nothing knowing what I did to achieve that happiness. Knowing that Punky was rotting away because of my betrayal.

For this reason, once my mom and Eva were settled, I came back here and picked up where I left things. I couldn't let it go. I couldn't move on with Punky being where he was. Rory and Cian were trying desperately to help Punky, but he still refused all visitors.

That is when Rory and I grew closer. We both shared the same pain—we missed Punky, and that's what we bonded over. We found solace in the other as it felt good being with someone who Punky once loved.

I eventually accepted that I may never see Punky again, and that's when I let Rory in. It was difficult at times; I suppose it still is. But being with Rory is easy. He has a very good job as an IT specialist. He had given up the life of crime because, without Punky, there wasn't a business to run.

And Brody Doyle, my *father*, ensured the Davieses and the Walshes knew their reign was over. It was his turn to rule both Belfast and Dublin. Without the Kellys, we had no choice but to start over. Most would say I should be thankful for the fact, but it's hard to forget someone who has given you so much to remember them by.

I have commuted back and forth between America and Northern Ireland for the past ten years. But when I accepted Rory's proposal, I knew I would call Northern Ireland my home, and I thought I was okay with that. But now that Punky is out…I don't know how to feel.

I never finished my performing arts degree because I couldn't commit to it. I've made it my life goal to help set Punky free. Because of this, I don't have a career like Darcy does. Back home, I work any job that pays.

As I only worked casual jobs, it allowed me to travel between here and America without having to worry about taking time off. I just quit and looked for another job when I went back home.

I shaped my life around Punky because deep down, I didn't feel deserving to live a full, prosperous life while he wasted away alone. But now that he's out, I can't help but look back on the last ten years with regret.

I would have done so many things differently. But I can't change the past.

"There ya are," Rory says, wrapping his arm low around my waist.

His colleague and wife stop talking and offer their congratulations to Rory. I feel horrible as I haven't listened to a word they've said.

Another group comes over, kissing our cheeks. Everyone is in good spirits, and I was too until a few minutes ago. Rory has picked up on my mood and politely makes up a lie as to why we have to leave. We walk through the packed room, and each step I take has my impending breakdown hastening.

Rory gently ushers me into the hallway, away from the guests. He hugs me softly. "Are ya all right?"

"Not really," I confess into his shoulder. "I didn't want Punky finding out this way. That's why I wanted to tell—"

But Rory cuts me off. "Ach, I know. I was wrong. I'm sorry. I didn't think Darcy would bring him here."

I can't help but narrow my eyes because I know she did that on purpose. But I don't let my anger show. "What's done is done. What did he say?"

I gently pull out of his arms, waiting for him to answer. When he sighs, I know the answer.

"He said he's happy for us."

"And," I coax, knowing there is more.

"And that I'm to treat ya right. Otherwise, he'll have no issues breakin' my arm."

I can't help but smile.

"I was wrong not to tell him sooner. Can ya forgive me?"

I cup his cheek. "Rory, there's nothing to forgive."

"I know the timin' isn't great, but we couldn't put our life on hold. We've already spent so much time—"

Now I'm the one to butt in. "I know. You're right. There's no need to explain."

Rory places his hand over mine, his love for me reflecting in his poignant green eyes. He and Punky are opposites. Punky always had the bad-boy image down pat, while Rory was more conservative. I guess that's why he, Punky, and Cian became best friends—opposites attract.

Rory's father, Cormac Walsh, comes over, not hiding his distaste for me. Rory assures me he does like me, but we both know he's lying. I think it's because he thinks his son is too good for me, and he's right.

His son deserves someone who isn't as fucked up as me.

"We're away to the ballroom. Let's toast the happy couple."

Rory nods while I smile, trying my best not to alert Cormac that I'm trembling inside.

Cian, Amber, and Hannah appear, wearing strained smiles on their faces. I know how hard this has been for Cian. He and Punky were always closer than Rory and Punky. I'd hate for him to think he has to pick a side.

Cian has been through so much. When his father took his own life, a part of him died too. We've all lost so much, and that's thanks to the man I refuse to acknowledge as my father.

He may have met his end of the deal, but that doesn't mean I'm grateful for what he did. He ruined our lives, and for what? For greed. He makes me sick. No wonder my mom wants nothing to do with him. And now that he's the most powerful man in Ireland and Northern Ireland, he thinks he can buy my love.

I have no idea what he wants.

He has Erin and Liam, children who actually want to know him, but that hasn't stopped him from sending flowers or texts, expressing his remorse for how things ended between us. He's delusional if he thinks I'll ever forgive him for what he did.

Thinking of his other child, Punky, the knot in my stomach only tightens.

Darcy and Punky make their way down the staircase, laughing about something. I hide my jealousy because he'll never laugh like that with me. We lock eyes before he dismisses me, returning his attention to Darcy, who looks stunning.

They look amazing together. On his arm, she shines.

Punky says something into Cian's ear. He laughs in response.

He doesn't seem too upset to find out that I'm marrying his best friend. *That's a good thing*, I remind myself. So why do I feel like bursting into tears?

I know the reason—because I don't feel the same way looking at him and Darcy together. I want to claw out her eyes.

I need to get over this. I need to remember that Punky is my half-brother.

A waiter zips past, but I stop him and grab two glasses of champagne off his silver tray. Rory thinks one glass is for him, but he's wrong. I throw back both, making a face as the alcohol hits my empty stomach.

"Let's go," Rory says, gently kissing my cheek, and when he does, I see something which pleases me immensely—Punky narrows his eyes, eyeballing the fuck out of Rory.

The sight gives me hope that he does care, that this is as weird for him as it is for me.

We know we can never be together the way we once were, but to see his mood sour this way shows me that I still affect him. I don't know why, but that makes me feel better. I don't feel like everything we experienced was all in my head.

Rory leads me toward the ballroom with our friends following close behind. I snare another glass of champagne from a waiter as we enter the room.

The moment we do, the room falls quiet before it explodes into joyous clapping. Everyone passes their congratulations onto us as we walk through the crowd, and suddenly, I feel claustrophobic. It's all too much.

I'm on autopilot, smiling and acting the part of the happy fiancée, but on the inside, I'm moments away from falling apart. Rory doesn't seem to notice and leads me to the front of the room where his mom and dad stand.

There is an elaborate white cake, feet away, and I suddenly realize, the next cake I'll see of this size will probably be my wedding cake. Sweat gathers along my brow as I wet my suddenly parched lips.

Our guests wait for us to speak, but Cormac takes the lead. "Thank you for comin' 'ere tonight to celebrate the engagement of our only son and his beautiful wife-to-be, Camilla."

The crowd erupts into applause while I try to smile even though I know Cormac is lying.

"Aileen and I are proud of you, son. Y've never backed down, and shown true strength in whatever life decisions y've made."

Rory nods in acknowledgment as Cormac raises his glass in salute.

"Yer a good man with a big heart. Yer willin' to overlook the past."

I shuffle uncomfortably because I suddenly feel like this speech is directed at me.

"Ye give people a second chance. And ya forgive. Yer kindness is somethin' ya got from yer ma."

The crowd chuckles while I gesture for the waiter to bring me another glass of champagne. This entire speech is Cormac's way of telling me that his son is perfect while I'm the whore who fucked her brother.

"So, let's raise our glasses and celebrate the happy couple. Cheers!"

The room clinks their glasses, drinking to Rory's and my engagement as I throw back my drink, suddenly light-headed from all the booze I've had in such a short amount of time.

Rory seems oblivious to the fact as he takes the microphone from his father so he can thank our guests. I stand off to the side, staring into the crowd, which suddenly looks double in size.

"Ach, that's a hard act to follow," Rory teases, looking at his father, who smirks.

I'm suddenly angered he would choose the words that he did because his passive-aggressive approach is not necessary. I know how he feels about me. He doesn't need to embarrass me in front of our guests—guests who have no right to judge me when Cormac isn't exactly an angel.

He once was best friends and in partnership with Connor Kelly, the biggest drug dealer and bad guy in all of Belfast. He has no right to make me feel bad for my past.

No right.

When Rory turns over his shoulder to look at me mid-speech, I realize I've spoken those words aloud. I try to act normal, but when my gaze falls on Darcy whispering something into Punky's ear, my ruse falters.

I quickly down another glass of champagne, hoping to suppress the need to throw up.

"To my beautiful fiancée, Camilla, I love you. I can't wait to spend the rest of my life with ya." Rory raises his glass while the masses follow and salute our happy union, all unaware of the conflict raging within me.

It's suddenly too much, and I'm going to be sick.

Before Rory has a chance to kiss me, I quickly excuse myself and make a beeline for the door, hand over my mouth to stop my vomit. Guests move out of my way, gossiping no doubt about my sudden departure. But let them talk. I don't care anymore.

The moment I find the nearest bathroom, I yank open the door and heave into the toilet. Gripping the toilet bowl, I dry retch, hoping to expel this emptiness I feel. But I only feel worse.

Something is seriously wrong with me.

Unrolling some toilet paper, I wipe my mouth and toss it into the toilet. Coming to a shaky stand, I flush it and make my way over to the basin. Peering into the mirror, I blanch when I see my pallid complexion. I look like shit.

My red ball gown would put any Disney Princess to shame, but I suddenly feel like a fraud. The thick jeweled bracelets confirm this as they conceal what I did. It's all too much, and I wonder if that is because I'm trying to make up for something that isn't there. I thought if I looked like a happy fiancée, I would surely feel like one.

But I don't.

All I feel is numb.

Turning on the faucet, I gulp down some water to clear my head, but the static isn't because I drank too much—no. I'm drunk on something, *someone* else, and I don't know what to do about it.

As I pop a mint from the conveniently placed glass bowl on the counter, there is a knock on the door. Before I can tell whoever it is that I'll be out in a minute, it opens, and who I see has me gripping the marble counter in fear I'll fall down.

Punky closes and locks the door. He doesn't move. He leans against it, watching me closely.

My heart begins to beat faster, and I'm suddenly animated in ways I never thought possible again.

"Some speech," he finally says, understanding why I left so suddenly to puke up my guts. "Don't let Cormac get to ya. He was always a self-entitled bastard."

I nod, embarrassed at how rapidly my breaths leave me.

Punky pushes off the door while I gulp, still clutching onto the counter for support.

"What's the matter, Babydoll?" he asks, his voice smooth, calm. "This should be a happy day."

"I-I am happy," I counter, but my falter proves me to be a liar.

He arches a smug brow, continuing his saunter toward me. "Happy days then."

When he gets within feet, he stops, watching me with those predatory eyes. I need to leave.

When I move to make a mad dash for the door, his hand snaps out, and he grips my forearm. The touch sets me alight, and I bite my cheek to suppress my moan. "Let me go."

Punky smirks, tonguing over his bottom lip. I'm instantly hit with the memory of how that bottom lip looked pierced. I whimper when I remember how it felt.

"So, Rory? I didn't realize ya felt that way about him."

"Neither did I," I respond sharply, trying to yank my arm

free. "But he was there for me when I needed him. When you refused to see me."

"That was awful convenient," he says, smirking. "I just find it…weird. I don't see ya havin' that much in common."

He's right.

We disagree on the smallest things, but opposites attract, and I love that he challenges me. That he isn't a yes-man.

"He's your best friend. You can't find it that weird," I argue, standing tall. "You know what a good person he is."

He reaches out while I forget to breathe as he runs a single finger along the seam of my mouth. "Aye, he's the best. I'm glad y've found yer happiness with him. When's the weddin'?"

"I-I don't know," I reply from around his finger. "We haven't set a date."

"And yer gettin' married here? Yer goin' to live in Belfast then?"

I nod, and my knees buckle when his signature fragrance hits me. He looks like my Punky, only older, harder maybe. I suppose being in jail for ten years does that to a person.

His blue eyes can still hold me prisoner, as does his entire being. He's built as the tux hugs his taut frame, allowing me to imagine his defined muscles beneath. His hair is longer, the dirty blond strands falling whichever way they flick naturally to give him a sexy bedhead look.

Even though he wears a tuxedo, I don't mistake him for a gentleman because he is anything but. And God strike me down, I like it. He still towers over me, even in my heels. I remember his weight pressed against me. I remember how I knew he could hurt me, but he never did.

He pushed me to the point of breaking, but that sort of pain had never felt that good. I grow wet between the legs at the memory.

My cheeks flush as I'm ashamed I can't control myself with him. I need to remember we're blood. I need to remember that I'm engaged.

"I think so. Rory and I haven't discussed the details. Now, if you'll excuse me."

But he doesn't let me go. Instead, he pulls me toward him, pressing us chest to chest. He peers down at me, the perfect poker face in play. "Why did ya not tell me Rory was yer fiancé when you came to see me?"

I lick my lips nervously.

I wanted to tell him, but I didn't know how. And I promised Rory we would do it together.

"I don't know," I confess, losing sight of what's right and what's wrong. "Why didn't you tell me you're Darcy's new pet?"

I regret the words the moment they leave me. But it's too late.

With a low growl, Punky shoves me up against the wall, holding me captive with his body. "I'm no one's pet," he snarls, inches from my face.

I laugh in response. "Could have fooled me. You're following her around like a little lost puppy."

He cups my throat, arching my neck back. "If I was, what business is it of yours?"

"It's not," I gasp as he squeezes tighter. "I don't blame you. After being starved for so long, anything will look appetizing."

Punky snickers while tonguing his cheek. "Ya think yer sweet pussy was the last I had, Babydoll?"

My cheeks instantly blush at his words. But they also heat because, what does that mean?

"I hate to disappoint ya, but yer cunt is a distant memory. There were quite a few who tended to me in more ways than one."

I don't let my emotions betray me, but does this mean he *did* see visitors in prison? Or that the prison staff crossed the line? Either way, I see red.

"Nice story. Tell it to someone who gives a fuck." I try to push him away, but he slams my back into the wall and raises my arms above my head. He secures my wrists in one hand.

"Good to see you're still a fucking asshole! Let me go."

He clucks his tongue as I fight him fruitlessly. "Still got a filthy mouth, is it. What else is still the same?"

He bends low and inhales deeply along the column of my neck.

Humming, he utters, "Sweet as always."

The low neckline of my dress exposes the tops of my breasts, rising and falling rapidly, betraying my arousal. The more he talks, the wetter I become, and the further I hate myself for it.

"Sweetness your best friend enjoys over and over again." I go on the attack, needing this to end before I do something I'll regret for the rest of my life.

Punky smirks, but there is nothing pleasant about it. "Fair play."

I'm expecting him to let me go, but he doesn't. He examines me slowly while I quiver under his watchful eye.

"Yer heart is racing."

"Is not," I uselessly argue because when he lets me go and places his hand over my chest, he can feel how my heart betrays me.

With the tips of his fingers, he gently brushes over the tops of my breasts. Millions of goosebumps prickle my skin. "Ya used to be such a good liar. That's something that has changed."

Instantly, I lower my gaze, embarrassed and ashamed. It's because of my lies Punky lost ten years of his life.

"Regardless of that big rock on yer finger, I know somethin' that's not changed."

"Punky, don't," I caution when he lowers his lips to mine. But the warning is weak because I want this—I want him.

"Don't what?" he asks, inches from my mouth as he places a hand against the wall. His breath is warm and sweet, and I want to be lost in it forevermore.

"Please don't do *this*." He needs to be the one to stop this because I don't have the strength to.

"Don't drop to my knees and bury my head between those parful legs of yours?"

A whimper escapes me because I want that and so much more.

"Don't lift yer dress and fuck ye up against this wall how we both want me to?"

He presses his erection into me, rubbing over me deliciously slow. My gown's thick material acts as a buffer, but I can still feel him, and my mouth waters at the sensation.

"No, we c-can't." But my resolve is failing.

"Why?" he questions, those blue eyes looking deep into my soul. "Because we're kin?"

Yes, that's a big reason, but I'm afraid if we cross that line, I will lose myself to him again, and this time, the damage we cause will be irreparable to so many.

"No, because Rory doesn't deserve this. Just because we're fucked up doesn't mean we have to take him down with us."

My confession has Punky squeezing his eyes shut. A moment later, he slams his fist against the wall. I flinch, afraid of what comes next.

He places a chaste kiss on my cheek before pulling away.

I wait for him to pounce, but he doesn't. He turns his back, his shoulders rising and falling with the deep breaths he takes. I should be relieved, but I'm not. I'm disappointed he stopped. That's how fucked up I am.

"Aye, yer right. Let's not speak of this again."

I wrap my arms around my middle, holding back the torrent of tears. Doing the right thing has never felt more wrong.

With a deep breath, Punky unlocks and opens the door, but when he hisses and instantly retreats back, guarding me with his body, my sadness is replaced with terror when I see what or, rather, *who* has caused him to respond this way.

"Ach, together at last," says Brody Doyle, our father—the man who destroyed our lives.

FIVE

PUNKY

My first instinct is to protect her.

And my second? Well, the second instinct is to rip out Brody's spleen and feed it to him.

Babydoll's accelerated breathing hints that Brody wasn't invited. She's just as surprised as I am at seeing him here. But Darcy seemed to know he was coming. I wonder how?

I can figure that out later because now, I need to salvage the last ten years of my life.

Brody enters the bathroom, closing the door behind him. He obviously wants privacy. My stance in front of Babydoll remains firm. He's going to have to go through me before he touches her.

I was seconds away from telling her the truth—that we're

not brother and sister. But when I asked her why we couldn't give in to what we both wanted, her response put everything into perspective.

"Because Rory doesn't deserve this. Just because we're fucked up doesn't mean we have to take him down with us."

She's right.

I lost sight of everything because all I could see was her.

I didn't care that my best friend was happy and living the life I wanted for him. All that mattered was giving in to temptation because my hunger for Babydoll has only grown, and I know that regardless of what's right or wrong, she feels this undeniable pull as well.

Her body responded to me just how it did ten years ago. She may love Rory, but it's clear our feelings for one another haven't diminished with time. Which is why I will never tell her the truth. If she believes we cannot be, then her feelings will eventually fade, and she and Rory can have a chance at living the life they both deserve.

Every part of me rebels at the thought, but what nearly happened is proof that together, we're on a collision course, bound to destroy anyone in our way. And I won't allow that to happen. I need to accept that Babydoll and I are better off apart.

The hunger she stirs in me is unbearable, but I won't let it win. I will treat her as if we are really related and forget that I want her more than I need air to fucking breathe.

"Bout ye, son?" asks Brody, smiling happily. "Look at ya.

Yer a big man now."

He almost sounds proud at the fact, that going to prison because he sent me there was a grand life lesson.

"How dare you!" Babydoll snarls from behind me. "You say that like it's something to be proud of. Puck was in jail because of you. You're not welcome here. Get out before I throw you out myself."

Brody chuckles, not at all intimidated by her demands. And why would he? He's the king of this fucking town.

"I'm a wee bit hurt ya didn't invite yer da to yer engagement," he says while Babydoll scoffs.

"You may have been the sperm donor, but you are not my dad. As far as I'm concerned, I have no father. And I'm totally fine with that."

Brody merely smiles in response. But what I say next wipes his smile clean.

"I thought y'd have better things to do, like trackin' down Sean. I mean, surely ya know he's not dead?"

Babydoll gasps while Brody's jaw clenches. "I can't say I do."

But he's lying.

Although he may not want to believe it, I'm certain he's heard rumors about the fact. However, without proof, he has merely passed it off as hearsay. I'm here to change that.

"I think we have some things to discuss in private."

"I'm not going anywhere," Babydoll argues, and I know this is a fight I won't win.

So, I put my plan into action as I confront Brody.

"We both know that's a lie, but I suppose honesty isn't a quality ya possess. Yer sloppy. And yer fucking arrogant. Yer not untouchable. You may think that ye are, but yer not. Sean is smarter than ya. He also has somethin' that you don't. And that's the Kelly name.

"Don't you ever forget that we once ruled Northern Ireland, and if Sean is intendin' to return, then ya won't stand a chance against him. He managed to fool ya once. The second time around, he won't be so generous."

"Ye know an awful lot, considerin' ya just got out of prison. Ya shouldn't be believin' everythin' ya hear."

I smirk, taking great pleasure in seeing him squirm. "Suit yerself. But don't say I didn't warn ya when he comes for yer head."

Brody folds his arms across his chest. "What concern is it of yers, anyway?"

"'Cause that cunt has fooled my wee brother, and for that, I will do everythin' to take him down. I won't stand back and let him ruin Ethan's life. He's cancer, a cancer which needs to be cut out."

Babydoll is silent throughout the exchange as I know this is news to her.

"So, what do you propose then?"

Levelling Brody, I detail my plans, knowing he'll listen because deep down, he's afraid of the power Sean still holds.

"I'm goin' to smoke him out. He believes I don't know of his plans, but he's underestimated my hatred for him."

As a twitch spasms under Brody's left eye, I see it. He's read between the lines—he realizes I've uncovered the truth. He knows I've found out who my real father is.

"And y've underestimated yer men. Y've given them more credit than they deserve, for Sean has recruited them. He's building an army, and he's waitin', waitin' for the perfect time to strike and bring ye down. And when he does, ya won't stand a chance."

Brody doesn't say a word, but for me to come to him with this information, he understands I have an inside source—Sean's journal. Written in his own hand, I have Sean's plans detailed in black and white, and with Hannah's sighting of him and Ethan's attack on me, I know he's putting those plans into action.

"Why are ya tellin' me this?"

"'Cause we both want the same thing. Sean dead, and for real this time."

"And ya think I need ye for that? If I wanted him dead, then I'd have it done. Things have changed, Punky. Yer no longer in charge. I'm the one in control now."

I burst into a cynical snicker. "Ach, is that so? Is that why Sean was able to fool ya into thinkin' he was dead? Or that ye'd actually be partners once ye were rid of Connor and me?"

Brody's cheeks flush in anger. "Ye cheeky wee hallion. Ya

don't know anythin.'"

"All right. You go on believin' that. But when Sean takes everythin' from ya, don't say I didn't warn ya."

I stand composed, knowing I've won.

"What do you have that a hundred men don't?"

Apart from the fact that this is personal to me, I have one thing that no one, not even Brody, has.

"Sean fears me," I state with confidence because it's true. "He knows I have nothin' left to lose. And I won't stop until one of us is dead."

Brody ponders over my words, realizing I mean every single one.

"I know my…uncle," I say, ensuring he understands the pause was intentional. "I know how he thinks, how he can win yer trust without ya even knowin' it. And when he has ya where he wants ya, he'll strike. Yer livin' on borrowed time."

"Ye want to work together, is it?" he asks with a deep snicker. That soon stops when I nod firmly.

"Aye. I want to form an alliance with ya. Ya need me, and I need you."

"How?" Brody questions, eyes narrowed. He has every right not to trust me, but for him to still be here, he knows I'm right.

"Ya need someone to remind yer men that *yer* the leader, not Sean. They've strayed, just how our men once did because yer no longer feared or respected."

Brody storms forward, fisting the lapels of my suit jacket

and drawing us nose to nose.

"Let him go!" Babydoll demands, but my grin hints that I'm the one in control. Brody losing his cool is a sure sign of this.

"Fuck ye. I should kill ya right now."

"Go on then," I challenge, never breaking eye contact with him. "But I have a sneakin' suspicion that if ya wanted me dead, I'd already be so. I'm alive 'cause ya know that ye need me. Ya always knew that I'm more valuable to ya alive than I am dead."

"If what ya say is true, then I'm just expected to believe ya won't double-cross me how yer *uncle* did?"

Tonguing my cheek, I don't take the bait. He wants me to explode. Wants me to confess I know that Sean is my dad, not Brody. But I will not.

"I want no part in it," I declare resolutely. "Besides, what allies do I have? Ten years is a long fucking time. I'd have to start from scratch, and I don't have the patience for that. I want revenge on Sean for killing Connor and for stealin' my life.

"That's it. You can have Belfast. All I want is Sean's head."

Brody lets me go, his anger palpable. But he believes me because he thinks I want revenge on Sean for lying to me about being my father and killing my ma. And I do. But I want my legacy back as well.

In saying that, however, I know he won't trust me, but he'll work with me because he needs me. And I need him. He knows I'm the only one who can take Sean down because I'm a Kelly. I think like a Kelly. And I'm Sean's son.

This partnership is similar to the one he entered into with Sean. If he had done the job right the first time around, he wouldn't be in this predicament. But I'm glad that he didn't, because now, I get to kill both him and Sean for the error of their ways.

"It's a lot to take in. Ye know where I am when ya make the right choice. But trust me, Sean is huntin' ya, and he will not stop until he gets what he wants. Look what he did to my ma. She double-crossed him, and in return, he fuckin' killed her."

Brody's eyebrows shoot up into his hairline. "Ach, so ye know the truth then?"

"Aye. I know he killed her because she had a secret that would destroy him. I know that he killed Connor because he wanted what is now yours. Don't ever mistake yerself as safe, 'cause yer not. None of us are."

Whether he knows I've uncovered that he's the third man who killed my ma, I do not know. But he will.

"This is all an interestin' story, but yer an…ex-Kelly, and I don't do business with Kellys." I *am* a Kelly, but he doesn't want Babydoll to know that. "I learned that the hard way. So, there is no deal. Enjoy yer freedom, and remember, if ya try to outsmart me, I'll kill ya."

A hoarse laugh leaves me. "You and what army? Yer men are traitors, and sooner or later, y'll see that ya need me. I know this because Sean did this to my da. His own flesh and blood. Can ya imagine what he'd do to you?"

Brody has heard enough, and that's because he knows I'm right. "Congratulations again, Camilla. I've left yer gift downstairs. Annette sends her wishes."

Annette? I'm assuming this is Brody's wife?

Before she can respond, Brody opens the door and exits, leaving me the winner. He'll be back. I've given him food for thought, and he'll soon see he needs me.

But now, I need to deal with the wrath of Babydoll.

"What the *fuck* are you thinking?" she questions, her horror over what she just witnessed clear.

I'm going to be as honest as I can. "I wish I could do this without him. But we're stronger together. And I won't let him slip past me again.

"Better I have one arsehole huntin' me than two, which is what will happen if I don't have Brody on my side. I will be fightin' him *and* Sean, and I know that I will lose."

"You think because he's your father, he's just going to trust you?"

I conceal my feelings because Babydoll has no idea how fucked up this entire thing is.

"You're wrong, Punky. He's going to kill you. You've just told him what he needs to know about Sean, and he'll deal with it accordingly. And what the fuck? Sean is alive? He…killed your mom? How do you know all this?"

She begins to pace, and I realize I haven't looked at her since Brody entered the bathroom. Turning slowly, I'm hit with her beauty, just how I am every time I lay eyes on her.

I give her time and space as I know it's a lot to take in. This is why I wanted to talk to Brody in private. But knowing Babydoll, there was no way she would let that happen.

"Ethan tried to kill me. I went to visit my ma's and Connor's graves, and he was there. Dressed in a balaclava, too fucking gutless to face me. Sean sent him, and it was a test Ethan failed."

Babydoll covers her mouth with a trembling hand.

"I let him go because I will not give up on him. Sean will not destroy his life as he did to mine. I let Ethan and Hannah down, but I'll make it up to them," I reveal, still feeling the guilt eat away at me. "And if that means sidin' with Brody Doyle, then so be it."

"I don't understand why Sean has waited this long. I mean, he could have taken Brody down by now. How do you even know he's still here? What's he waiting for?"

"I know he's close because predators stay where they're comfortable. Belfast is his home. He's waitin' for the right time, Babydoll. He almost had that, but he never saw us comin'. We ruined his plans, and he won't have that happenin' again."

"Why can't you just kill them both?"

"I wish I could. But the truth is, Brody's men know where Sean is hidin'. They will surely tell me where. If not, I'll carve out their tongues. If I kill Brody, what happens then? I need him alive so I can steal his allies and the few men who are still loyal to him.

"I know this plan is far from perfect, but it's easier if I work with Brody than against him. We both want Sean dead. He will see that I won't stop until I get what I want."

"What's going to happen?" Babydoll asks, her eyes filling with tears.

"I suspect Brody is going to confront his men and make an example of a few. But it's too late for that, just how it was for us. Sean managed to steal everythin' from Connor, and his plan would have worked if it wasn't for us.

"We were the force he didn't see comin'. If I hadn't asked questions and Brody hadn't used ye to infiltrate us, Sean would have won."

"That doesn't excuse what I did," she cries, unable to look at me. "You lost ten years of your life because of my lies."

Stepping forward, I gently lift her chin with my pointer. "Naw, that was my choice. Don'tcha be blamin' yerself for that."

Her lower lip quivers. "What do you mean?"

Sighing, I shake my head. "Now is not the time. Rory will be lookin' for ya."

Something I can't quite place overcomes her, and she subtly removes herself from my touch. She's angry I won't tell her the truth. "This makes no sense. Why can't you go to the police?"

"How did that turn out the last time the peelers were involved?" I pose. "I understand this is reckless and fucking dangerous, but I have no one. I need to start from scratch."

"You have me," she professes in a whisper.

"I won't be havin' that. There's no way I'll allow ya to risk yer life—again."

She pulls back her shoulders. "That's not for you to decide. I'm involved, whether you like it or not."

"Or not," I counter, forgetting just how stubborn she is. "This isn't yer fight. Rory will agree with me on that."

She narrows her eyes as she knows I'm right. "Fuck you both. I'm my own person. Neither of you has the right to tell me what I can or can't do."

"Aye, yer right. But I don't need ye." And what I say next has the impact I suspected it would. "I don't want ya."

She blinks once, her surprise clear. She's taken it how I knew she would—personally. But this is the only way I can keep her safe.

"But you want Darcy? Is that it?"

My silence is all the response she needs.

"Fine. Have it your way then. You always do." She pushes past me and opens the door, slamming it shut behind her.

Once she's gone, I stare into the mirror, my knackered appearance confirming I look as shit as I feel. I can't have Babydoll involved in this. She and Rory have a shot at happiness, and I won't stand in the way of that.

A knock sounds on the door before it opens, and Cian appears. "What happened?"

With a laugh, I turn toward him and shake my head. "It's times such as this that I miss solitary confinement."

"Ach, stop bustin' my bollocks. I told ya I was sorry. And I promised Rory."

I understand the predicament Cian was put in. He was caught in a very uncomfortable position because it wasn't his place to tell me Rory and Babydoll were engaged. But I still can't help but feel it's me versus the people I once trusted with my life. Except for Darcy.

She's the only one who's been honest with me this whole time.

"I saw Brody leave. What did he want?"

"It doesn't matter what he wants. This is about gettin' what I want. And I have no doubt that'll come about awful soon."

"Ya told him the plans?"

"Aye. He'll come around," I say, having complete faith. "Now that I've planted the seed, it'll grow."

Cian's cheeks billow as he exhales loudly. "So what do we do now?"

"Now, ya go and enjoy the festivities. I'm goin' home."

Cian appears guilty for the fact, but I won't have it. This is a happy time for Rory. He deserves at least one friend here to help him celebrate. Before Cian can protest, I bring him in for a loose hug and leave him behind.

"There ya are," Darcy says as I walk down the hallway.

I was hoping to remain undetected, but she is technically my date, so I suppose I owe her an explanation. "I'm goin' to catch a taxi home. You stay, though."

She shakes her head. "Naw, I'll take ya. Besides, I don't think I'm welcome here anymore."

I know that's because she brought me here.

I don't argue as I want to ask her how she knew Brody was going to be here. We leave without saying goodbye.

When the valet brings the car around, Darcy gestures with her head that I'm to drive.

"I don't have a current license," I say, but Darcy smirks.

"Since when have you ever followed the rules, Puck Kelly?"

"Aye, I suppose yer right," I reply, ignoring good sense and getting behind the wheel.

The moment Darcy buckles in, I plant my foot onto the accelerator and speed down the drive. She yelps, reaching for the grab handle, but I don't slow down. I've not driven for so long. I've forgotten the thrill of being in control.

Darcy turns down the radio as if I need the silence to concentrate, but it only has me going faster.

"Y've obviously not forgotten how to drive," Darcy states, white-knuckling the seat belt across her chest.

Her fear only spurs me on.

"How'd ya know Brody was comin' tonight?"

"My dad does business with him."

Turning to look at her, I ask in horror, "What?"

"Keep yer eyes on the road!" she exclaims, recoiling back in her seat when I aggressively overtake the car in front of me.

But I'm in control.

What I'm not in control of, however, is Patrick Duffy doing business with the man who played a part in Connor's death and the end of the Kelly name.

"The fuck is yer da doin' business with that arsehole?"

Darcy appears regretful for the overshare. "Just like everyone else in this town, he's afraid of Brody Doyle. If yer not with him, then yer dead. There's no way around that, which is why…" Her pause has me gripping the steering wheel in anticipation.

"Which is why I needed to get ye out of prison. Yer the only one who can stop him."

I'm not surprised Darcy had an ulterior motive. Nor am I angry at the fact either. But I don't understand why she's so confident that I can put him down like the sick dog that he is.

"Is that right?" I question, interested to know her reasoning.

"Yes. I know he's afraid of you. I've heard him speak to my father about ye. How he's glad ya were in prison because yer the only worthy opponent capable of bringin' him down. But ya were in prison 'cause of him. He was braggin' 'bout that. And that is why I needed to get ya out.

"He stole Belfast from ya. These past ten years have been hell without ya, Punky. Everyone lives in fear. At least when the Kellys ruled, they looked out for us. But now, no one trusts anyone anymore. Brody rules with fear, while Connor, he ruled with respect."

I clench my jaw because her claim makes me feel

uncomfortable. To speak of Connor this way reveals that even though he lost the respect of most of his men, he made those he did business with feel safe. They trusted him, and that's why his associates never turned on him, which is why Sean needed Brody to help beat Connor.

"Brody was talkin' with my da, and I casually mentioned the engagement party and that I was bringin' ya as my date. I knew Brody would take the bait."

Darcy is far more cunning than I ever thought she was. Because of her plotting, I've been able to plant the first step in my plans. Brody and I were able to talk without violence because he knew better than to cause a scene with so many witnesses on hand.

"Thanks, Darcy. Y've done so much for me. For my family. I don't know how to repay ya."

When she gently places her hand on my leg, I try to remain calm. "Just kill that fucker, and make sure he suffers. That's all I want."

"Why is this so personal to ya?"

When she removes her hand, I realize there is so much more to this story. "Let's just say yer not the only one who has a vendetta against the Doyles."

"What did they do to ya?" I ask, turning to look at her.

She dips her chin, attempting to hide her tears. But I see them, and I know they've hurt her. "I didn't know who he was, but I should have known us meetin' wasn't a coincidence."

"Who?"

She turns to look out her window, unable to face me as she confesses, "Liam Doyle. He seduced me so his father could become close to mine. And when both Doyle men got what they wanted, Liam dumped me.

"He humiliated and lied to me," she admits. "And for that, I want him to pay. If it wasn't for me, maybe my dad would never have gotten into business with Brody. I blame myself for it."

"Don't be blamin' yerself," I say, assuring her. "The Doyles are poison and would have infected yer da with or without yer help."

"But they did have my help," she argues, quickly wiping away her tears with the back of her hand. "And I'll never forgive myself for it."

I suddenly see Darcy in a different light. She too wants to make right the wrongs of her past, and I respect her for that. So I'll help her.

"I thought he really loved me," she professes with a tremble before covering her face with her hands. "What's wrong with me, Punky? Why do I fall in love with the wrong men?"

I don't know what to say as most would say something comforting like the right man is out there. Or it's not you, it's them. But the truth is, sometimes, life is just unfair.

I pull up the drive of my house and park the car, a million thoughts racing around my head. Darcy realizes the answers she seeks are not here and gets out of her car. She doesn't say a word as I get out as well, only for her to slide into the driver's seat and pull away, leaving me with more questions than answers.

Freedom is suddenly not what I thought it would be.

SIX

PUNKY

I'm quiet, lost in my thoughts and thinking about Darcy and what she revealed about Liam Doyle.

Cian is helping me clean out the castle, and when he tries to playfully tackle me, I strike out and punch him in the jaw. It's a knee-jerk reaction, one which I learned being locked behind bars with the depraved.

"Fuck!" he curses, cupping his chin. "I was just playin'."

"I'm sorry," I quickly apologize, flinching when I see I've busted his lip open. "Bad habits die hard, I suppose."

"What happened to ya in there? Yer…different."

Of course, he'd assume Riverbend House is a "normal" prison where officers look out for the well-being of prisoners. But there is nothing normal about that place.

"Whatever ya believe Riverbend House to be, it is not. The officers are more depraved and corrupt than the inmates."

I understand he's curious about what my life has been like for the past ten years. But the truth is, I don't feel comfortable sharing that with him yet. I don't want him knowing all the vile things I did and enjoyed doing.

"I want to know what happened to my best friend," he presses with sincerity.

I appreciate it. "Maybe one day, but not today."

He nods, accepting my reply.

"Let's throw out the boggin' couch next," he says, changing the subject.

Cian has offered to help me clean the castle up because it's more than a one-man job. A builder Hannah found online is coming out today to look at the damage. I'm expecting the worst.

I've told Cian not to stray too far without me. Not because I'm worried the unstable structure will collapse and render him unconscious, but rather, I don't know who is lurking in the shadows—take your pick, it could be anyone.

The crunching of gravel has both Cian and I turning to see a police car coming up the drive.

"The fuck they want?" he asks while I shrug.

The guns and knives Cian brought over are hidden away, so we're in the clear. The weapons are hardly the arsenal I need, but they'll do until I can get my hands on something that packs a little more heat.

We wait for the officer to exit the car. I have no idea who he is, but when Cian curses under his breath, it's obvious this peeler is known to him. He adjusts his belt, ensuring we see his gun. I roll my eyes at his desperate attempt to flaunt his authority.

"Mornin," he says, eyeing us closely when he notices Cian's bleeding lip.

"Hi," Cian replies while I don't bother.

It's obvious he sees me as nothing but a criminal.

"I wanted to introduce myself," he explains. "I'm Constable Shane Moore."

I merely look at him, hinting if he has a point, then to make it.

I don't realize the significance of his surname and Cian's reaction to him until he says, "Donovan Moore was my father."

Cian waits for me to respond, and when I chuckle, he sighs, knowing this won't end well.

"Ach, the chief constable's son, here in the flesh. To what do I owe this pleasure?" I sarcastically say because this arsehole is not welcome here.

His father is the reason I was thrown into prison so he could climb the ranks, uncaring I was rotting in hell. I don't fail to notice his use of past tense.

"What happened to him then? I'd love to catch up on old times over a pint."

Cian conceals his snort of laughter behind a cough.

Shane's cheeks turn a brutal red. "My da died two years ago. Heart attack."

"Only the good die young," I quip, ensuring Shane knows I'm happy that the bastard is dead. "So, what do ya want? Yer here to lend a hand?"

The corded veins in Shane's neck reveal he is trying his best to stop from using his hands to choke the life from me. "I'm 'ere 'cause I want ya to know I'm keepin' an eye on ya."

"Are ye the welcomin' committee?" I say, never breaking eye contact with him. "I'll run some fifteens over to the cap shap to express mi thanks."

If this arsehole thinks he can come here and intimidate me, he is sorely mistaken. I've dealt with far worse monsters than him.

"Yer da was awful attentive toward the Kellys too. Like father, like wee son. Now, if y'll excuse me, we've been up to ninety since half seven. I've got to throw away ten years' worth of filth, so I better get back to work. And I'm sure yer busy, chasin' crime, so y'are."

My words are dripping with innuendo and sarcasm, something which Shane doesn't appreciate.

He advances forward but soon remembers he's wearing a uniform and stops. His nostrils flare, expressing his anger. "I'll be seein' ya around, Puck Kelly."

"All the best, Stuart," I say with a wave, deciding to bait him further by deliberately using a different name.

He doesn't correct me and storms off. He rakes down the drive, leaving dust in his wake.

"Thon wee fella has a face like a bulldog chewing a wasp," Cian says, shaking his head.

"Aye, he's a waste of space, just like his da. He made a mistake comin' here. I now know he's watchin' us. We've got to be careful."

Cian nods. "What a wee want. He came here to whip out his cock when he should have stayed hidden."

"There's no cure for stupid, Cian, and Shane Moore's gene pool is drownin' in stupidity. He wanted to assert his authority, but he's small fry. Now we know the peelers aren't on our side."

"Who is?" Cian asks, expressing his concerns.

I don't reply because honestly, I don't know. There are so many unanswered questions, but I'm certain about one thing and that is: I have no doubt Brody will be in touch soon. Once he is, we can get the ball rolling.

A truck turns into the drive, alerting us that the builder has arrived. He parks the car, and when he exits, both Cian and I turn toward the other, shook.

We know him.

Ronan Murray.

I'm transported back in time to when Ronan was tied to a chair, begging for his life. Rory, Cian, and I decided to let him go even though he was a traitor. He was the scapegoat we needed and was used to throw the Doyles off course.

But that all turned to shite.

"The fuck ya doin' here?" Cian says, half in awe, the other in anger. "We gave ya one chance, and ye fucked it up."

When he goes to retrieve the gun from the small of his back, I stop him. I want to know why Ronan would come here willingly. This address is known to him, and I'm certain he heard I was out. So why would he risk it?

"What's the craic, Ronan?"

Ronan keeps his distance. "Hi, Punky. Y've grown."

"Aye, that's what happens when ten years pass," I reply, not interested in small talk. "Why would ya come here when ye knew the consequences?"

Ronan looks at the ground. "'Cause I want a second chance."

Cian scoffs, while I cannot believe the bollocks on Ronan. "Second chance with what?"

"I want to regain yer trust and help rebuild yer empire. Northern Ireland is rightfully yours. Yer da would be turnin' in his grave. God rest his soul."

A laugh leaves me, but it's not a happy sound. "Why the fuck would I trust ya? After everythin' y've done. I should cut out yer tongue and feed it to ye for speaking such filth."

He knows I speak the truth because he was there when I cut off Aidan Doyle's lips.

"You were happy to sacrifice my siblings to save yer own arse. I don't do business with people like ya."

The memory of Ronan using the twins as bargaining chips still enrages me as it did ten years ago.

"I would not have done that to them," he frantically explains. "I would have said anythin' to get out of there."

His excuses have me curling my lip in disgust. "Yer weak, and yer also a fucking traitor. Away ta fuck, before I finish what I started ten years ago."

Ronan doesn't move, however, and that's because he has something or, rather, *someone* I want. "I know where Sean is."

And just like that, Ronan has signed his own death warrant.

"How would ya know that?" I ask, folding my arms across my chest.

"Because he approached me, askin' if I wanted back in," he reveals in a rushed breath. "I told him I was on the straight and narrow. That my business was goin' well. He said if I ever changed my mind, that he was havin' a meetin' tomorrow."

I take a deep breath. "Where?"

"I don't know yet."

Cian scoffs as he's clearly heard enough. "Well, what good are ye then?"

He takes off into a sprint, chasing after Ronan, who uses his truck as a barricade. "But he said he'd send a text an hour before. I can tell ya where then," Ronan pleads.

"Cian, enough," I say lightly as they're making me seasick with their running around.

"Ye surely don't believe this dick," Cian exclaims, looking

at me. "He was workin' with Sean *and* Brody. He is a double-crossing fuck who cannot be trusted."

And he's right. But Ronan is the break we need. Even if this is a trap, it'll get me face-to-face with Sean. "Why would ya want to help me?"

"It's because of Sean and Brody that I was exiled, forced to leave Belfast when they wanted nothin' to do with me," he declares, his sincerity clear. "Youse could have killed me, but ye spared me. I owe youse my life. This is my way of sayin' I'm sorry. Of payin' ye back so I'm no longer indebted to ya.

"This is my way to say sorry to yer da."

I will probably regret this decision, but I believe him.

"Punky, no," Cian says, reading my expression instantly.

I understand his concerns, but this is my choice. If he turns around and leaves me to deal with the repercussions on my own, there would be no hard feelings. But I know Cian—he'll never let me down.

"If yer lying, and there's a good chance that y'are, know that I will make ya watch as I torture and then kill yer family. Every single one of them."

My threat isn't empty. I mean every single word.

Ronan nods calmly. "I understand. I will not let ya down."

"Again," Cian adds, shaking his head.

With that settled, Ronan opens the car door, but I arch a brow. "Where are ya goin'?"

Ronan freezes, lost in translation. So I decide to clarify.

"Yer a builder, are ya not?"

"Aye. I am."

Gesturing toward the castle, I smile. "Then do yer job. I called ya out here for a reason."

Cian curses under his breath, while Ronan quickly reaches into the back of his truck for his toolbox.

"Don'tcha think 'bout rippin' me off now. Otherwise, I'll return the favor. But I'll be rippin' out yer spleen."

Ronan smiles, but it's strained, for he knows he's walking a thin line. However, if what he says is true, then he'll prove to be one of our biggest allies. Lucky, we didn't kill him, after all.

Ronan's quotes are very reasonable, but I'm pretty sure he gave me a discount, fearing for his life if I wasn't happy with the price.

Cian reminded me every chance he got what a stupid idea trusting Ronan is—in case I had forgotten—but this is happening. I have no other way to get to Sean, and even if this is a setup, at least it'll get me in the same room as him.

He is too much of a narcissist not to end me himself. He wants it to be his face I see when he finishes what he started ten years ago. That's how I can be so certain that he will be there. He wouldn't allow anyone else to kill his son.

Reaching for my whiskey, I gulp it down, needing to wash away the reality that Sean Kelly is my dad. It's still a hard pill to swallow. Father hunting son. Son hunting father. Ironically, I never called Connor my da, and I will never call Sean that either. But looking back, I realize Connor will always be more of a father than Sean ever will.

My phone rings, thankfully interrupting this pity party for one.

It's a private number, which raises suspicions. So I decide to let it go to voicemail. Once the screen lights up, alerting me I have one voice message, I go through the prompts to listen.

At first, all I hear is background noise, like the caller is at a pub with a rowdy crowd, but through that, there is no mistaking a voice I'd recognize even in the pits of hell.

"I don't know what I'm doing anymore," Babydoll slurs before the line goes dead.

I listen to the message three more times, in case I missed anything, and when I hear the faint tolling of a bell tower, I know where she is. I have no idea what her message means, but I'm not about to wait around to find out.

The sensible thing to do would be to call Rory, but if Babydoll called me without him knowing, then I don't want to upset either of them. Grabbing the truck keys off the wooden dining table Hannah surprised me with today, I quickly sprint to Cian's truck.

I don't have a current license, but I don't care. I have a

sinking feeling in my guts that something is wrong. All that matters is getting to Babydoll. I don't think twice as I slip the key into the ignition, put the truck into gear, and rake down the drive.

The tolling bell hints that Babydoll is somewhere near Queen's Square. There are many pubs around there, but I will search every one until I find her. I could message Hannah and ask for Babydoll's number. But I don't want anyone involved in this.

I try my best to keep to the speed limit, but the farther I travel, the more anxious I become to find Babydoll. The drive takes me half the amount of time it would if I drove legally, and I park in the first space I find.

Locking the car, I quickly use the map on my phone to locate the nearest pubs as things have changed in ten years. There are places I can remember, and others that I can't.

I start at the first pub I can find and work my way through a dozen or so, coming up empty. But that doesn't deter me as I continue searching for Babydoll. She's got to be here.

I notice a lot of places I used to know are closed down. I wonder what happened as some businesses have been here for decades.

One place which still stands is Bull and Crow, an Irish pub that has been around for generations. The place is jammers— just as I remember it being. Cian, Rory, and I frequented this pub, and when I scan the room and see her sitting in a red booth alone, it seems Babydoll does as well.

Half a dozen empty pint glasses litter the table, and I wonder if she's alone. Maybe she's here with friends? I decide to wait just in case.

I sit at the bar, discreetly watching Babydoll, who nurses a pint as she stares blankly ahead. It appears she's lost in another world.

"Puck Kelly?" a familiar voice says in awe.

Peering up, I see Ollie Molony, the owner of Bull and Crow standing behind the bar.

Ollie was a good friend of Connor's, but he never once outed us when we came in here, drinking underage. For that, we respected him.

"Ollie." I smile, extending my hand and shaking his over the bar. "Good to see ya again."

"I don't believe my eyes. Look at ya," he says, his brown eyes taking in ten years' worth of change. "Let me get ye a pint."

But I wave my hand. "Naw, I'm here to pick up my friend."

He arches a brow, and when I turn my attention to Babydoll, he sighs. "The wee lass has been 'ere for hours. I thought Rory would be comin', but she's been drinkin' alone…which is never a good thing."

"That's the truth, so it is," I agree, looking at her. "It was good seein' ye, Ollie."

I go to stand, but he reaches across the bar and grips my wrist. I peer down, confused. There is a desperation beneath his touch.

"Could I trouble ya for a moment?"

"Course. Is everythin' all right?"

Ollie ensures no one is earwiggin' as he leans in close. "Are ya back?"

He doesn't want to say too much as no matter how careful one is, someone is always listening.

"Maybe. But it's a long road ahead. What Connor left behind…it's gone."

"We want to help," he shares softly, his eyes darting around the room.

"Help?"

Ollie nods. "That fucker, Brody Doyle, he's bleedin' us dry. But if we don't do business with him, then yer the enemy. Just take a look around, Punky, and y'll see what happened to those who rebelled."

That explains what happened to the businesses which are no more.

"What's he want with youse?"

"With the Kellys gone, we've been at the mercy of other rival families, wantin' to take control. Brody has offered us protection, for a fee, of course."

"That fucker," I mumble under my breath. "How much?"

"Half of our monthly earnin's," he reveals with regret. "We're barely pullin' through. But if we don't pay, we'll end up like the rest of them who said no to the Doyles. Liam Doyle is just as bad as his father."

The Doyles are offering "protection," but the truth is, this is an extortion racket. Ollie doesn't pay, and he's open to attack from the Doyles, as well as others who want to take over Belfast.

"What a fucking mess," I say, running a hand through my hair.

I never knew what Connor actually did for this town. I now see it was a lot. When he ruled, there were no rivalries because everyone knew not to fuck with the Kellys. But everything has turned to shite since his death.

I never respected the aul' lad, but that's starting to slowly change.

"We never wanted to side with him, but my wee grandkids—"

"It's all right, Ollie," I say, cutting him off. "There's no need to explain."

There are no hard feelings. No one knows the truth. They all thought I was sent to prison for organizing the death of many men, including Sean and Connor. I'm sure my friends defended my honor, but with Brody tainting my name and putting the fear of God into friends and foe, I was soon a forgotten memory.

"I never believed what the papers said. We all knew ye'd never steal from yer da and hurt him."

"Thank you, Ollie. I appreciate that. Yer right. Brody Doyle set me up. He blackmailed me. I didn't have much of a choice but to disappear."

I regret that decision as I should have fought harder. But at the time, I believed I deserved to be sent to prison as punishment for the deaths of Sean and Connor. Sean knew me too well and realized this was the only way to get rid of me for good.

If only I knew the real story, how things would have turned out differently.

"I fucking knew it!" he declares, slamming his fist on the bar. "Y've always been a good lad, Punky, and now, yer a man, a man yer da would be proud of. Whatever ya need from me, know that my loyalties are with ya."

I don't know how to respond to his claim, so I nod, needing a moment to take it all in.

If Brody is extorting Ollie, I'm certain he's doing it to many others, and this is what I need to use to reinstate the Kelly name.

Connor never exploited his friends—he took care of them as well as Belfast. But now, this town is a fucking mess. Brody has no ties to Belfast. It's merely a place of business for him. But this is my home, and I'm taking it back.

Ollie is someone I trust. He has no reason to lie to me.

"Tell those who will listen that I'm back," I state firmly, adrenaline and hope coursing through my veins. "And that I'm goin' to return Belfast to her former glory. I'm the new leader now, and I will protect yousens against them Doyles, and any other fucker who wants to take what is rightfully mine. What is ours."

I can't let Ollie know about Sean.

"Now we're suckin' diesel!" Ollie hollers, his eyes wild with excitement.

"A'll be in touch soon. There are a few things I need to arrange. But don'tcha be worryin' 'bout anythin'. Brody Doyle's days are numbered."

I shake Ollie's hand, as this conversation is over for now. When we talk next, it'll be away from prying ears.

I leave Ollie smiling, the man I knew returning because I've just given him something we've all been robbed of, thanks to Brody Doyle—hope.

Someone who isn't smiling, however, is Babydoll, who still hasn't noticed I'm here. She simply sits like a statue, occasionally sipping her pint.

Taking a seat opposite her, I lean back in the booth. "Drinkin' alone is minus craic, Babydoll. And from the looks of it, I think y've had enough alone time."

She snaps from her daze, her glassy eyes attempting to focus on me. She is completely blootered. "What makes you think I'm alone? And I'll be the judge of when I've had enough."

She draws the glass to her lips, spilling most of the pint down the front of her dress as she attempts to act like she's in control.

"All right." I reach over the table and lower her hand. "That's enough. I'm takin' ye home."

She recoils violently, her drink sloshing all over her and the table. She's a mess—both inside and out.

"Why are you even here?" she slurs angrily, wiping her lips with the back of her hand.

"'Cause ya called me," I retort softly.

"I did not," she argues, but we both know that's not true. "I don't even know your number."

"Fine then, ya didn't call me and yer not absolutely hammered. Let's go."

I go to stand, but Babydoll leans back, folding her arms across her chest in defiance. "I'm not going anywhere with you. I hate your stupid face."

"Aye, I hate my stupid face too," I agree, wishing for this conversation to be over with. "So the sooner we leave, the sooner ya can stop lookin' at it."

She merely turns her cheek, refusing to budge.

Leaning across the table slowly, I grip her chin and turn her face so our lips are inches apart. A breathless whimper escapes her. Every part of me wants to eat her alive.

"You can either come willingly…"

"Or?" she challenges, her sweet breath tempting me to lean forward and steal it from her.

"Or I'll throw ya over my shoulder and carry ye out, kickin' and screamin'."

"You wouldn't dare," she snarls, eyes narrowed.

A smirk spreads from cheek to cheek, as this dare is one I will take great pleasure in seeing through.

When I lunge for her, she yelps and scoots across the booth. "Don't touch me you fucking savage."

The moment she stands, she almost falls on her arse. I reach out and grip her forearm, ignoring the way my body responds to her because right now, all I need to focus on is getting her out of here. We've caused enough of a scene.

She thankfully lets me help her through the crowd as we walk toward the exit. The moment we're outside, she shrugs from my hold and commences a stagger. I stand back, shaking my head in amusement at the spectacle.

She groans in annoyance and leans against the wall as she fumbles, attempting to take off her high heels. All she manages to do is sway from side to side.

"Ach, let me help."

Before she can protest, I drop to a squat and roughly take off one shoe. She has no choice but to place a hand on my shoulder for balance. I repeat the action with the other shoe, but when I look up, I'm left speechless because the look in her eyes sets me on fire.

She doesn't remove her hand from my shoulder. Instead, she slowly moves it toward my nape and toys with my hair. Her touch is everything I want and need, and I surrender before her.

I place my hand over hers, interlocking our fingers behind my neck. She licks her lips, her cheeks turning a scarlet.

"I'm sorry," she whispers so softly, I almost didn't hear her. "I lied. I did call you. And I don't hate you. I like your stupid face. A lot."

I don't know what to say. I thought keeping the truth from her would keep her safe, but as I run my thumb over a raised scar on her wrist, I realize I've done the complete opposite. She tries to pull away, but it's too late.

Furiously yanking her wrist in front of me, a hiss leaves me as I see the pain I've caused, in the shape of a three-inch scar. There is a matching scar on the other wrist.

"What's this?" I ask, gripping her wrist tighter as she tries to escape. "Answer me!"

"Let me go!" she exclaims, writhing madly.

But I will not.

"You did this to yerself? Ye…slit yer fucking wrists, is it?"

Every sense is sharpened as the thought of any harm coming to Babydoll has me losing control.

"Are ya all right, love?" someone asks, their concern clear.

But all I see is a threat, yet another person trying to come between Babydoll and me. I spring to my feet, shoving the man against the brick wall, ready to rip out his fucking throat.

"Punky, no!" Babydoll cries as I feel her frantically trying to pry me off the Good Samaritan.

But I can't stop.

Rage overtakes me, and until I can hurt someone to expel this pain inside me, I'll never stop. I elbow him in the face, blood instantly gushing from his nose. The sight only feeds my demons, and they're hungry for so much more.

Just as I raise my fist, ready to punch away my anger and pain, Babydoll wraps her arms around me and presses her chest to my back.

Her frantic heart is in sync with her words as she pleads, "Please…stop. I can't lose you again. I'm so sorry. For everything. Please don't do this."

Her shaky breaths match mine, and as she squeezes me tighter, begging me to see reason, her demons subdue mine, and I let the man go. He slumps to the ground, groaning in pain.

Ollie appears, obviously hearing the ruckus just outside. "A'll take care of it," he orders, looking at the bloody man. "Go before the peelers come."

He's right. I can't be caught here.

Babydoll takes my hand, and we rake down the street, everything a blur as I lead us toward my truck. She's breathless, and I realize she has no shoes on, but she doesn't stop or whine. She follows me, protecting me, just how she always has.

I open the door and practically throw her in, sighing in relief when she's safe. I get behind the wheel, and the truck roars to life as I start it and drive away from a mess which I should have avoided. I know better than to lead with emotion, but this is what happens when Babydoll and I are together.

Our love is toxic and causes nothing but destruction.

No one speaks. We both need a moment to process what just happened.

Babydoll leans her head against the window. "I'm sorry, Punky."

"Stop apologizin'," I snap, clenching the wheel. "Y've nothing to be sorry for."

"Yes, I do," she argues, a tremble in her voice. "When you left, you took a part...no, you took *all* of me with you. I was so lonely without you, and the worst thing was, I had to stop myself from feeling that way because of what we are.

"I felt so helpless. I wanted to help you, but I didn't know how. Each letter, each visit which you refused to acknowledge, I just...I lost myself. I know that's pathetic and weak when you've been nothing but strong, but I just...I just missed you. So much."

I let her vent because I need to know why she'd attempt to end her own life.

"I was at the lowest point in my life, and I thought...I could make the pain, the constant void go away. This was something I *could* control. So like a cliché, I slit my wrists in the bathtub. It's something I'll regret for the rest of my life. I was so selfish. I didn't even leave a note for my mom or my sister. I'm a coward."

My stomach turns in anger and also, in sadness.

"Rory found me, and he called an ambulance. He saved my life. I owe him everything," she says, still refusing to look at me.

I now understand what Cian meant when he said Babydoll worked until it made her sick. She was at the end of her tether because of me. I also understand why she and Rory bonded. He did what I could not—he saved her and kept her safe.

I failed her. I failed them all.

"I fell in love with him because, how couldn't I? He saved my life."

The break in her voice hammers away at my heart because the thought of her not being here is a life I don't want to live.

"Yer not a coward," I say when I think it's safe to speak without my words betraying me.

"Then what am I?" she asks, turning slowly to face me.

Her desperation for validity wounds me. My world has been filled with nothing but darkness; Babydoll was the light I needed to guide me through the dark. Her light is now snuffed out because she is lost. So lost.

But now, it's my turn to be her light and help lead her through the dark times.

"Yer human, Cami," I say, using her name for the first time. "And yer a fighter. You being alive is proof of that."

She bursts into tears.

Thankfully, the castle is near, and I turn into the drive, heading straight for the stable yard building. The moment I kill the engine, I drag her over the console and onto my lap. She comes willingly, weeping into my neck as she wraps her arms around me.

"Shh, it'll be all right," I assure, rubbing her back and allowing her to cry. "I'm sorry for leavin' ya. But I had to."

"W-why?" she stutters, her body vibrating with her

shudders.

I never wanted to tell her this, but she was honest with me, so I will be honest with her.

"'Cause Brody threatened yer lives if I spoke to youse again. If I didn't take the fall, if I didn't give Belfast to him, he'd kill everyone I…love. I wouldn't hurt youse like that. Better I suffer than yousens. I deserved the punishment for everythin' I did. I just wish I could have stopped yer pain," I confess, hating how many people I've hurt. "So, if anyone is a coward, it's me."

Babydoll's cries cease, as do her breaths, and she becomes frozen solid.

"What?" she wheezes when she can speak, gently pulling from our embrace to face me. "He blackmailed you?"

I nod. "Among other things."

She squeezes her eyes shut, the tears cascading down her cheeks. "That motherfucking asshole. I hate him. I hate them all."

She opens her eyes, and what she says next has me barely holding on. "Hugh, he did things to…me."

"What things?" I ask, dangerously low.

"He never, he never crossed that line, but he was…sick. He didn't act like we were brother and sister." She chews her lip when realizing what she just said. "I want Liam and Brody dead, just how Hugh is. Did he suffer?"

Nodding, I wipe away her tears with my thumb.

"What did you do to him?" When she reads my hesitation,

she presses, "Please, I need to know."

With a sigh, I reveal the real me. "I tortured him, and then I set him on fire."

She's silent, and I'm afraid I've said too much. But with the slowest of movements, she lowers her lips to mine, kissing me.

I refuse to give in to temptation because this isn't about that. This kiss is letting go. "Thank you," she whispers against my lips.

The kiss isn't a lover's kiss but, rather, a kiss filled with love. It's the first chaste kiss we've shared, and I realize it's because by telling me the truth, she has let go.

"Can I stay with you tonight?"

"What 'bout Rory?" I ask, brushing the hair from her cheek.

She leans into my touch, her lips parting. "I'll deal with him tomorrow. Now, I just want to be with you."

Against my better judgment, I nod, condemning us both to a fate that was always sealed with a bloodied kiss.

I open the door with Babydoll still clinging onto me. She's so delicate, so light. I walk us toward my home and unlock the door. "I'm sorry the place is a mess," I say, kicking aside the mop and bucket.

She merely snuggles closer to me.

I walk us toward the bedroom, wishing I had something nicer to offer her. All that's in here is a double bed mattress on the floor. "I haven't had a chance to get a proper bed," I explain, but she shakes her head.

"I don't care."

I lower her onto the mattress, and she untangles herself from my arms, slipping under the blankets sluggishly. Her long brown hair contrasts with the white pillow. She looks too perfect in my bed.

Needing a breather, I go into the bathroom and grip the sink, taking a moment to compose myself. Looking into the mirror, I wrestle with my emotions—should I tell her the truth? Should I tell her Brody is not my father?

I thought keeping the truth from her would spare her further pain, but the scars on her wrists detail the pain she carries is a part of her always. I decide to sleep on it because telling her when she's half-cut is not the best plan.

Brushing my teeth, I undress down to my boxers because I can't sleep with anything else on. Switching off the light, I pray that Babydoll has succumbed to sleep, but when I walk into the bedroom, I see she's wide-awake.

She turns her head to look at me, and with the full moon beaming in from the window, it allows her to see I'm only in boxers. She quickly averts her gaze, embarrassed.

Pulling back the blankets, I slip into bed and shift onto the edge, needing to put as much space as possible between us. My back is to her, which I know is rude, but it's been so long since I shared a bed with anyone, I don't know how to act or feel.

"Ex favilla nos resurgemus," she whispers, reciting the tattoo across my chest, reciting our parting words to each other ten years ago. "From the ashes we will rise. It's so appropriate to what's happened over the past ten years."

When I got the tattoo, I felt connected to it as I could relate to every word. It seems Babydoll can as well.

"Do you think we will ever live a normal life?"

I ponder over her question. "I thought gettin' married to the man of yer dreams is supposed to be normal?"

There is no sarcasm behind my words, just genuine curiosity. When she sighs, I risk turning over to look at her.

She appears torn, and I wonder why. "Rory is everything I could ever ask for. He's such a good man. He loves me."

I try not to let my hurt show.

"But he's not that."

"Not what?" I ask, confused.

She licks her lips before inching toward me. Like two magnets, we're drawn to one another without choice. "Not the man of my dreams."

I don't ask who is because I know.

She places her hands under her cheek and rests on them, looking at me closely. She's waiting for me to reply, but I don't. I won't do that to Rory. He deserves happiness, and Babydoll once believed she could find happiness with him.

Me being back has just brought up old memories which are better left buried.

I need to be strong. If I surrender to what I want, I will hurt my best friend. I'll also hurt the only woman I'll ever love.

Babydoll's breaths are uneven. I know she's nervous. I also know if I were to give in to temptation, she wouldn't stop me. But come morning, she'd feel nothing but guilt for betraying Rory and also, herself.

Instead, I offer her what I can.

Gently drawing her toward me, I wrap my arms around her and hug her tight. "Sometimes, the wrong choices bring us to the right places. Rory is the right place for ye, Babydoll."

She sighs, understanding that I will always be the wrong choice…no matter how right this feels.

SEVEN

Cami

"**W**here've ya been? And where are yer shoes?"

Closing my eyes, I brace the door handle, wondering if I still have time to make a run for it. But I'm done running.

Shutting the door, I forget about why I fled Punky's house early this morning and walked back to Rory's flat, needing the fresh air to help clear my head. I owe Rory an explanation.

"I'm sorry I didn't call. I got caught up," I explain, turning around and trying my best to smile.

Rory's hair is sticking up like he's run his fingers through it over and over again. His eyes are bloodshot, hinting he's not slept a wink. "Caught up doin' what? We had dinner plans with my parents. Did ya forget?"

No, I didn't.

The thought of spending an evening with Rory's parents while pretending that everything is okay literally drove me to drink.

I can't shift this weight in my chest. It's been here since Punky returned. I can barely breathe.

I shouldn't have called him last night, but they say the truth comes out when you're drunk, and boy, did I disclose a lot of truths last night.

The words spilled from me before I could stop myself, but I didn't regret them. I wanted Punky to know how I feel. He may be able to pretend that everything between us is fine, but I can't. I can't stop feeling the way I do about him.

I've tried. I've tried so hard, but it seems the more I do, the further detached I feel from this new life I built without Punky in it. And that life includes marrying Rory.

I want to love him how I do Punky, but I just don't. My heart belongs to a man I can never have because he's my half-brother.

This morning, I woke up in Punky's arms. It was the most peaceful slumber I've had in ten long years. But when I realized it wasn't his arms I should be in, guilt overrode me. In some sense, I had cheated on Rory, and he didn't deserve that.

I fled Punky's home, not caring I had no shoes. I just needed to get out of there. The farther I walked, the heavier Rory's ring felt. I realized marrying him isn't fair; I don't love him the way he deserves. And he needs to know that.

"Rory, I can't do this."

"Do what?" he asks, cocking his head to the side.

"This," I clarify, gesturing a finger between us.

I wish I could sugarcoat this to spare his feelings, but he deserves more than that.

Rory's cheeks billow before he exhales loudly. "I don't understand. Y've got cold feet, is it? A'll wait. A'll wait forever for ye, Cami. I love ya."

I turn my cheek, guilt eating at me as he confesses his love because I don't feel the same. "I don't have cold feet," I explain softly. "I…I can't marry you, Rory, because I don't love you how you deserve."

Even though it's the truth, it doesn't make me feel any better for breaking his heart.

"Where were ya last night?" He knows, but he asks me anyway. "Cami! Answer me."

I jolt, not used to his tone as he's never raised his voice to me before.

My silence has him filling in the blanks. "He's yer brother, ferfeckssake! It's sick."

"It's not like that," I cry, angered.

"How is it then?" he challenges, folding his arms across his chest.

He's livid, and he has every right to be. But forcing me into this isn't doing him any favors. "I know I can't be with him," I state, pushing my sadness aside. "But I don't have those feelings for you. I don't think I ever will."

"What feelin's? Yer talkin' rubbish! You had those feelin's for me when ya said yes to bein' my wife. Why has that changed?"

Biting my lip, I shrug. "I don't know. It just has."

Rory sighs, messing his hair up further as he runs his fingers through it. "Puck bein' back has confused everyone," he shares, the first time he's openly spoken about him to me. "I understand. But y've got to let him go."

"I can't," I confess, shaking my head. "He's a part of me. I've told you that."

Rory snickers, his anger rising. "Aye, that's 'cause he's yer brother."

"I know that," I reply, not appreciating his snide remark. "But it's more than that. You wouldn't understand."

"Don'tcha do that," he scolds, eyes narrowed. "Don't act like I wasn't there. He was my friend too."

"*Is* your friend," I amend. "You're the one who's pushed him away. You won't even talk to him."

"What would ya have me say, Cami? Ten years is a long time. I've changed and so has he. I don't even know what to say to him anymore."

"What about, hi, how are you?" I offer as I know there is more to this. "You were inseparable once upon a time."

"We're not those people anymore," he states firmly. "None of us are. Nothin' but trouble follows Punky. I don't want that life. I'm glad we're out."

"You're *out* because Punky went to jail so we all could live a normal life," I say, in case he needs reminding. "He sacrificed his freedom so we could have ours."

"Ach, don't be makin' a martyr outta him," he snaps. "That was his choice. And besides, if he wasn't so fucking thran, none of this would have happened."

I pull back, stunned he would say that. "Are you fucking serious? Have you forgotten we all had a part to play in this?"

"Naw, I cannot forget. Ya won't allow it."

"What's that supposed to mean?"

"It means ya won't leave things where they belong—in the past! Ya can't be happy 'cause ye thrive on the drama."

He may as well have slapped me with his insult. "That's bullshit. The 'things' you speak so flippantly about is a man who lost ten years of his life, rotting alone in a cell because my father forced him to!"

"What d'ya mean?" Rory questions as he doesn't know the truth. But he's about to.

"Brody gave Punky an ultimatum—take the fall for the mess we *all* had a hand in and give Belfast to him, or he'd make sure we all paid. Punky went to jail to protect us. So that we could live a normal life, away from crime, away from him!"

"I was there. I heard what was said," Rory exclaims, arms out wide. "But why did he refuse to see us? Why did he not let us help him when we could?"

"Because we only heard part of it. Punky told me what was said when we left—that he was to cease contact with us or Brody would kill us all," I explain, the truth still angering me beyond words. "If Punky tried to get out of jail, we would pay.

"So, he stayed in there to ensure we could live the life he could not."

Rory's shoulders sag as he hears the truth. We were all angry with Punky for refusing to see us, thinking he was just being stubborn. But the truth is, he couldn't. If he did, Brody would have killed us all.

This whole time, we thought Punky had given up, but he never did. He sacrificed himself to save us. My love for him just grows.

"Fucking hell," Rory says, clearly surprised.

I decide not to tell him what else I know about Sean being alive, as this isn't my news to share.

"Cami, I love ya. No matter what's happened, please see sense. Yer actin' crazy!"

His disrespect for my feelings maddens me, and it's out before I can stop myself. "I will never love you how I love him."

Once the truth surfaces from me, it leaves a bitter aftertaste, one I wish I could wash away. But I can't. He doesn't see it now, but I'm saving Rory a lifetime of heartache because he will always be second best.

Rory tongues his cheek, appearing to weigh over what I just spewed forth.

"I'm sorry," I say, shaking my head as this isn't the way I wanted this to go. "The love I feel for Punky, it goes beyond that. I can't explain it. I don't expect you to understand because I don't understand it myself."

This is the best way I can explain something which doesn't make sense.

"I don't know what ya want me to say. Ya tell me yer still in love with my mate and expect me to be okay with it?" he states, his disgust clear. "I wish y'd told me this before our engagement party. I look like a buck eejit."

"I wanted to be honest," I explain, realizing that doesn't make a difference.

"Ach, I wish ya were honest before ya agreed to marryin' me."

He has every right to be mad at me. I'm mad at me. He's a good man who loves me and provides stability, but it's not enough. And I won't string him along, hoping my feelings will change. That's not fair to either of us.

"I'll just pack my things."

He doesn't stop me.

I don't have that much stuff here, so everything fits into my overnight bag I left at the flat. Thinking back, I wonder if I knew it would always come to this. I always made excuses as to why I never left more stuff here. Rory wanted me to stay with him when I came to Belfast, but I always felt more comfortable in a hotel.

I should have known why that was.

Once I have everything, I slip on a pair of black Chucks and take one last look at the flat because I do have happy memories here. It's just not enough.

Rory is sitting on the couch, head bowed, hands interlaced between his splayed legs. "Don't do this, Cami. Ya don't have to marry me. Just don't leave me. We're good together."

Toying with the strap of the overnight bag over my shoulder, I shake my head. "No, Rory, *you're* good. I'm the fucked-up one. You deserve so much better than me."

There's no point prolonging the inevitable, so I slip the ring from my finger and place it on the coffee table. Rory's shoulders shudder as he inhales sharply. I just broke his heart.

With tears in my eyes, I leave behind the best thing that has ever happened to me.

But once I step onto the sidewalk, I feel like a weight has been lifted from my chest. I know that I should never have agreed to marry Rory. I wanted so desperately to believe that I would be happy by being his wife, but it never felt natural.

My smile, my laugh, it was always forced. And even though I will probably live the rest of my life alone, I'm okay with that as I won't settle for second best.

With a sigh, I flag down a passing taxi because there is something I have to do.

I haven't been able to stop thinking about what Punky revealed—Sean is alive. And he killed Cara Kelly. But what I don't understand is, why?

What reason did Sean have to kill her?

Punky's hatred for Sean is far deeper than that toward Brody, so this makes me think that whatever Sean did, Punky sees it as a bigger betrayal than that of Brody, who he is willing to work with. Both are as corrupt and vile as the other, but for Punky to be hunting Sean instead of Brody, it's safe to assume Sean has done something else to Punky.

But what?

Once we arrive at the destination, I pay the driver and take a quick look around before exiting the taxi. It's quiet, but I know the Doyle spies are never too far away. As I make my way down the street, I take in the stores which used to thrive, but now, they're nothing but a ghost town.

And that's thanks to my father.

I enter Ron's Butchers, and when I see Ron Brady behind the counter, I smile and wave. "Hi, Ron. How are you?"

There are no customers in line, which answers my question. "Cami, bout ye? Is everythin' all right? Yer brother called by this mornin'," he says nervously, wiping his hands on his apron. "I already paid him."

I shake my head, horrified. "Oh no, that's not the reason I'm here."

It disgusts me that my brother and father are okay with exploiting people for their own gain. They offer protection from the "bad guys," but they *are* the bad guys. People like Ron pay—in fear for their lives if they don't do what the Doyles say.

Which is why I've come here.

"Can I speak with you? In private," I add in fear of being overheard by the two workers.

Ron narrows his eyes in suspicion but nods. "Aye."

He removes his apron and grabs a pack of cigarettes off the counter. We walk outside where Ron heads toward the back of the store. I follow.

When we're in the alley, he lights his smoke.

Clearing my throat, I hope to God this works. "I know you respected Connor Kelly. You called him a friend," I commence, watching for any signs. But he continues smoking.

"When we came to speak with you—Cian, Rory, and I— Puck was in prison," I say because I know he's wondering where I'm going with this. "But he's just been released. And I—"

Before I can go on, he shakes his head, eyes wide. "Hush, love," he whispers, peering up and down the alleyway. "Don'tcha speak his name."

"Why not?"

"'Cause y'll get us killed," he warns, and he isn't being melodramatic. He means every word.

"Killed?" I question. "I don't understand."

Ron tosses his cigarette onto the ground and turns to leave. But I latch onto his forearm, begging him to explain.

Ron and a dozen other men and women loyal to the Kellys were beside themselves when they found out what had happened to Punky and Connor. They didn't believe Punky was guilty of the charges he was accused of and wanted to help any way they could.

But over time, Brody and Liam forced them to see that if they weren't willing to work with the Doyles, then they would suffer the consequences. So, with a family to feed and fearing for their lives, they submitted. Their loyalty was with a new family—mine.

But that loyalty isn't genuine, as my family doesn't care whether Ron and others like him live or die. They are merely dollar signs. Each person represents money Brody can extort from them.

It wasn't that way with Connor. He actually gave a shit about them, and that's because most of them were his friends. I came to learn a lot about Connor Kelly when trying to free Punky. Although he didn't take any shit and wouldn't think twice about killing someone for double-crossing him, he actually made people like Ron feel safe.

He never exploited them and often helped them. If their kids were buying drugs from him, he would usually give them a lecture about how their decision would affect their parents. He never refused to sell to them, as that would be bad business, but he always made clear that the drugs he sold would fuck up their lives.

It was their decision in the end, but to know he cared enough to speak up reveals what sort of a man he was.

He was an asshole, but he wasn't a fucking asshole.

Cian and Rory told me they too operated this way. They never knew Connor did, though. There was a lot of things they didn't know Connor did.

I know he was hard on Punky, but I think he was trying his best to parent a man just as stubborn as he was.

"Punky is back," I continue softly. I'm going to help him, even if he doesn't want me to. "And he's going to right the wrongs which have occurred over the last ten years."

I know Punky believes he needs to work with Brody, but I won't stand back and watch him demean himself and work with the man who killed his mom. Punky has forgotten, I'm a Doyle too. People know who I am. And they fear me because of my surname.

He needs allies. And I plan on getting them for him.

"It's only a matter of time. Brody's days are numbered. He is no match for Punky. Belfast belongs to him, to a Kelly. Not a Doyle."

I don't care that technically Punky is a Doyle. He is known as Puck Kelly, because that's who he is.

Ron sighs, running a hand over his bald head. He's torn. I know Punky is worried Sean has been recruiting behind the scenes, but I came to Ron because he expressed his dislike for Sean. He would never do business with him.

This is why I can trust him.

"Does he know that Sea—"

But I nod, cutting him off as I refuse to give that vile human the satisfaction of saying his name aloud. "Yes. He knows that that asshole is back. But he never left, did he?"

Ron nods slowly. "I will not go into business with him. It's gettin' into bed with the devil. It'll be like leavin' one gobshite for another. But if what ya say 'bout Puck is true, then aye, I want to help. As will others who were friends with Connor.

"We owe him that."

I smile, happiness and relief overcoming me. "Do you think you could spread the word? Put the feelers out to see who's onboard?"

"I'll get it sorted," he says, the first sign of life reflecting in his green eyes. "I'll be discreet, don'tcha worry."

"As will I," I reply. "Don't go to Punky. For the moment, come to me with everything."

Ron arches a brow but doesn't argue. "If anyone can save us, it's thon boy. He's more like Connor than he thinks. Both are awful thran, but they're loyal. They'll do what's right."

"Yes. And that's all Punky wants—to make things right. And to make those who betrayed him pay," I add, while Ron grins.

"Good craic. We've been waitin' for a miracle. Looks like our prayers have been answered. Thank you for comin' to me, Cami. Y've given me hope."

Tears prick my eyes and I don't know why. It's only when I shake Ron's hand, flag down a taxi, and direct the driver to the closest hotel in town do I understand why.

Punky is hope.

He may not believe it, but we do. He doesn't realize the impact he has on this world. His strength and loyalty give those who have lost their way a reason to smile again.

Once I check into the hotel, I collapse face-first onto the bed and smile. If I can help people like Ron while destroying my father and helping Punky, then I will make it my mission to ensure my plan doesn't fail.

Punky believes he's in this alone, but he's not. He believes everyone has forgotten him, but someone like Punky isn't easily forgotten.

My cell chimes and when I see it's Brody, I decide to answer in case one of his henchmen saw me talking to Ron. "What?"

"Ya answered," he says, his surprise clear.

"Yup, and I already regret it. What do you want?"

Brody chuckles that confident laugh which I hate so much. "I need to speak with ya." Before I can protest, he adds, "It's about Punky," as he knows I will never say no to that request.

"Fine then. Speak."

"Naw, what I have to say can't be said over the phone. I'm at the pub. See you soon." He hangs up, knowing he's won this round.

With a groan, I punch the mattress, frustrated this asshole wields so much power over us. But with no other choice, I get up and organize a taxi to meet me downstairs.

As I lock the door, I decide to send a text in case this is a trap, and I'm willingly walking into my death.

Daddy dearest wants to see me at The Craic's 90. If you don't hear from me, assume that I'm dead. I'll check in later. Ps. Last night was a mistake.

Turning off my phone, I regret nothing.

EIGHT

PUNKY

"It would be easier if we rip this wall out," says the tradesman, as he attempts to convince me for the third time to destroy part of the castle as it'll make his job easier.

"And it'd be easier if I rip yer tongue out," I counter, standing firm.

He pales, knowing my threat isn't empty. "This will cost another—"

But he soon stops in his tracks when I arch a brow.

"All right, we won't change a thing."

"Grand," I reply, thankful he's finally clued on.

There is no way I'm going to be tearing down walls, or adding a fucking theatre room just because. This castle has belonged to the Kellys for generations. It was the place my ma treasured. Even though I only remember bits and pieces from when she was alive, I do recall the pride she took in her home, especially her gardens.

I intend to restore it to its former glory to honor my ma and Connor.

Ronan has sent his colleagues to commence work on the castle because tonight is the meeting with Sean. We both agreed it's too dangerous to be seen together, especially if Sean has eyes on the castle. We can't let on that we're onto him.

So far, I haven't seen him. But that doesn't mean he isn't watching. Underestimating Sean is what got me here. I think about all that he's done, how I thought him killing Nolen Ryan was a favor to me. But he did that because Nolen was a threat. He was going to tell me the truth, but Sean killed him before he could.

He has always been ten steps ahead.

As I'm clearing the debris from the master bedroom, I dig into my pocket for my mobile to check my calendar as I'm still getting used to keeping track of days and weeks, but when I read over the text from Babydoll which was sent over two hours ago, I forget about everything but her.

I need to get to Dublin.

I woke alone. I was hoping it was because she saw reason. That she went to Rory after realizing she and I can never be. She clearly left without saying goodbye because she was angry with me. But that's nothing new. We're constantly angry with one another. And now she's gone to Dublin just to show me how fucking angry she is.

"Fuck!" I curse when I dial her number, only for it to go to voicemail.

Jumping into my truck, I rake down the drive, not bothering to tell anyone where I'm going. All I care about is getting to Dublin. I don't know why she's gone to see Brody, but what I do know is that this can't be good.

I decide not to call Cian. The fewer people who know about this, the better as Brody Doyle seems to leave a trail of destruction wherever he goes.

Looking at the clock on the dashboard, I realize that Ronan will be calling soon with information about where tonight's meeting will take place. But I can't worry about that. This, getting to Babydoll, takes precedence over everything.

She is all that matters.

Slamming my fist against the steering wheel, I seem to understand Connor more and more every day.

"Rule with the cruelty I taught ya because it's the only way to survive in our world."

That's what he said to me before he took his last breath. He knew of the repercussions of falling in love. Look what his love for my ma did. He knew that love can be used as collateral, and in the hands of the wrong people, love can destroy kingdoms.

It has.

He didn't want that for me, so he taught me how to hate instead.

But I rebelled when I should have listened because I will crawl to hell and back to keep Babydoll safe. She is my one weakness, and that makes her valuable to my enemies. That puts her in danger, and to someone like Babydoll, where trouble seems to follow her, I need to keep her within arm's reach.

The drive to Dublin takes longer than I want, but I keep to the speed limit, not wanting to alert the peelers to anything suspicious, especially with Constable Shane Moore on the scene.

I thought being released would be simple—find Sean and kill him, and save Ethan. But every corner I turn, I'm faced with one obstacle after another.

The world isn't what I remember it to be, and I realize it was easier once upon a time because of Connor. He ensured everything was kept in order. Aye, he strayed from the path and lost the respect of his men in the end, but that's because he trusted the wrong person—Sean.

Everything comes down to him. We all trusted him, and for that, we now pay the price for our foolishness. Finding him and making him pay, and pay painfully slow, can't come soon enough.

Once I'm in Dublin, I try Babydoll's phone again, but it's still switched off. Dread churns in the pit of my stomach.

Finding a space, I park the truck and slip the hood low over my brow. This place will be crawling with Doyle spies. I want to remain as incognito as I can.

Dublin has changed some since I was last here, but I suppose that's what happens when ten years pass. It's still bustling with people, which has always left me with the question—why would Brody bother with Belfast when he has Dublin?

My phone rings, and when I see it's Ronan, I'm disappointed and relieved in the same breath. I don't stop walking. "What's the craic?"

"Punky," he says. "I got the text."

"What did it say then?" I ask, allowing my frustration to show as I don't have time for these theatrics.

"Y'll never believe it. The meetin' is happenin' at Kellys' Aluminum."

I stop dead in my tracks, certain I've misheard Ronan. "Catch yerself on!"

"I swear it," Ronan cries, reading my disbelief over his claims. "Why would he do that, knowin' yer back?"

It's at this moment the churning in my guts has me almost dropping to my knees. Once again, Sean has outsmarted us all.

"Cami!" I cry, hanging up and running toward the pub.

So many emotions are running through me, emotions Connor warned me about. But I didn't listen, and now, so many people's lives are at stake.

My boots pound against the footpath, and when I see Brody out front, smoking a cigar, I clench my fists, ready to end his life once and for all. With the devil in my corner, he doesn't see me coming, allowing me to connect with his jaw.

"Ya fucking bastard! Where is she?"

I don't allow him to reply as I punch him again. The crack in his cheek sings to my depravity, and I won't be satisfied until he is dead. "Answer me! Where is Cami?"

Brody spits out blood, having the nerve to smirk in response. "Sorry, lad, what was the question? I didn't hear ya over the lamping in my gob."

This is no time to be making jokes. "I'll ask this once and once only. Where is Cami? Answer carefully 'cause yer life depends on it."

Brody senses the seriousness to my question, and his smugness soon fades. "She's inside, having a pint. But I don't think she wants to talk to ye."

"What did you say to her? If y've hurt her—"

"She's fine. Don't believe me, go look for yerself. Why?"

"Ack, quit the bullshit. I know you and Sean are up to somethin'. That's why ya asked her here. That's why Sean has the bollocks to call a meeting at Connor's factory. He doesn't want me there and knew I would come here to save her. What have ya done with her?"

However, the more I divulge, the more evident it becomes that Brody has no idea what I'm talking about.

"Brody!" a man calls out from down the street.

We both turn and see a deliveryman pushing a trolley filled

with kegs.

Brody is so distracted by what I just revealed, he waves the man into the pub without saying hello. He smiles as he passes us, and when we lock eyes, I get the feeling something is very wrong.

"I have no idea what yer yakking on about," he says, wiping his bloodied lip with the back of his hand. "If what ya say is true, then why the fuck are ya here? Ye should be back in Belfast, getting rid of our problem."

His comment only cements the sinking feeling in the pit of my stomach.

If Brody is telling the truth, then it's safe to assume Sean is having a meeting at Kellys' Aluminum because he wants me to know that I *chose* to be somewhere. He wants me here in Dublin so he can shite all over me and prove he's still in control.

I could have confronted him, but instead, I came here to save Babydoll.

So, the question is, why does he want us all together?

"Why did ya order another delivery?" Erin says as she pokes her head out the door. She does a double take when she sees me. "Away with yerself!"

We haven't officially met as she knew me as Mike from America, not Puck Kelly. She looks how I remember her.

"Not now, Erin," Brody barks. "Yer brother probably placed the order. Go back inside."

But she stubbornly stands her ground and steps onto the

footpath. She looks at her injured father, then at me, shaking her head in disgust before slapping my cheek.

"Ya bleedin' arsehole. Ye lied to me. Ya used me…*Mike*."

"Ach, so I did," I reply, moving my jaw from side to side. I don't make apologies because I would do it again.

"I actually liked ya," she reveals, turning up her lip, repulsed. "And yer my brother. That's sick."

"Naw, I'm not," I counter sharply, done playing this game. Nothing good has come out of this lie, and I intend to tell Babydoll the truth, regardless of the consequences. "I'm not a Doyle. I *am* a Kelly, but Connor Kelly isn't my father. Sean Kelly is. Isn't that right, Brody? Ya played along for whatever reason Sean told ya to, makin' me believe that ye were my da."

Erin's mouth hinges open while Brody stands rigid.

"I know a lot more than ya think I do," I state, eyeing him closely. "And I know Sean wanted us all together for a—"

"*Why did ya order another delivery?*"

The reason he wanted me here detonates inside me before everything explodes—literally.

"Move!" I scream, desperate for Erin to move aside so I can go inside to save Babydoll, but it's too late.

My world is set on fire as *The Craic's 90* shatters the silence and is engulfed in black smoke and an earsplitting *BOOM*. I dive for cover behind a parked lorry on the road, but the stinging in my arms and legs is a sure sign I've been hit.

Car alarms blare, adding to the chaos, as do the disorientated people who stagger along the footpath, bleeding and looking for missing limbs. I don't bother to look at my injuries. My legs and eyes work; that's all I need as I push past patrons who are stumbling from what is left of the blown-up pub.

The smoke is so thick, I can barely breathe, so I place my forearm over my mouth and nose and run inside. There are small fires where debris has caught alight, but the mess is far worse from the blast of the bomb Sean planted inside those kegs.

"Babydoll!" I call out, coughing madly as I inhale the suffocating smoke. The liquor is the perfect accelerant—it'll only be a few minutes before this place explodes once again.

Twisted, bloody bodies are strewn everywhere. Innocent victims who never wanted a part in this war. As my boots slip and slide during my frantic search for Babydoll, I realize it's because I'm traipsing through blood and guts. The thought turns my stomach, and I want to be sick.

But I don't have time.

When I see a head with brown hair a few feet away, I pray harder than I've ever prayed before that this isn't Babydoll. I know for a fact that this person is dead because the head is no longer attached to a body.

Dropping to a squat, I hold my breath as I cup the head in my trembling hands and turn it over so I can see the face. A sigh of relief leaves me when I see that it's not her, but that's soon replaced with regret for this poor lass whose life has been cut short.

Someone's jacket is within reach, so I wrap her head in the garment and place it on a table. It's the only thing I can do to honor her in death.

Sirens sound in the distance, hinting help is on the way, but it's too late. No one in here is alive. It's eerily silent. No moans for help. Just death lingering in the air.

The back of the building has been blown out because of the blast, so I frantically race toward it as it leads out into the alley. There are people slumped against the brick wall, coughing, crying for help. I pass a man who is pushing his entrails back into the gaping wound in his body.

I see a woman cradling her dead baby.

I see the destruction my father caused because he wanted to send a message. He has eyes everywhere, and the gloves are off. Nothing, *no one* is off-limits. He doesn't care who he kills to get what he wants.

"Please, help me." A woman tugs at my jeans with one hand; the other has been blown off.

This is a war zone.

"Help is comin," I assure her because she needs medical assistance, something I can't provide.

A man who is missing both his legs screams for help, and when I look his way, I see her—Babydoll.

She has collapsed on the ground. She's covered in soot and blood. I almost trip over my feet as I desperately run toward her. Dropping to my knees, I cradle her lifeless body against me.

"No!" I cry, rocking her in my arms as I'm blinded by my tears. "Please, no. Wake up, Babydoll. Please."

But she doesn't wake.

With Babydoll in my arms, I look at the carnage around me, promising to avenge each life Sean took.

"Come back to me, Cami. Please don't leave me. All I wanted was to protect ya, but all I've done is get ya hurt."

I kiss her temple, her brow. I promise if she wakes, I'll never allow her to be hurt again.

Brushing the matted hair from her cheeks, I kiss her lips. "I love…you. So much."

A guttural sob fills the air, and I realize it's come from me.

If I could trade my life for hers, I would, and when her chest shudders, it seems my wish has been granted. But both our lives have been spared—for now.

"Punky," she wheezes, trying to open her eyes. "I can't feel my…b-body."

And just like that, I feel like I can breathe again.

"Shh," I assure her gently, kissing her cheeks frantically. "It'll be all right. I've got ya, and I'll never let ya go again."

I wrap her arms around my neck and come to a stand with her securely against my chest. I cradle her close as I leave the carnage behind. I want to help, but I need to get Babydoll somewhere safe.

As I walk down the alley with my eyes downcast, not wanting to draw attention, I see a blood-splattered Brody sitting in his car with his phone pressed to his ear. Erin's bloody body lays twisted in a heap, feet away. Brody locks eyes with me, and with a simple nod, I know that he's in.

I need Brody to regain what is mine, and he needs me to kill Sean. We can work out the details later, but this attack is personal and has allowed Brody to see that it's only a matter of time before Sean finishes the job.

This was a warning. Next time, we won't be so lucky.

Brody's allies are no more. Sean is the new king, and he has no qualms about spilling innocent blood.

With Babydoll pressed to my chest, I run toward my truck. Ambulances, police, and fire engines line the street, but I can't be here because they'll ask questions I can't answer.

A tender caress against my face has me peering down to see Babydoll touching my cheek. "You're bleeding," she deliriously slurs. "I liked your piercings. Will you put them back in?"

"Aye, whatever ya want, Baby."

She smiles, her hand slipping from my cheek as she doesn't have the strength to hold it up. But that's all right—I'll be the strength she needs.

She's passed out by the time I gently place her into the truck and speed away.

I can't help but glance at her every few seconds to ensure she's breathing. She is.

She needs to go to the hospital as I don't know the extent of her injuries. Everything looks to be attached, but it's the unseen which worries me.

"It's going to be all right. A'll take ya to the hospital."

"No," she groans, attempting to shake her floppy head. "No hospital. Too many questions. I'm okay now. I can feel my legs. I think."

She's right about the questions, but I won't risk her life.

"Take me back to Belfast," she breathlessly pleads.

My heart hurts because, of course, she'd want to be with Rory. As much as it pains me, I dial his number, but Babydoll reaches out and winces as she disconnects the call.

"Ya don't want Rory?" I ask, confused.

And what she says next confirms what a bastard I truly am, because these are the words I've wanted to hear for ten long years.

"I think…I think I'm broken because I have a man who could make me happy, yet…I still want you. I *always* want you." She closes her eyes and slumps against the chair.

She's breathing. She's just exhausted.

I'll heed her wishes, and we'll go back to Belfast. I'll call an old doctor friend of Connor's. He's surely retired by now, but I'll make clear this request isn't optional.

"She'll be all right," Dr. Shannon says, packing up his supplies. "If anythin' changes overnight, give me a call."

"Thank you, Doctor. I'll make sure ya get paid."

He nods, coming to a stand. "I'm glad yer back, Puck. Yer father would be happy that yer fixin' this place up."

"I'm tryin'," I confess, running a hand through my hair as I sit vigil by Babydoll's bedside.

"I've left some medication for you too," he says, gesturing to the tablets on the nightstand.

"I'm all right, but thank you."

Dr. Shannon insisted he look over my injuries once he examined Babydoll. I had shrapnel embedded in almost every part of me, but it was an easy fix, and he stitched everything up. Besides, my injuries are the least of my worries.

Babydoll has a few broken ribs and a sprained ankle. She also sustained a nasty gash on the back of her head. Like me, she had shrapnel in every part of her, but the doctor could remove it without her needing to go to the hospital.

Dr. Shannon didn't ask any questions, nor did he insist we go to the hospital, as he knows better. He's seen enough during his time being on call to Connor.

Babydoll is sleeping soundly as the doctor gave her

sedatives. She is a fucking warrior because not once did she cry out, or hint the real pain she was in.

"A'll see myself out." The door closes a few moments later.

I've not let go of Babydoll's hand since Dr. Shannon said I was able to be with her. I wish I had the chance to fit my bedroom with a proper bed, but since I got out of prison, life has been a fucking shitshow.

The soft sighs slipping from her parted lips as she hugs my pillow reveal she doesn't seem to mind, however.

I won't leave her until she wakes, but I need to make some calls. So, I quietly reach for my phone and see I have a text message from Brody. It's a link to a news report.

Reading it over, I snicker as the peelers are saying gangs are responsible for the bombing. This has me wondering if Sean has them working for him too as this was an inside job.

I'll bet my life that Sean was the one who planted that bomb. The unexpected delivery was the perfect ruse as it didn't raise any suspicions until it was too late. The Doyles welcomed Sean into their pub, underestimating him and his need for power and control.

Babydoll was lucky to be outside when the bomb went off, as there is no way she'd be alive if she were inside.

My phone rings and I quickly answer it, not wanting to wake Babydoll.

"Bout ye," I say to Cian.

"Have ya seen the news?" he says on a rushed breath. "The

Doyles' pub was bombed. The peelers are saying it's some gang." The doubt in Cian's voice reveals he too knows the truth.

"Aye, I was there. I'm all right," I add as I know he's about to panic. "So was Cami, and Brody. It wasn't some gang. This is Sean's doing. He wanted us to be in the same place, at the same time."

"Fucking hell," Cian curses. "I knew it. Is Cami all right?"

My pause is all the answer he needs. "Punky, have ya called Rory?"

"She asked me not to," I reply, looking at a sleeping Babydoll. "Dr. Shannon has just been. He's looked after her. Now, she just needs to rest."

"She can rest at Rory's flat," he says. "I don't want to be involved in this."

"Then don't," I snap. "This isn't yer business. Cami is a big girl. I'm not about to throw her out. She's always welcome in my home. When she wakes, she can decide what she wants to do."

Cian is quiet as I know he sees this as the bad idea that it is.

"I've got to go. I've to call Brody. He's on our side after what happened. Sean will pay for what he did."

"All right then, call me later and let me know what the plans are. No matter if yer a buck eejit, I still want to help."

This is Cian's way of telling me he doesn't want to choose sides, but if push comes to shove, he'll side with me. He won't tell Rory where Babydoll is.

"I owe ya everythin'. I'm sorry for puttin' ye in an awkward position."

"I've yer back, Punky. Always."

He hangs up, while I exhale loudly, absolutely knackered.

I decide to send Brody an ambiguous text, as I'm sure he's dealing with the peelers and I don't want to alert them onto anything suspicious.

Where ye ended my life is where we'll meet tomorrow. The hills have eyes...

It's too dangerous meeting anywhere public as Sean has proven that he has eyes everywhere. I decide to meet at the place which kickstarted this entire ordeal, the place where I watched Connor take his last breath.

It's a deserted road and allows easy access if we need to flee. Out in the open is far safer than somewhere where potential victims are.

Brody replies a moment later.

Those eyes are about to be blinded.

I take his response to mean that I'll see him tomorrow.

There's no way Brody will take this lying down. If he felt confident he could do it alone, I'd already be dead. But he realizes he needs me, as I am a Kelly, after all, and what better ally to have; the son of the man you want dead.

"Thanks for not calling Rory." Her croaky voice startles me as I thought she was asleep.

Looking down at Babydoll, I manage a strained smile. "No bother. How are ya feelin'?"

Babydoll winces as she shifts onto her side. "I'm okay. Dr. Shannon was great. He said my injuries are minor. Are you all right?"

She looks at my arms which are stitched up, as is the gash across my eyebrow.

"I'll live. You should rest."

But I know better than to order her to do anything as she shakes her head. "Sean called me minutes before the bomb went off. That's why I was outside."

I don't know how to respond, so I allow her to continue.

"He told me to take the call in the alleyway. When I asked what he wanted, he said he had a message he wanted me to pass onto you."

"What was it then?" I ask, my breathing measured.

She licks her dry lips. "That you're starting a war you won't win. That he's giving you one chance to back out. If you choose not to, then everything that happens from here on out is on you. After that…everything went black."

I clench my fists.

"Why would he save me? That's what he did by calling me, right? He led me outside on purpose."

I tip my face to the ceiling, taking three deep breaths before

I explode.

"Punky?"

When I think I can speak without punching something, I lock eyes with her and state, "He saved ya to show me that he's in control. That all our lives are in his hands. What else did he say?"

When she averts her eyes, I know there is something else she's not willing to share.

"His message proves that he's scared. He knows I'm the only person who can beat him. He could have killed all of us, but he didn't, and that proves he still needs us alive."

I don't know why that is, but I'll die finding out if need be.

"So Brody is still alive?"

I nod while Babydoll sighs. I don't know if it's in relief or sadness.

"Erin wasn't so lucky."

Images of her mangled corpse will forever haunt me. Even though she was a Doyle, she didn't deserve to die that way.

"Why were ya at the pub in the first place? What did Brody want with ya?"

She chews her bottom lip, clearly torn. "He told me that I shouldn't trust you."

"Ach, well I've been tellin' ya that for years," I state firmly.

She ignores me. "That you're not the person I think you are. What does that mean?"

This is the time I tell her the truth. But the words don't

come. I don't know how to tell Babydoll that we're not kin. What does that mean for Rory? I don't want to sound conceited, but her comment about always wanting me confirms that Rory will be the one who suffers from my confession.

My loyalty to him has me sighing.

"Never mind," she says, shaking her head. "We've all got secrets, right?"

Looking at her closely, I cock my head to the side. "Aye, so we do."

She indicates we're done talking when she turns her back to me.

I understand she's mad. She also almost lost her life. It's a lot to take in, so I leave it be.

Exhausted, I sit in the chair by her bedside and watch as her shoulders shudder. She's crying, but she doesn't want me to see. So, I don't console her. I let her cry tears for me too.

NINE

Cami

The tweeting of birds alerts me that it's morning.

I finally passed out in exhaustion after crying my eyes out. I should be used to tears when Punky is involved. He isn't who I thought he was. We all harbor our own secrets for whatever reason, but Punky's secrets are damaging in ways I sometimes doubt I'll ever recover from.

All my things are at the hotel I checked into before I went to see Brody. I literally only have the clothes I'm wearing, which, thanks to being burned to an almost crisp, have seen better days. I desperately want to shower and brush my teeth, so I decide to clean up before catching a cab to retrieve my things from the hotel.

Punky is slumped in a chair by my bedside. He looks

awfully uncomfortable. Good.

Pulling back the blanket, I slowly come to a stand. I'm in my underwear and a T-shirt, so when I peer down at my legs and see the numerous stitches, I sigh. Walking will hurt, but I push past the discomfort as I reach for the pain meds Dr. Shannon left for me.

Popping two pills, I hobble toward the bathroom and sigh in relief when I see the shower. I don't even think twice as I strip off with great difficultly and turn the faucets on. When the water is scalding, I step in.

The warmth unknots the aches in my body and I stand under the spray, wishing it could wash away this ache in my chest.

In just a few hours, I uncovered so much about Punky. I don't know what to think. I don't want to believe what I heard, but deep down, I know that it's true. He lied to me. I know I did the same thing to him, but this pattern between us, when will it stop?

I scrub myself clean and only turn off the faucet when standing becomes too uncomfortable, thanks to my ankle being the size of a balloon. Opening the shower door, I lean forward and reach for the towel on the rack, but thanks to being unsteady on my feet, I lose my balance and tumble out the shower and onto the bathroom floor with a yelp.

"Fuck," I curse, slamming my fist against the tiles, frustrated.

As I'm desperately trying to stand, Punky appears. My yelp

must have woken him as he looks like he's still half asleep. But that soon changes when he sees me sprawled out on the floor, naked and wet.

The blue to his eyes is soon replaced with a menacing black.

This is wrong, but when Punky is involved, I've come to realize there is no right. It's now my turn to be bad. It's now *his* turn to feel the pain that I have.

I stop trying to rise and remain perfectly still, locking eyes with Punky. He doesn't look away when he knows he should. The fact that he wants me this way stirs this constant hunger inside me. It's the reason I shuffle back to lean against the wall, not bothering to cover my nakedness.

"Let me help ye," Punky finally says when he realizes he's staring. He reaches for the towel, but I shake my head.

"You can help me another way," I purr, opening my legs to expose my sex to him.

His gaze sets me on fire as he's clearly wrestling with looking away. But he can't. "No," he states, but the fact that he's looking at me like I'm his next meal contradicts his claim.

"No?" I question with a smirk as I cup my breasts and run my thumbs over my erect nipples. "No, you won't help me?"

"We can't, Baby," he says, still ogling me.

I love it when he calls me baby. The term of endearment from anyone else would piss me off, but not when Punky says it. But I refuse to let him know that.

"Oh? 'Cause you're my brother?"

He clenches his jaw.

"Brother or not," I state, slowly gliding my hands toward the junction of my thighs. "You're the best fuck I've ever had. No one can make me come like you can."

I'm being crude on purpose because I want to see him squirm, and squirm he does when I slip two fingers into my sex. I'm wet, thanks to the shower, but also because Punky is here, watching me as I start to get myself off.

My injuries are long forgotten as I sink my fingers in and out of my pussy, locking eyes with Punky as he's the perfect material to get off to. He watches as I play with myself slowly, humming in approval as I see him responding to what he sees.

"Stop it," he says, but he doesn't mean it.

"You can always walk away," I gasp, pushing out my breasts to enhance this torturous show for him. "But you can't, can you?"

When he doesn't answer, I grin.

"Get on your knees."

My demand shocks him. I can clearly see him weighing over my order, as he knows this is wrong. But temptation wins, just how I knew it would when he slowly drops to his knees. He doesn't speak. He just watches me as I open my legs wider and increase the tempo of my fingers.

"I used to think of you when Rory fucked me. It was the only way I could come. Don't get me wrong, he fucked me good and hard."

Punky clenches his fists and jaw while I smirk.

"But it wasn't his cock I wanted in my mouth. In my pussy. And my a—"

"Stop talkin' like that. This isn't you."

"How do you know?" I challenge, cupping one breast as I continue playing with my needy center. "You don't know me anymore. You're too busy getting to know Darcy Duffy to care."

"She means nothin' to me," he declares, still on his knees. The sight is fucking glorious. He deserves to be on his knees after what he's done.

"Is that so? Do you just fuck women to get what you want? Is that it?"

"I never fucked her," he says, curling his lip. His confession appeases my curiosity. "What's the matter? Why are ye actin' this way?"

"I don't know what you're talking about." A gasp escapes me as I feel my orgasm approaching.

"Don'tcha fucking lie to me."

Laughing, I arch my back and open my legs wider. "That's rich, coming from you."

"Watch yer tongue, Babydoll," he warns, his anger palpable. It's exactly what I want. He's fallen into the honeytrap.

"What are you going to do about it?" I challenge with a snicker. "I'm your sister. You can't—"

Before I can finish my sentence, he's on top of me, heatedly jerking my legs out from under me. The moment my back hits the cool tiled floor, he's between my legs, replacing my fingers with his mouth as he eats me out violently.

A loud moan slips free because every part of me is stimulated. His stubble scratches my sensitive skin in just the right way as does his skillful tongue. He isn't gentle, but I don't want him to be. I've wanted this for ten years.

What I said about Rory was true. No matter what he did to try to please me, it was never enough because he wasn't the man I wanted. The man who is fucking me senseless with his tongue, mouth, and fingers is.

Punky's hot breath sends a shiver straight through me, and I tug at his long hair, pressing him deeper into my pussy as I want to slather myself all over him and mark him as mine, because he is. He belongs to me. And I belong to him.

"Oh God," I pant, squirming as he feels so good.

He spreads my legs out farther, leaving no part of me untouched as he stokes the fire inside me. He reaches up and plays with my pert nipples, just how he knows I like. He knows my body better than me.

I ride his face as he twirls his tongue deep inside me. The animalistic sounds coming from him are everything I need, and I come so hard and fast tears leak from my eyes. Punky milks every last shudder from me before he places a hot kiss over my aching sex.

He crawls off me while I lay on the floor, sprawled out, breathless and spent. When I think I can speak, I come to rest on my elbows and marvel at a wanting Punky.

"You want to fuck me?"

"Naw, Babydoll," he says, licking me off his lips with a hum. "I don't want to just fuck ya. I want to break ye in two."

The impressive bulge at the front of his pants reveals the truth of his claims.

"But you can't? 'Cause you're my brother? And because of Rory?"

"Aye, 'cause of Rory," he says, leaving out our relationship on purpose, which infuriates me.

"Maybe I can give him a call to come over and you can watch me fuck him then? I mean, you've fucked me in every other way."

"What are ya talkin' about?"

"Do you want to fuck me?" I question, shuffling toward him.

"Ye know the answer to that." He remains perfectly still as I climb onto his lap, straddling him.

"Tell me."

"Cami, I want ya, but I can't."

I wrap my arms around the back of his neck and arch my back so my breasts are inches from his mouth.

"Why? No one has to know." I commence rocking against his erection, grinding my pussy against him as he clenches his jaw, his sense of morals diminishing by the second.

"It's wrong. I won't do that to Rory. Oh, fucking hell," he

groans when I lick the seam of his deceitful lips.

"I suppose fucking your sister is also wrong," I state, reaching between us and unfastening his zipper. When I wrap my hand around his hot shaft, he throws his head back and moans. "Okay, I'll stop."

But the reason behind why I started this is finally revealed.

"Naw…yer not. Yer not my…sister. Sean is my dad. Not Brody."

Tonguing my cheek, I shake my head, unbelieving I had to find out the truth from two immoral pieces of shit, and not Punky.

"I know," I spit, angered. "I just wanted to hear you say it. I wanted you to admit that you've been lying to me this entire time, you fucking asshole!"

Jumping off him, I rip the towel from the rack and wrap it around myself.

Punky's passion is soon replaced with confusion. "Ya knew? How?"

"Brody called me to the pub to tell me he wasn't your father. That's why he said I shouldn't trust you, for you to keep such a life-changing secret from me proves that *you* don't trust me. He wanted to make amends and thought by ratting you out, I'd see you were the bad guy, not him.

"He thought by telling me, my alliances would shift, and I would be on *his* side. I would lay my claim to being a Doyle just like he's always wanted me to do. He knows I'm an enemy he doesn't want to have."

Punky quickly does up his jeans before coming to a stand. But it's my turn to talk.

"I didn't want to believe Brody. I mean, making me believe that you were my brother is just cruel, especially since we were moments away from fucking at my engagement party! Do you know how fucked up I've been?

"Having these sorts of feelings for someone who I believed was my brother?"

"I'm sorry," he says, trying to explain, but the time for explanations has come and gone.

"But when your father called me and confirmed what Brody told me, I knew it was true. That's why Sean called me. To pass on the message to you, but to also tell me the truth—that *he's* your father! You've lied to me this entire time. How could you?"

"Baby—"

I can't stop myself and slap his cheek—hard. The moment I do, I instantly regret it because this won't be solved with violence. That's why we're in the position we're in.

"You're nothing but a liar."

"Aye, that I am," he replies, rubbing his cheek. "I didn't want to tell ya 'cause yer better off without me. Trouble only follows me. I don't want that for ya. I want ya to be happy. I want ya to be safe."

"Oh, grow up!" I snap, not accepting his excuses. "I'm a grown-ass woman and can make my own choices. I don't need protecting. This isn't nineteen twenty. Chivalry is fucking sexist."

Punky exhales loudly. "I fucked up, so I did. But yer happy with Rory, and I knew if I told ya the truth, ye'd—"

I chuckle, incredulous. "I'd what? Swoon at your feet? Follow you around like a lost little puppy? Please. Give me a little credit."

"Ye can't deny the attraction is still there. It never went away," he states, which has a bubble of happiness floating to the surface. I soon pop it, infuriated.

"I was afraid if I told ya, I'd fuck up everything. Rory is my mate, and I didn't want to hurt either of ya."

"Are you even listening to yourself?" I question, arching a brow.

"Tell me y'll go back to Rory, now that ya know the truth," he challenges, but the joke's on him.

"I left Rory before I found out the truth. Get over yourself, Puck Kelly!"

He takes a step back, speechless.

I stab my finger into my chest. "That choice was mine to make, not yours."

I omit the fact that I left Rory because of my feelings for Punky as that isn't the only reason. Rory is a wonderful man, and he'll make some lucky girl happy one day, but that girl isn't me.

"Ye broke off the engagement?" he asks softly.

In response, I hold up my ringless finger.

"Why? I thought Rory made ya happy. I don't understand it."

"Yeah, well, I don't either," I reply, but Punky doesn't buy it. "It seems I'm happier on my own. Now, if you'll excuse me, I need to fetch my things from the hotel."

"Babydoll," Punky says, reaching for me.

For the first time in my life, I recoil from his touch. "Don't. Thank you for saving my life, but I am done. You should have told me the truth, and now, I don't trust you."

He lowers his eyes, my words wounding him.

I know I'm a hypocrite for being angry, as I lied to him once, but this is totally different. I lied because I didn't have a choice, but he did. The ball is, and has always been, in Punky's court.

Pushing past him, I grab a pair of his sweats and cuff them at the ankle since they're about three sizes too long. I slip on my ruined T-shirt and Chucks and grab my leather backpack, which I'm thankful I still have.

"Baby, please don't leave. Yer still hurt. I'll go get yer things," Punky says, walking into the bedroom.

"No," I firmly state. "I need time to think. Away from you. I didn't want to believe them, but to finally hear the truth come from you…I wish you really *were* my brother, so I could fucking stop loving you."

A heavy sigh leaves him.

Not bothering with goodbyes—as we've had enough of those—I walk out the door and don't look back. Sadly, the person in front of me isn't any better.

"Hi," Darcy says, getting out of her car.

"He's all yours," I reply, storming past her.

She doesn't know what to say.

"Babydoll!" Punky screams, chasing after me.

But I don't stop.

"Cami!"

He knows better than to touch me, so he runs in front of me, forcing me to stop as he blocks my path.

"Please don't go. Let me explain."

"The time to explain has come and gone. You made your choice, and this is me, making mine."

I attempt to walk around him, but he stands his ground. "Y've always been my choice!" he cries, arms out wide. "I thought I was doin' the right thing. I'm sorry."

A part of me softens as I can read his sincerity. But the stubbornness within scolds me for being so weak. "Well, you thought wrong. I'm not some damsel in distress who needs rescuing."

"I know that," he counters angrily. "I just wanted ye to be happy. You and Rory. I can't offer ya that."

"Oh, enough! I've had it with your self-sacrifice bullshit," I exclaim. "A man without friends is a man without power, and where I'm standing, you're fucking powerless!"

"Ya don't think I know that?" he barks, running a hand through his snarled hair. "Why do ya think I'm prepared to work with the man who killed my ma! The man who ruined my life."

"There are other people who can and want to help," I inform him. "But you're so fucking stubborn and self-absorbed in your own shit, you won't let anyone else in. I want to see Sean and Brody pay too. They fucked me over as well.

"They destroyed all our lives!"

My chest is heaving as I'm fuming.

Punky interlaces his hands behind his neck, clearly frustrated that I'm not submitting. "I know that, but it's hard for me to ask this of ye. To put yer lives in danger for me."

"You're not asking, Punky. We want to help. You're the one who doesn't want it."

"If anythin' were to happen to any of youse, I'd never forgive myself," he reveals, swallowing deeply. "I already failed Hannah and Ethan when I swore to protect them. They're wains, Cami, and they're messed up in shite that no one their age should be."

"Hannah can handle herself," I say, my anger simmering. "She was the one who got you out of jail. She and Darcy."

Darcy is standing by her car, giving us privacy, which surprises me. I thought she'd be eager to be the shoulder for Punky to cry on.

"I know that. I'm just…fucking scared," he confesses, surprising me. "Not for me, but for youse. What if I can't stop

Sean? What if all of this is for nothin'?"

To see Punky exposed is a rare thing. He wants to save and protect us all, but he can't do that alone.

"This will never be for nothing," I reply, meaning that in every way possible.

Punky nods, understanding the innuendo.

I'm about to tell him about my visit with Ron when my cell rings. Reaching into my backpack, I don't recognize the number. I answer with dread.

"Hello?"

"Hi, sis."

"*Eva*? Whose number are you calling from?"

"It's my new number," she replies. "Surprise! I'm here in Belfast."

"What?" One word has never held more weight than it does right now. "Where's Mom?"

"Back home. Can you come pick me up from the airport? Or I can catch a cab to where you are?"

"Why are you here?"

"I thought you'd be happy," she says, saddened.

"I am, I just…What happened with Mom?" There is a reason she up and left without telling me because I would have never said yes to her coming here alone.

Punky listens closely, ready to spring to command if need be.

"Nothing, I just needed to get away. So can you come and

get me?"

"Sure," I reply, as I can hardly say no. "I'll be there in twenty minutes. And, Eva, don't get into a car with any strangers, okay?"

"Okay, Mom," she teases, but little does she know the danger she's put herself in by coming here.

I hang up, shaking my head in defeat. "I've got to pick my little sister up from the airport."

"What? She's here? Now?"

"Yes," I reply, before quickly adding, "you don't need to tell me what a bad idea this is. I know. I think she had a fight with my mom. She's eighteen going on twenty-nine."

"Is yer ma all right?"

"I think so, but I'll find out the full story when I see Eva. I've got to go."

"Of course," Punky says. "Do ya want to take my truck?"

"No, it's okay. I'll catch a cab. If I turn up in your truck, Eva will ask questions, and I don't have the energy to explain it to her right now."

Punky nods, understanding that I mean she'll ask where Rory is.

This conversation will have to be put on hold for now as I have yet another drama to deal with.

"Be careful," he says with a sigh.

"I always am. You too. Are you seeing Brody today?" I know Punky, and he will want to strike as soon as possible.

He nods. "Aye. It's time to set the rules."

"Rules Brody will break."

"Not if I break him first," he counters quickly, and I know that he will.

I don't know what to say, so I smile briefly before turning my back on him and walking away, hoping it's for the last time. But I know better. Things with Punky and I have only just begun.

TEN

PUNKY

I watch Babydoll walk away with a lump in my throat as I can't help but think she won't be back.

I fucked up, so I did.

I thought I was doing the right thing, but I was so very wrong. I should have told Babydoll the truth as hearing it from her father and Sean was the worst possible way she could have found out. I hurt her, and she has every right to hate me.

I suppose whatever fate is headed my way, I'll accept, as I've brought this onto myself.

"Bout ye, Darcy?" I ask as I walk up the drive.

"I'm sorry I didn't call first," she says, brushing a strand of hair behind her ears. "But I heard about *The Craic's 90*. I wanted to make sure yer okay, but I can see that yer not."

When she reaches out, attempting to examine the stitches across my eyebrow, I recoil. It's a force of habit with anyone, bar Babydoll.

I don't want to be rude to Darcy as she's the reason I'm a free man. But I can only offer her friendship. "I'm fine. I've got to go, though. I'm sorry."

Darcy pretends my brush-off doesn't affect her and smiles. "That's all right. Is there anything I can do to help?"

I'm about to tell her no when I get an idea.

"Do ya think ye'd be able to get information on the real estate Brody owns?"

Darcy smirks. "Absolutely. I'll get it to you today."

Another thought occurs. "What about abandoned properties? Or buildings which should be abandoned but yer da turns a blind eye to?"

Darcy nods. "Aye, I can get that organized for ya. Why would ya be wantin' that?"

She is helping me, so I do owe her an explanation. "'Cause there's someone besides Brody I'm huntin'," I explain, not wanting to reveal too much. "I need to know if he's using any of yer da's buildings as his own personal headquarters."

Sean is somewhere close. I know it. The best way to find out where he is, is by having a list of possible locations. I can't wait for him to call Ronan with the next meeting details. I need to strike now.

"I'll get everything over to ya as soon as I can," Darcy says, knowing better than to press.

"Thanks. I really appreciate it. I don't want to scare ya, but…be careful, will ya?"

"I don't scare easy, but I will," she replies, getting into her car. "I'll be in touch once I have everythin' ya asked for."

Nodding, I watch as she starts the engine and descends the drive. Once she's gone, I sigh as I'm already knackered, and it's not even ten o'clock yet. My phone sounds, and I see it's a text from Brody.

Noon. Come alone.

Ironically, I trust Brody because we want the same thing, but working with him kills me. To get what I want, I have to trust the man I hate just as much as Sean. But Brody is less dangerous. Sean has the ability to cause irreparable damage.

He already has.

Walking into my empty house, I send Hannah a text and bend to her wishes of decorating my home however she wishes. I don't expect Babydoll to be back, but just in case.

Hannah texts back an array of happy emojis.

I know she'll work her magic, and when I return, I won't recognize the place.

I shower and get ready for my meeting with Brody, not that I can prepare for the unexpected. Even though I doubt I'll need it, I reach into the chimney of the brick fireplace where I've hidden the bag of weapons and grab the flick knife.

Placing it into my boot, I leave my credit card for Hannah in the bedroom and lock up. She has her own key, so she can come over when she's ready. Jumping into my truck, I commence the journey I never thought I'd travel again.

I'm on edge, checking my surroundings to ensure I'm not being followed. Sean's ballsy attack proves he's not afraid to make his motivations very public. But I think he's laying low, waiting and watching to see how I respond to his attack.

I too am waiting as today's meeting will determine the future.

The moment I turn down the deserted road, a flood of emotion overwhelms me. It was here, a new chapter commenced. It's not changed much in the past ten years. I begin to think about the day that changed my life forever.

I would have done so many things differently, like not trust Sean. But he is a master manipulator, making me believe he actually gave a fuck about me. I wonder when my ma found this out for herself. I clench the steering wheel at the thought.

Her memory has faded over time, and I don't know if the things I do recall are genuine memories or if it's my mind making up accounts of her. But something that hasn't faded is the need to avenge her, and at this moment, I realize it's to avenge Connor as well.

He took his last breath here trying to protect me.

"Don't trust...Sean."

He went to the grave not privy to the fact that Sean is my real father. He believed it was Brody, or whoever else Sean brainwashed him into believing it could be. But something twigged at the last minute for him to use his last dying breath to utter those words.

It has me wondering if that's why he left nothing to Sean in his will.

There is only one man who can answer that, and he's the reason I pull up behind the black BMW parked on the side of the road. I don't want to be here, making a deal with the devil, but he's merely a means to an end—a bloody end where those who wronged me, and those I love, pay with their lives.

The door opens, and out limps a wounded Brody Doyle. The sight pleases me immensely.

He reaches into the car, and when he retrieves a cane, I smile. This fucker suffering is not even a sliver of what he deserves. But his karma is coming…

I exit the truck and meet Brody halfway as he continues hobbling along the gravel road. Folding my arms across my chest, I remain poker-faced because I can't guarantee that both of us will be standing by the end of this conversation.

Brody's dark sunglasses hide his eyes, but they don't conceal the small red wounds all over his face. They're too small to be stitched up, but they're obvious enough for me to see he too suffered as I did. However, I thankfully don't need a cane for assistance.

This has made Brody weak, something he no doubt hates.

"Is Camilla all right? She will not answer my calls," he says, which surprises me because it sounds like he actually cares for her well-being.

"Do ya blame her?" I counter, shrugging. "All y've done is hurt her."

"Ach, I know that," he spits, angered. "But with two of my children now dead, she and Liam are all that I have left."

"Ya should have thought about that before ye used her for yer own sick games." I'm not touched by his newfound revelation. It shouldn't take the deaths of his kids to realize this. Does he really think she'll forgive him after everything he's done?

He clenches his jaw but doesn't retaliate.

"Yer dad is going to pay for what he's done," Brody promises, gripping the gold topper of his cane.

"Finally, somethin' we agree on. Let's hope it's not too late."

"And what's that supposed to mean?"

"It means, for Sean to be able to blow up yer pub, he's in deeper than I thought. It won't be long until he takes ya down."

Brody curls his lip, livid, but he knows I speak the truth. "So what do ya suggest I do?"

"First, yer goin' to answer some questions, and yer goin' to be honest."

Brody reluctantly nods.

"Before Connor was killed, he said there was a deal made

between ye? I want to know what it was."

"We had a deal. Why would ya break it? Why now?"

That's what Connor said to Brody before shit hit the fan. I want to know why Connor would make a deal with Brody. It'll help me understand him better. It'll also make me feel a little less guilty for doing the same thing.

"Connor came to me after yer ma…died." He decides to use the less gruesome term, knowing I will rip out his tongue for the fact that she was murdered because of him. "He didn't want any more bloodshed, so we made a deal—he would not seek retribution for Cara only if I promised to stay out of Belfast forever.

"Our families have been at war for generations, but Connor had power like no other Kelly we'd seen before. I knew if he found out the entire truth, he'd put an end to the Doyles for good. That's why I agreed to help Sean deal with yer aul' man."

On instinct, I punch him straight in the jaw.

Brody's head snaps back with a crack, and I rein in the urge to punch him again. "Don't you dare speak so casually 'bout what ye did," I warn, ensuring he knows my threat isn't empty.

"Ya wanted the truth, so here it is," he says, spitting out a mouthful of blood. "Connor would be fine with me fucking his wife, but if he knew I was workin' with Sean, that would be unforgivable. Sean had that over me.

"But I agreed because I knew it would hurt Connor, and after he hurt my family for generations, I was more than happy to give him what he deserved."

Clenching my fists, I take three calming breaths. I wanted the truth, and no matter how painful it is, I need to know it. "Why would ya trust Sean? He is a Kelly, after all."

"Sean offered me a partnership, and I couldn't say no. Once yer ma was gone, Sean took a step back. I think he was worried yer da would find out he was the one who organized it. But his greed could only lay dormant for so long.

"The rest, ya know how that goes. We worked together as we were stronger. We could put our differences aside as working with Sean was more profitable than him being dead.

"But then he got greedy."

"Ya both did," I amend, disgusted with them both. "I can't believe the aul' lad didn't see it. How did he not know Sean was goin' behind his back?"

"Sean is a very good liar," Brody says. "He's also a fucking psychopath."

"So he is," I agree. "I suppose I didn't see it either."

"No one did. People are just playthings to him. Once they stop being valuable, he disposes of them like nothing but rubbish. That's what he was planning on doing to me."

"Ack, dry yer eyes," I spit, not interested in his sob story. "Ya made yer choice. Ya got in bed with the devil once ya agreed to kill my ma. Sean had that over ya. He's always been ten steps ahead of us all."

Brody's nostrils flare because the truth hurts. "I don't trust ya, bucko."

With a chuckle, I reply, "Good, ya shouldn't."

I want to make that clear. Just because we're forced to work together doesn't mean he's going to leave this with his life intact. Once I get what I want, he'll go down too.

"If this is going to work, then we both need collateral on the other," he wisely says. "So what happened with Sean won't happen with you."

"All right, sounds fair."

Brody smirks, and I know what he's about to say next will change the course of everything. "So, whose life do ya want to gamble with?"

Money, land, and possessions are all meaningless to us because this collateral has to be one worth fighting for.

It seems fairly obvious what choice I'll make. "Mine."

Brody's eyebrows shoot up into his hairline, surprised by my choice. "Yers?"

"Aye, no life is more important than mine," I reply firmly. This is true to some degree. But I'm not prepared to gamble with the lives of those I love.

"If I double-cross ya…and ya catch me," I add with a smirk. "Then I won't fight ya. A'll go down without a fight."

Brody doesn't seem too happy with this bargain, but too bad. This is my final offer. However, I don't plan on getting caught.

"I'm just meant to trust ya, is it?" he asks, incredulous. "Ye killed my son and my brother, and God knows who else. I need more."

"There is no more, Brody. My life for yers. Seems fair as ya took the life of my ma. A life for a life."

Brody weighs over my demands, realizing there is no room to negotiate. "If ya fuck me over, lad, y'll pay."

"Same can be said about ye."

Brody cocks his head to the side, watching for any signs of deceit. He won't see any.

With reluctance, he offers me his hand. Peering down at it, I accept his offering, sealing our fate forevermore.

With that done, I get down to business because I want this done now. "I want ya to organize a meetin' with yer men. I also want names and addresses. Today. Let me know when yer ready."

"Why?"

"'Cause they need to know we're not fucking around. Each day is just another chance for Sean to brainwash more of yer men. We need them to know there are consequences if they wish to betray us. And those consequences will be paid with their lives."

"I don't think there's many of them," Brody naïvely states.

"Underestimating anyone is fucking stupid. It'll cost ya yer life. Trust me, I know this firsthand. It only takes one of them to open their mouths, braggin' 'bout how grand Sean is and what he can offer them that you can't. There is no loyalty. Men will go where the money and security is. And I'm guessin' a lot of these men used to work for the Kellys?"

Brody nods.

"Well, in that case, yer fucked. It's just a matter of time."

Brody inhales sharply, not accustomed to being told what to do. "The men in Dublin won't appreciate taking orders from a Kelly. If anything, that'll push them away. They'll see me as a traitor for workin' with the enemy."

What he says is true, which gives me an idea.

"You let me take care of that. Just make sure ya send me what I've asked for."

Brody shakes his head, his cheeks turning red in anger. "Don't forget I'm still the one in charge," he snarls, eyes narrowed. "Yer helpin' me deal with a problem. Ye can disappear without a trace, so don't think we're in this together. Once Sean is gone, it's fair game."

"Ach, if that were true, I'd already be gone," I arrogantly argue. "If Sean were merely a problem, he'd be dealt with by now. But he's more than that. And ya know I'm the only person who can take him on."

Brody reaches into the small of his back and pulls out a gun. He trains it on me, nostrils flared. "I should kill ya where ya stand," he says, waiting for me to react.

I just stand still, unamused.

"Hurts, doesn't it?"

"What does?" he barks, never taking the gun off me.

"The unknown," I reply, stepping forward and pressing the gun to the middle of my chest. "If ya wanted me dead, I'd be dead already. So stop yer theatrics. Yer embarrassin' yerself."

"Fuck you," he spits, shoving the gun into me.

"Not today, thanks. So if yer done, how 'bout we stop wastin' time. Or have ye forgotten what Sean did to Erin? And how he's belittled ya in front of yer men?"

Brody's jaw clenches as he wrestles with not killing me where I stand. He needs me, and he fucking hates it. No doubt, there have been whispers about Sean throughout the years, but Brody is so fucking arrogant, he never believed his empire could crumble.

But now that it has, he realizes to win this war, he's going to have to side with the enemy—me.

With utter hatred, he slowly retreats, keeping the gun in his hand. "I'll be in touch about tonight."

With a smile, I bask in the victory. It feels good to kick a dog when he's down.

Brody hobbles off toward his car, clearly done with this conversation. He speeds away while I sarcastically wave goodbye.

Once he's out of sight, I tip my face to the heavens and inhale. The first step toward revenge has been taken. I won't count my chickens before they hatch, however, as Brody may still try to kill me. It's obvious he'd rather work with anyone but me, but he needs me. As I need him.

Tonight's meeting is for me to gauge who has been led astray because those are the weak men. They will crack under pressure, and I intend to bleed them for any information on Sean. I also hope to see some familiar faces because they're traitors for siding with the Doyles, and they'll be dealt with accordingly.

My mobile rings, interrupting visions of bloody revenge, but when I see it's Rory phoning, I wonder if that's the reason he's calling.

"Bout ye?"

"Hey, Punky," he says, his unease clear. "I wanted to clear the air with ya. Cami and I broke up. I wanted to tell ya. I also wanted to say how sorry I am for being a fucking eejit. I was angry with ya. Everythin' went to shite when ya left. Everythin' changed. Some for the better, but mostly for the worse.

"I can't force Cami to feel somethin' she doesn't. I always knew that. I just thought one day, she'd stop lovin' ya. But she didn't."

I sigh as I hate hearing my friend so low. I decide not to tell him that I know what happened between them. I don't want to cause Babydoll any more pain. But what I do need to share is that Babydoll and I aren't related.

"Can ya meet me at the castle in about an hour?"

"Of course," he replies, and his acceptance makes me happier than I care to admit.

"Grand. I'll phone Cian as well."

"Just like old times, so it is," he says, but we both know those times have come and gone.

"I'll see ya soon." I hang up and send a text to Cian as they both have a right to know what I'm planning.

However, I need to do something else first.

Jumping into the truck, I look into the visor mirror and grin—a sinister grin that has laid dormant until now.

My mum's voice echoes softly, a reminder that her memories are still present. I just need to know where to look.

"I want ya to be someone else. I want ya to pretend yer anywhere but here. Whatever ya see, whatever ya hear, I want ya to know it's not real because yer not really here."

"All right, Ma. One more time."

I'll give it to Hannah, she has good taste because the moment I step foot inside my house, I think I'm at the wrong address.

I don't know how she pulled this off, but she managed to deck my house out with everything I'd need and so much more. The kitchen is sparkling with brand-new appliances, some of which I have no idea what they do. The living area is fitted with a comfy black leather couch, a coffee table, and a huge TV mounted on the wall.

The king-size bed is covered in silk and satin. But it's what hangs above it that makes this house my home. It's the drawing I sketched what feels like a lifetime ago. I suppose it was.

"Y'll always come back to me, will ye not?"

That's what I asked Babydoll when I drew this picture for her. This abstract piece is one of my favorites and that's because it's how I see Cami—free.

I haven't drawn in so long. It's weird looking at this piece and remembering the way I felt, sitting behind the easel and letting go. I wonder if I could still do that now? I also wonder where Hannah found this drawing?

All questions are put on hold, though, when Rory announces his arrival.

I try not to let my guilt show when I walk past the bathroom—the place where I devoured his ex-fiancée without remorse—and into the living area to greet Rory. He smiles, but it's strained. This is fucking weird for us both.

"Hey."

Rory whistles, taking in the grand state of my house. "Ach, yer gaff is class."

"I've Hannah to thank," I reveal. "I have no idea what half the shite does."

Rory laughs, turning around to face me.

I remember a time when us three boys were thick as thieves. But now, so much has changed. I don't want to drag Rory into my bullshit, but I want to be honest with him. Babydoll is right—a man without friends is a man without power.

I can't do this alone.

If he wants nothing to do with this, then I'll respect his choice because he made it. Unlike Babydoll, whose choices were taken away from her. No wonder she's fucking angry with me.

Fuck.

"Rory, no more small talk. I need to tell ya somethin.'"

Rory swallows, placing his hands into his pockets.

"Cami and I…we're not brother and sister," I declare, and the truth has never felt sweeter. "Connor wasn't my father. But neither is Brody. Sean is my dad."

He blinks once, obviously surprised by my admission. I don't blame him. No matter how many times I say it, I still have a hard time believing it.

"Are ya sure?" he asks when he can finally speak.

"Aye. I've got it in Sean's handwritin'. He set me up. He also killed my ma."

"Fucking hell," Rory gasps, shaking his head and turning white.

I go on to tell him the full story, leaving out the details of Babydoll and me. That's her story to tell. Once I'm done, Rory is sitting on the edge on my sofa, interlacing his fingers in front of his mouth.

I know it's a lot to take in, so I let him process it while I dig into my pocket for my phone and send Babydoll a simple message.

I'm sorry.

I don't expect a reply, but I'll continue apologizing for the rest of my life.

"I can't believe this." Rory suddenly jumps like the couch is on fire and starts pacing the room.

I stand back and wait as I realize he may need some time. But when he stops in front of me, that spark reigniting behind those eyes, I know he's made his choice.

"There's no way yer doin' this alone," he states with conviction. "I'm sorry for bein' such a buck eejit. I failed ya. I was supposed to be here for ya."

"I won't be havin' that," I say, cutting him off. "There's nothin' for ya to be sorry for. Ya wanted to live yer life. I wanted that for ya."

"I know, but I let ya down. I should have fought harder."

I don't know in what context he is referring to. Fought harder not to fall in love with the woman I love? Regardless, none of that matters.

"What's the craic?" Cian asks, but when he sees Rory, he looks between us frantically.

"What's happened now?"

"Why didn't ya tell me all this?" Rory asks Cian, who pulls in his lips, weighing over what to say.

"It wasn't his place to tell ya," I answer for Cian because it's the truth. "Things weren't right between us. But I want to be honest with ya. No more lies."

A look I can't place comes over Rory. "Does Cami know?"

I simply nod but won't elaborate any further.

"Fuck," he curses under his breath.

Without a doubt, he's wondering if she knew this before or after she ended their engagement.

"I can't deal with that right now," he reveals. "But if I get to hurt someone today, then please count me in."

Cian is still in the dark about what happened with Brody, so I fill him in as I did with Rory. Once he's up to speed, he nods firmly.

"Aye, I second that, Rory. It's time to spill some fuckin' blood."

On cue, I get a notification on my phone. I have an email and a text message.

The email is from Darcy. She came through. I now have a list of all the properties that belong to Brody. I also have "places of interest."

The text message is from a number I don't recognize.

Check yer letter box.

Sounds as ominous as it probably is.

"I'll be back in a second," I say to the lads, who nod.

Jogging out the door, I make my way down the drive, and when I open the letter box, I see a yellow envelope. It's unaddressed. It feels like there is paper inside, so I rip open the seal and unfold the piece of paper.

When I see the names and addresses, some of which I recognize, of over a hundred men, I know Brody has agreed to play by my rules—for now. There is also an address and time.

It's showtime.

Jogging back to the house, I enter to see Rory and Cian arguing over the fancy coffee machine. "It's this button," Cian insists, pressing it, only for steam to shoot out, almost burning him.

"Ya buck eejit," Rory says, shoving him aside.

I stand back, amused by my two friends. It almost feels like old times—almost. What I hold in my hands, however, is a sure sign things have changed.

ELEVEN

PUNKY

The address has led us into the Republic.

No word of a lie. It sickens me that my men, men who were loyal comrades of Connor, can come here and serve another leader. But I need to get past that for this to work.

During the car ride, I applied my "mask," as I promised Brody the men wouldn't recognize me. And what better way to do that than by reverting to where this started.

The moment I circled my fingers in the face paint, I was at home. I haven't worn this face in so long, but that doesn't mean it isn't as much a part of me as my usual face. I see myself wearing both, split right down the middle.

But the darkness has always won.

Cian turns over his shoulder to look at me from the passenger seat as I'm adding the final strokes to my lips. Hunting through my backpack, I open the box and hold the silver hoops between my fingers. My mask isn't complete without my piercings.

I don't have time to wait and see a piercer, so finding the small, closed-over hole in my nose, I press the post of the hoop and pierce the skin. Cian shudders, cursing under his breath.

"Don't be such a pussy," I tease, doing the same for the hoop in my bottom lip. "Yer nose is pierced."

"Ach, that it is, but I got a professional to do it. I didn't do it in the back of Rory's car."

"What's wrong with my car?" Rory asks, lightening the mood.

Once my piercings are in, I suddenly feel like the old me, but I'm not. None of us are who we once were.

"Let's do this."

We're in the middle of nowhere, surrounded by nothing but greenery. The old abandoned farmhouse up ahead is where we're meeting.

"This is how every horror movie starts," Cian says, using the light on his phone to help guide us up the drive.

He's not wrong. This place is fucking boggin'.

Cars are parked behind the house, and when we turn the corner, I'm surprised to see there is electricity. A few men stand outside the back door, plumes of smoke filling the night air as they finish their fegs.

When I get closer, one of the men nudges his friend with his elbow, hinting he's to look in my direction, and when he does, he almost swallows his cigarette.

"Time for you boys to make yerselves scarce," I instruct as no one can know they are here. If anyone recognizes them, they'll put two and two together and assume Brody is working with me.

Nodding, they walk to opposite ends of the property, guns in hand just in case we have any unplanned visitors.

"What's the craic, lads?" I ask as I walk past Brody's men.

One of them, however, doesn't seem too happy that I'm here. "Yer not welcome here," he spits, gripping my forearm to stop me from taking another step.

Reining in the need to break his hand, I smile. "Oh, is that so? This a private party, is it?"

The man doesn't let go. "Aye, and yer away in the head if ya think yer comin' in here lookin' like that."

"Like what?" I sarcastically question, arching a brow.

"Like a fucking molly. Get outta here before ya break a fingernail."

His friends all laugh, egging him on as they think his joke is fucking hilarious. I'll give them something to laugh about.

I join in with their laughter, confusing them, but my amusement is due to me quickly striking out and punching him in the esophagus. He chokes mid-laugh, his eyes bugging out of his head as he cups his throat, gasping for air. But I'm not that generous.

Cupping his throat, I force him to squeeze his larynx. He turns a lovely shade of red as he struggles to breathe. His friends' laughter soon dies.

"Anythin' else ya want to say to me?" I question inches from his face.

He quickly shakes his head, begging me to let him go.

"Are ya sure now? It seemed ye couldn't stop talkin' a few seconds ago."

I ease the pressure on his throat, allowing him to wheeze in air. "Sorry."

"What was that?" I ask, placing my ear near his mouth.

"Let him go," demands one of the men. When he tries to pry me off his mucker, I elbow him in the face. His screams echo in the distance as he cups his broken nose.

"Now, what was I sayin'?"

"Sorry, sorry," he wheezes, his eyes pleading I let him go as he slaps at my hand at his throat.

"I don't believe ye," I scold, forcing him to his knees.

"Yer welcome to stay."

Peering down at him, I smile. "Ach, that's awful kind of ya. Thank you."

I finally let him go.

He collapses forward, gasping for air on his hands and knees. I roll my eyes 'cause this response is a little dramatic. As he attempts to stand, I push him back down with my boot.

"I think y'd much prefer the view from down there, do ya not think?" I suggest, ensuring he understands if he attempts to stand again, I'll break his kneecaps.

His head jerks in a half-hearted nod.

The last man standing doesn't get in my way as I walk past him and into the farmhouse. The place is gutted. The only thing which stands is the structure. There doesn't appear to be as many men here as Brody sent me on the list.

The men who are missing will be considered traitors and dealt with accordingly.

As I scan the room, I see Brody and Liam talking to a group of men. This is the first time I've seen Liam since I got out. He looks even more arrogant than I remember. When we lock eyes, his narrow, making clear he isn't on board with the deal I made with his father.

He shoves the men he's speaking with aside and comes my way. "Y've got some bollocks on ye, comin' here with yer face painted like that. After what ya did to my uncle. And my brother," he spits, fists clenched.

I decorated Aidan and Hugh's faces before I killed them. It was my finest hour.

"Y'd prefer a different color?" I mock, pursing my lips in contemplation.

He advances forward, the veins in his neck pulsating, hinting at his rage. "I'd prefer it if ye were dead," he states bitterly. "Just 'cause my dad thinks this is a good idea, doesn't mean I do. If ya do anything to piss me off, I'll kill ya."

"Yer goin' to have to be a little more specific," I counter smartly. "What pisses ya off, Liam? Just so I know."

He growls, ready to end the agreement between his father and me. But Brody steps in, grabbing Liam.

"That's enough, son," he warns softly, not wanting to alert anyone that something is wrong. But that was the case long before me.

"This is yer idea of concealin' who ye are?" Brody asks.

"Aye. I thought y'd like it."

He exhales, clearly holding back the urge to kill me.

"What the fuck?" Liam curses, looking over my shoulder.

Turning to see what's going on, I snort when I see the arsehole who tried to act like a tough guy enter the room on his hands and knees. The guy whose nose I broke stands by his friend with blood dried on his face.

When they see me standing with Brody and Liam, they instantly avert their eyes.

"Your doing?" Brody asks while I smirk in response.

"Good thing they don't know who I am."

Liam is about to clock me, but Brody grips his bicep.

"I said enough." His tone is firm, hinting if Liam continues to defy him, he'll suffer the consequences. "Our men need leaders. Not to see us arguin' like a couple of aul' weemin."

"And ya think this cunt can do that?" Liam spits, looking at me.

"Flynn and Grady seem to think so," Brody replies, looking at the two men I encountered earlier.

Liam doesn't reply because his aul' lad has a point.

"This all of them?" I ask, looking around the room.

"Naw, some are workin'. I couldn't get everyone together on such short notice."

"Blah, blah, fucking blah," I exclaim, shaking my head. "You're the boss, and last I checked, yer workers do what ya say. No wonder yer up shit creek without a paddle."

Before they can give me their excuses, I clear my throat loudly, interrupting the soft chatter amongst the men. "Can I have yer attention, please?"

Some men give me their attention while others turn their lip up at me and continue talking. These men are like uncivilized animals that need taming.

Reaching into the small of my back for my gun, I find an uncouth animal laughing joyously, aim for his leg, and fire. The sound ricochets off the walls, as do the screams of the pussy who drops to the ground like a sack of potatoes.

The room suddenly becomes so still, I could hear a pin drop.

"Ya fucking cunt! Ya shot me!" he cries, rolling from side to side as he grips his leg.

"So I did," I reply, using the butt of my gun to scratch my temple. "To be fair, I did ask for yer attention."

"Brody! Who is this nutter?" someone asks, as Brody has

obviously fallen into the good cop category.

"He's my new partner," he replies, and I can only imagine how that stung to say aloud. "Rumor has it some of youse have forgotten what loyalty is."

Anger is replaced with nervousness as the men look between each other. Brody steps aside, indicating the floor is mine.

"That's right," I agree, folding my arms. "Now, before ya go denyin' it, I want ya to know yer all guilty until proven otherwise."

A ballbag steps forward, attempting to assert some authority. "What's yer name?"

With a smirk, I counter, "Ya don't need to know my name. We're not friends. We're not goin' to go out and 'ave a pint. I know your names, however. I know where ya live. Who yer family are. I know what I need to."

The men look amongst one another, clearly shaken up that a stranger has come into their territory and threatened them.

"If I discover any of youse are double-crossing us"—I pause and tongue my cheek—"it won't end well for ya. I promise ya that. I'll be keepin' a close eye on youse. I'll know when you eat, sleep, and when ya take a shite because that's what a good leader does.

"They know where their men are."

Brody clears this throat, clearly not impressed with my choice of words. But this is his fault, as it was Connor's. I can't help but compare this speech to the one I made to Connor's men. I learned my lesson, though, and will not make the same mistake again.

"If I find out yer loyalty lies elsewhere, and I will find out, I'll torture ya until ye speak, and when ya do, I'll kill ya. Consider this yer first and only warnin'. Yer lucky I'm givin' ya that. There are no second chances."

They hate me, and that's what I want. But above that, I want them to respect me. Fear only gets you so far, but earn the respect of a man, and he'll be willing to die for you.

"Go home. Count yerself lucky ya came. The same can't be said for the men who can't follow orders."

The men look confused, unsure if this is a trick. When I aim my gun, they realize it's not.

They scatter like scared mice, not looking back as they make a dash for the exit. The man I shot is helped to his feet by his friends and hobbles out the door. Some men stand aside, clearly wanting to talk to Liam and Brody about what the fuck is going on.

One man is hovering. I know he wants to speak to me because he used to work for us. The way he examines me, I'm certain he knows who I am.

When everyone is out of earshot, he walks over. "Punky?" he whispers, desperately searching for any clues that it's me.

The face paint is a great disguise for those who don't know me, but a familiar face would easily recognize who I am. And that's what Logan Doherty has done.

I knew this was bound to happen, but I didn't expect the anger I feel to be so predominant. This arsehole is a fucking traitor, and the urge to hurt him is almost unbearable.

"I always knew ya were a weak pussy, Logan," I mutter, eyeing him fiercely. "So I'm not surprised to see ya here."

"Ach, I knew it was you," he says, almost jumping on the spot in excitement. I don't know why. I'm about to break his nose for being here. "Yer speech reminded me of—"

I give in to temptation and punch him square in the nose.

He knows better than to retaliate or cry out. He simply accepts his punishment and reaches into his pocket for a tissue.

"Have ya no loyalty?" I question softly, clenching my fist. "We were good to ya, and this is how ya thank Connor? By working with the fucking Doyles?"

"What would ya have me do? I needed to feed my family."

"These are excuses I have no interest in listenin' to. I'm here to right the wrongs of the past."

"Yer uncle is goin' to be—"

But he quickly stops as I arch a brow.

"My uncle is goin' to be what?" I question, hinting if he lies to me, I'll cut out his tongue.

He nervously peers around the room. "Yer uncle is goin' to be so happy yer back," he reveals, which hints that Sean hasn't let our old colleagues onto the fact that he wants me dead. "He's tryin' to restore Belfast to her former glory.

"But there is pushback. People want nothin' to do with the Kellys after what happened." He soon stops, realizing what he just said.

I gesture he's to continue.

"Connor was the one they listened to. The one they respected. Sean was always his second. Well, third."

When I arch a brow, confused, he clarifies.

"We always expected you to take over, not Sean, which is why he's havin' problems gatherin' the support he needs to overthrow Brody. People don't think Sean has the bollocks to fill Connor's shoes. And they're right.

"This is why Brody is still in control. Men don't have faith in Sean. They don't trust him, not after he resurfaced when we all thought he was dead. He should have done more to save ya, but instead, he let ya rot. We're angry with him for doin' that.

"He was the one who should have gone to prison, not you. When we found out he was alive, we were certain he would get ya outta prison. But when he wanted to be the new leader, and not save ya, the men saw him as nothin' but a traitor.

"He let ya take the fall. What man does that? Certainly not a leader. But you, Puck. Whatcha did…the men would follow ya into war. Yer Connor's son, after all."

This is a lot to take in as I never realized how loyal some men still are to Connor.

"He's workin' with some men, but he doesn't have the manpower to win. He's tryin' everythin', but Brody is still in charge because Sean doesn't stand a chance against him. But with you back, that'll change. I can't wait to tell him."

I grip Logan's forearm, a gentle warning of things to come if he doesn't listen very closely. "Yer not gonna tell anyone I'm back, especially Sean," I state calmly. "This is goin' to stay between us. Y'hear?"

"Aye, but I—"

"Don't make me cut out yer tongue," I interrupt because he doesn't seem to understand me.

His head bobbles as he nods, fearing for his life.

"I want ya to compile a list of names of the men who used to work for us. I want to know who is loyal to Brody. And who you think can be swayed back to our side."

"And what will ya do to them?" he questions with a gulp.

"They made their choice, Logan. It was the wrong one. Think ya can manage that?"

He doesn't press any further. "All right. I can do that. Aye. I'll give ya all the names of the men who used to work for the Kellys and whose side they're now on."

"Grand. That'll be most helpful. Thank you."

Logan won't fuck with me because I know where he lives, who his children are, and that he is probably still fucking his wife's best friend. If he goes behind my back, I'll make sure he pays for his betrayal.

I release him, and he exhales in relief.

"Sooner rather than later, yeah?"

"Of course. I'll run it over to ya tomorrow."

He doesn't stick around and quickly exits while he still can.

Brody is still talking to a couple of men, but he makes eye contact with me as he saw the exchange between Logan and me. I need to be very careful now that I know he wields more power than I thought.

My phone rings, and when I see the caller is Hannah, I answer.

"It's Ethan," she blurts out, her panic clear.

She doesn't need to say another word as I'm out the door, running toward the car. Cian and Rory are following in hot pursuit, understanding the urgency. Rory deactivates the car alarm, and I almost rip open the door as I jump into the back seat.

The boys are in the car within seconds, and we're speeding down the road toward Fiona's house. No one speaks.

I've wiped my face paint off by the time we arrive. I don't take the time to look at Fiona's new house because I don't care. She is standing in the front garden having a feg. She doesn't recognize Rory's car, but when I get out, she shakes her head, snickering.

"So typical of Hannah to call her knight in shining armor," she quips, blowing out a puff of smoke.

"Where is she?" I question, not interested in getting into an argument with her, but she has other ideas.

"Yer not welcome here, Puck. Go, before I call the peelers."

"Listen to me, Fiona, whatever issues ya have with me, get over them. I'm here to help Ethan."

She scoffs in response. "Help? Since when have you helped anyone but yerself. Just how ya helped yerself to *my* money. I've struggled since yer father died, bein' a single mum, but no one seems to give a fuck about that!

"They're all concerned about you!"

I don't have time for her melodramatics, so I walk past her, as she's past reasoning. But she grips my arm, stopping me. "If you set foot in my home, I'll fucking kill ya."

"Mum, enough!" Hannah scolds as she opens the front door. "Thanks for comin'."

Eyeing Fiona's fingers, I give her the option to remove them on her own accord, or I'll remove them for her. She gets the hint and lets me go. But not before she lets me know what she thinks of me.

"Yer the reason Connor is dead. I wish it was you who died."

Time hasn't been kind to Fiona—I hardly recognize her. Some may be happy that their stepmum is suffering, but not me. I feel sorry for her.

"I wish that every day," I reply, meaning every word.

She feels nothing but hatred and anger for me, and I know that'll never change. There is no point trying to revive something that was dead long ago, so I walk past her and gesture to Hannah to take me to Ethan.

She walks down the short hallway and opens the last door on

the left. She steps aside, and I see the boy I no longer recognize curled up on the single bed. He's not under the covers. It looks like he passed out where he dropped.

"I found him like that," Hannah whispers, working her bottom lip. "I think—"

"Ya think what?" I coax when she pauses.

She merely shakes her head, unable to say the words, but she doesn't need to.

Walking into Ethan's bedroom, I notice how bland things are in here. For a young lad, he barely has anything in here to indicate this is a seventeen-year-old boy's room.

His chest rises and falls listlessly; it looks like he's in a coma, and that's because he is, in a sense. Dropping to a crouch by his bed, I gently pull up the sleeve on his hoodie and see what I suspected would be there.

Track marks.

Hannah muffles a cry behind her hand when she too sees what I do. She must have suspected he was using, but to be confronted by the truth is a hard pill to swallow.

A heavy sigh leaves me as I look at my baby brother. He's been brought into this world because of me. Rory, Cian, and I never touched the shite we dealt as we saw what it did. It turned functioning people into zombies, which is what Sean wanted.

I have no doubt Sean was the one who encouraged Ethan to try heroin because that's what Ethan is addicted to. I know this because, with heroin, there isn't simply one time. One taste, and you're hooked. And judging from these track marks, Ethan has been lost for a very long time.

Vomit rises, but I hold it down.

Reaching out, I brush back the matted hair at his brow. Where has my innocent brother gone?

He stirs, a whimper leaving him. Even in his drug-induced state, the pain still lingers, which is dangerous to any user. They use more to numb the pain, leaving them with an even bigger addiction.

His backpack lays by the foot of the bed, so I reach for it and search through it. I find his stash, as well as some prescription drugs. This is worse than I thought. If he continues this way, he won't live to see his eighteenth birthday.

Maybe that's what he wants.

"The fuck," Ethan slurs, his eyes flickering open as he attempts to gauge where he is.

"Hi, Ethan," I say gently.

It takes him a moment, but when he realizes where he is and that I'm really here, he springs up onto his knees, pressing his back to the wall. With urgency, he scans the room for a weapon no doubt. He thinks I'm here to hurt him.

Quickly rising to my feet, I raise my hands in surrender, wanting him to know I mean no harm.

"Ethan, I phoned Punky. He's here to help," Hannah says from behind me.

Ethan curls his lip in anger. "Always stickin' yer nose in

where it doesn't belong. Yer nothin' but a nosy little bitch!"

"Away on! Y'll speak to yer sister that way? Where are yer manners?" I scold, unbelieving he would speak to Hannah this way.

"Fuck you," he replies, not interested in anything I have to say as he comes to a shaky stand. When he sees the bag I hold with his drugs, he lunges for me, but I step back. "That's mine. Give it here."

I shake my head. "Ye should have killed me when ya had the chance, cub, 'cause I'm about to be yer worst nightmare."

He reacts how I knew he would.

With a roar, he advances forward, ready to spill blood for the drugs he loves more than me. Hannah yelps while I keep him at arm's length. He's scrawny and doesn't stand a chance, but that doesn't stop him from trying to take me down.

"Give them back!" he screams, kicking and punching thin air. He's still strung out, so his blows don't connect with me.

"I will not," I firmly state. "This is what I think of yer dope."

Gripping him by the back of the neck, I drag him out of the room and toss his arse into the bathroom. He slips and slides on the floor as he desperately attempts to get back what's his, but it's in vain as there is no way I'll let him put this filth in his body ever again.

Flipping open the toilet lid with my boot, I dump the pills and the baggie of heroin into the bowl. Ethan cries, fighting me, but he won't win.

"No! Ya fuckin' cunt! Naw!"

I ignore him and smash his syringe against the wall. "Ye won't touch this shite again. A'll not tell ya again."

As he continues to fight, I force him onto his knees and shove his face inches from the bowl.

"Is this who ya wanna be? Is this who ya think Connor would be proud of?" I question, my fingers clutching the back of his neck to keep him down.

"Fuck you, and fuck Connor! He's fucking dead. I wish you were too!"

I allow him to vent because this is going to get a lot worse before it gets better.

"I'm sorry I left ya, Ethan, but I had no choice."

"Yer pathetic!" he screams, still fruitlessly fighting. "Yer a coward! I fucking hate ya!"

"Aye, I hate myself for doin' this to ya," I say, keeping calm. "I'll do everythin' I can to make it up to ya."

"I don't want yer help," he spits, struggling on the tiled floor. "I have all the help I need."

"From Sean?"

"I don't know what yer talkin' 'bout," he replies, protecting Sean as I knew he would.

Gripping his arm and twisting it back at a painful angle, I look at the tattoo on his wrist, which confirms he's in so deep, I'm afraid he'll never be found.

"Ya know what this means?" I ask, bending his arm harder

so he answers me.

He screams as I'm hurting him, but I need to be cruel to be kind. "Aye! I'm just like you now, *brother*."

A hiss leaves me. "That's not somethin' to be proud of, Ethan. I don't want that for ya."

"I don't care what ya want. This is my life, and I'll live it how I want."

"Yer happy bein' Sean's errand boy, are ya? Ya think he gives a fuck about ye? He cares only about himself. Why can't ya see that?"

"Ethan, p-please," Hannah sobs, but her pleas are lost to her brother because he is lost himself.

"Shut up! I fucking hate you! Yer runnin' to this loser, thinkin' he can help. He can't even help himself," he spits out. "Ye better sleep with one eye open because—"

He doesn't get to finish his sentence because I shove his head into the bowl and flush the toilet. He gags on the water, slapping the porcelain in his attempt to get up. But I hold him down.

"Y'll never threaten yer sister again," I warn, forcing his head into the water. "So help me God, I will fuckin' end ya myself."

"Punky!" Hannah screams, concerned I'm drowning Ethan. But I know what I'm doing.

"From now on, I'm yer shadow, and it'll stay that way until ya remember who ye are. Got it?"

When he doesn't reply, I dunk his head deeper.

"I'll not tell ya again. The choice is yours."

He nods quickly, slapping the edge of the bowl, admitting defeat, and only then do I lift his head so he can breathe again. He slumps onto the floor as I let him go, gulping in mouthfuls of air.

"So ya do want to live?" I question, peering down at him, unmoved. "Ya were fightin' for yer life. There's still hope then."

Ethan crawls across the tiles, slamming his back against the wall as he attempts to catch his breath. The hatred is still reflected in his eyes, but now, I see something else—fear.

I leave Ethan to ponder on that as I exit the bathroom and raid his room for any remaining drugs. What I find, I tip down the kitchen sink. Fiona is sitting at the table, staring blankly ahead.

"This is yer fault," she says, numb. "He would have never turned out this way if Connor was alive. Ya failed him. Ya failed us all."

"Aye, that's one thing we agree on, Fiona," I reply, watching the shell of the woman I once knew cup her face and sob into her trembling hands.

I leave her alone because I don't know what else to say. She has every right to hate me. I hate me for what I've done.

Cian and Rory are outside, waiting in the garden. They don't ask how I am, or how things went. They heard it all.

"He's comin' home with me," I announce. "That's the only

way I can protect him. I won't send him to some clinic where they talk about their feelin's."

"Course, mate," Cian says. "Whatever help ya need, we're here."

"He's goin' to pay for what he's done," I snarl, clenching my fists and looking into the night sky. "I swear it."

The front door opens, and Ethan sheepishly comes outside. He understands he can come with me on his own accord, or I'll drag him out. Hannah stands behind him, a bag packed with his things slung over her shoulder.

This is tearing her apart, but I made her a promise. I won't break it.

I'm thankful Hannah fitted my house with everything I need because I intend on spending a lot of time here, helping Ethan heal.

He's going cold turkey. I know what that involves. It won't be pretty, but I'm here every step of the way.

Ethan is passed out on the sofa. I'm sitting in the armchair, watching him, too afraid to leave his side. He sleeps for now, but when he wakes, things are going to get ugly. He will lie, cheat, and steal to get his next fix.

I have to be strong because there is no way he's going to

touch that shite ever again.

A soft knock on the door has me reaching for the gun beside me.

"Punky, it's me."

Placing the gun in the small of my back, I quietly walk to the door. When I open it, I see Babydoll standing in the dark.

"Hannah called me," she explains. "She's worried. About both of you."

I don't say a word and open the door wider, permitting her entry.

She brushes past me, her touch soothing me in ways I still find impossible. But I don't have time to think on that. Closing the door, I walk into the living room where Babydoll stands, peering down at Ethan. She places a hand over her mouth.

"He's so skinny," she whispers, tears in her eyes.

"That's 'cause he's a druggie," I bluntly state, not seeing the point in sugarcoating it.

"This isn't your fault," she says, always defending me. "We all should have done more."

I appreciate her words, but they don't make a difference because it is my fault Ethan is here.

"Can I talk to you?"

I arch a brow but nod.

Not wanting to wake Ethan, I make sure the front door is locked and gesture she's to follow me into the bedroom. I leave the door open in case Ethan stirs.

She exhales, clearly gathering her thoughts. Her response has me bracing for the worst.

"The gangs Brody is offering protection against are his own," she says, confirming what I already knew to be true. "I went to see Ron Brady. He is one of the many businesses which pay a hefty fee to Brody. He told me he and many others won't work with Sean. But they will with you."

I take a moment to process what she just shared because this changes everything.

"They don't have a choice. They pay Brody because they see him and Sean being as bad as the other. They need hope. And that's you.

"I don't know how many, but from what Ron said, you've got the support of those who were loyal to Connor. They're loyal to you now."

"Ya shouldn't have gone on yer own. That was dangerous." But what she says, this now changes the course of everything. I know what I have to do.

She pulls in her lips, reminding me she can look after herself. "Every day is dangerous. It's time we stopped it. I'm sick of living in fear. So are many others."

Running a hand through my hair, I exhale, utterly knackered. This kind of exhaustion is unlike anything I've ever felt before. I feel this all the way to my very core.

Slumping onto the end of the bed, I cup my forehead, needing a minute. It would be so much easier to surrender because the fight in me is withering. Every corner I turn, I'm just confronted with more shite. But I didn't come this far to give up now.

With the softest of touches, Babydoll runs her fingers through my hair. I can't help but sigh because it feels so good.

"The biggest enemy you'll fight is yourself, Punky," she whispers, reading the turmoil inside me.

And she's right.

She gently places a finger under my chin, coaxing me to look at her. A mix of emotion is reflected in her eyes as she's supposed to be mad at me for lying to her. But the love we feel for one another seems to always win in the end.

"You want to save the world," she says, stroking over my jaw. "But who's going to save you?"

With nothing but sincerity, I reply, "You have. Ye were the only thing that gave me strength when I wanted to give up time and time again. I've made so many mistakes in my life, but yer not one of them."

She blinks back her tears.

I wrap my fingers around her other wrist and place her hand against my chest, where I nestle into her palm, lowering my guard. She strokes my cheek with trembling fingers.

"What are we going to do?" she asks, and I know we're no longer talking about this war we never wanted a part of.

She's vulnerable and scared, and even though I know she can look after herself, all I want to do is protect her. "I don't know."

"I should hate you. It would be easier if I did."

"I know."

"But I don't," she confesses, looking away. "I don't want to fight anymore. I feel like I've been fighting for ten years."

Her sincerity has me slowly rising to my feet.

She stands before me, her breaths uneven. She's nervous.

"I know what ya mean," I admit, wanting her to know I'm tired as well. "I don't know why ye continue to help me…but I'm thankful that ye do."

She lifts her chin, working her bottom lip as she knows what's about to happen.

"I do it because I—" She suddenly pauses, realizing if she says the words, there's no turning back. "It's not like this with others."

With a heavy sigh, I surrender, sealing our fates forevermore. "I know."

Before she can say another word, I press my lips to hers and make her breaths mine. Instantly, she softens against me, humming into my mouth as I devour her whole.

She stands on her toes and wraps her arms around the back of my neck, meeting me stroke for stroke as our tongues move with a languid speed. Even though this kiss is passion-filled, it's slow, hungry for so much more because we've realized nothing, *no one*, stands in our way.

This is finally our time where we can be Puck and Cami.

I can't get enough of her. I never will. Placing my hands low on her waist, I draw her to me, pressing us chest to chest. Our mouths tangle in a union of utter perfection because this is it. No more lies, no one standing in our way.

The only people to fuck this up is us.

"I want you," she whispers against my lips. "I can't stop."

"I want you too," I confess. "I always will."

But there's something I need to tell her before we do this. Something which will change the course of everything.

With one final kiss, I pull away, smiling when she pouts as she doesn't want me to stop. "Before we do this, I need to tell ya what I've planned, and if ya still want me afterward, well, then…I'm yours. Forever."

Her slender throat dips as she swallows deeply.

"Some things have changed, while others have remained the same. I didn't know what to expect when I got out. But what I did know was that workin' with Brody was the only way to find Sean.

"But Sean isn't as powerful as I thought he would be, which is why he's still in hidin'. He knows he can't beat Brody. He knows that the loyalties he was certain he would gain after Connor's death actually see him for the piece of shite that he is.

"It's because of this that the plan has now changed. It's because of you, because of yer fearlessness that I'm going to do somethin' I should have done a long time ago."

Babydoll nervously licks her lips. "What are you going to

do?"

I never thought I'd ever utter these words. "I'm goin' to kill Brody, but I want to make sure yer okay with me doin' that. He's a fucking bastard, but he's still yer dad."

She takes a moment to process what I've just shared because she understands when I say I'm going to kill him, I mean now. No more waiting. I thought I needed him alive, but I don't. There is no undying loyalty for either Sean or Brody because neither could ever be the leader Connor once was.

The men can be swayed given the right price or circumstance. Or, given the right leader.

If what Babydoll says is true, then the only person who can build an army with loyal men is me. It doesn't matter that Connor isn't my father. His colleagues and friends will always see me as the eldest Kelly son; the rightful ruler of Northern Ireland.

They are waiting for change, and that change is me.

I will kill Brody, making an example of him in case anyone else dares challenge me for my throne. This means it comes down to two people—Sean and me. And I won't lose.

"So, Baby, do ya still want me, knowing I'll have yer father's blood on my hands?"

Babydoll's breathing is shallow, and I worry she's gone into shock. I understand if she needs time. Or if she begs I change my mind.

But when she steps forward so we're inches apart, I realize

she doesn't need time. The only thing she needs is…me.

"Yes. I want you. Always. Forever. I…love you…so fucking much, it hurts to breathe."

Closing my eyes, I bask in her admission because I've not heard it in so long. To be loved is a gift. But to be loved by Babydoll—that is nothing short of a miracle.

"Then I'm yours."

She doesn't have a chance to speak because I'm on her, cupping the back of her neck, holding her prisoner as I kiss her passionately. She allows me to dominate her, her body molding to mine because we've finally come home.

I circle my tongue with hers, deepening the angle as I lead her to the point of no return. She moans when I bite her bottom lip, before sucking it gently. Even though we're pressed front to front, it's not close enough, so I lift her, coaxing her to wrap her legs around my waist.

She does, her pussy snug around my erection as I slam her back to the wall. Our mouths never miss a beat as we devour one another like it's the last day on earth. In some ways, I suppose it is because this is the start of something fucking beautiful.

She rubs herself against me, whimpering in need. I want nothing more than to fuck her senseless, but with Ethan in the next room, I know we'll have to raincheck on that thought. But I won't leave my girl wanting. She's waited long enough.

Walking toward the foot of the bed, I toss her onto the mattress, relishing in her yelp of surprise before she scampers onto the pillows, her eyes never leaving mine. Her taste lingers on my lips, but the sweetness I crave lays between those parful legs of hers.

Her skirt has ridden up, teasing me as I can just see the black lacy triangle covering her lovely cunt. She enjoys seeing me riled up, so she merely leans back on her elbows and opens her legs wider with a sassy grin.

Ethan won't wake for a while as he's still fucked up on the shite in his system. So I kneel onto the end of the mattress, taking in the goddess before me. Her choppy breaths reveal her nerves, and no matter how many times we've done this before, it always feels like the first time.

With an unhurried pace, I crawl toward her, coming to rest at the junction of her thighs. Her body trembles with anticipation as I gently rub over her underwear. She's wet. I'm hard. A deadly combination.

She lifts her hips, allowing me to slip off her underwear. When I see her pretty pink cunt, I lick my lips, ravenous beyond words. I don't bother taking off her skirt because I can't wait. Pushing it aside, I lower my mouth to her pussy and lay a single kiss over her hot flesh.

With a whimper, Babydoll lowers herself onto the pillow and opens her legs wider. I always feel so appreciative she'd allow an animal like me to touch her. I run my tongue along the seam of her pussy, humming when her sweetness hits me low.

She opens her legs wider and threads her fingers through

my hair, a silent plea I give her what we both want. I surrender because I need her as much as she needs me. She's still injured, so I'll try to be gentle.

I lick her slowly before parting her flesh with my tongue. She moans, arching her back and opening herself up wider to me. I take the offering, using my mouth, tongue, and fingers to work her over until she is quivering uncontrollably.

She is slathered all over me, and I love it. I love her, and one day, I will have the guts to tell her. But for now, I just want to make her come.

She tosses a leg over my shoulder and bows her back, moaning as I eat her out like she's my last meal. When I bite over her clit, she cries out and presses the heel of her foot into my back, holding me prisoner. But I come willingly because I am hers. And she is mine.

"Love me," she pants, "like only you know how."

I understand what she means. This attraction between us is unlike anything either of us has ever experienced before. To find such a pure connection in a world filled with violence and hate is an anomaly, but that's what Babydoll is.

She is in a class of her own.

There are no words to describe her, or my love for her because no single word exists. She is my everything, and so much more.

I suckle her flesh, working my tongue in and out until she is squirming in need. I'm sure to leave bruises on her thigh as

I grip it, holding her captive as I softly bite over her clit. I don't give her a chance to recover as I alternate between my tongue and finger, fucking her with skill.

Her body tightens, and I know she's close. "I love you," she cries, tenderly running her fingers through my hair. "It's always…been you."

Her admission touches me in ways I never thought possible, and emotion weighs heavily in my chest. I know she wants me to reciprocate, and I will. But I want to say it when the time is right; not just because she said it first.

Now, however, I can show her how I feel by giving her the best orgasm of her life.

"I want to…" she pants, but suddenly stops.

"Ya want to what?" I coax, my hot breath coating her damp skin.

"I want to ride your face," she confesses, her embarrassment apparent. But there is no need as there is nothing hotter than your woman making demands of you in the bedroom.

With one final lick of her pussy, I roll onto my back and take her with me. She doesn't waste a second and crawls on top of me, straddling me as she places her knees on either side of my face. When she's on all fours, she lowers her hips and rubs her pussy against my lips with a moan.

Instantly, I wrap my hands around her waist and encourage her to rock against me as I want her to ride me hard. She begins to move faster, rocking up and down as I fuck her with my tongue and mouth. I show no mercy as I bite, suck, and lick.

She groans, fucking my face without apology. I'm certain to leave fingermarks on her hips as I hold her, urging her to move faster. And she does.

Usually, I would feel uncomfortable being caged in this way because Babydoll is all over me. But not with her. Never with her.

"Oh, fuck," she curses, grinding herself against my mouth. She tears at the blankets beneath her, using them as reins as she rides me hard.

I encourage her to move faster so I can fuck her deeper with my tongue. A heavy whimper escapes her, which pleases me. She rocks wildly against me, chasing her release and when I flick my tongue over her swollen clit, she comes with a guttural moan.

Her pussy trembles over my lips, and I rub my face from side to side, wanting to shower myself with her sweetness. When the last tremor rocks her body, I flip her onto her back and steal her breaths as I kiss the living fuck out of her.

She whimpers, sucking on my tongue and writhing under me.

She presses both hands against my cheeks, the touch filled with nothing but love.

"See how grand ye taste?" I ask her, rubbing my lips across hers. Her cheeks instantly turn a deep scarlet.

"Let me take care of you," she says, fumbling with the

button on my jeans.

"No, Baby, this is all for you."

Kissing the tip of her nose, I roll off her and draw her into my arms. She comes willingly, and it feels incredible. We stay this way for minutes, both basking in this newfound freedom of being together without any reservations.

But there are some things we need to discuss.

"I don't want to rub this in Rory's face," she says softly. "We need to be discreet."

"Aye, I agree." Rory has just come around, and seeing me with the woman he loves will just push him away again.

A pensive silence embraces us, and I ask something which has nagged at me for a while. "Why did ya steal my ma's brooch, only to give it back?"

It feels like a lifetime ago, and in some ways, it is.

"Brody ordered I do something which would spark your interest in me, so I knew stealing from you would get under your skin," she reveals, snuggling closer to me. "But when I saw the brooch, I knew it held sentimental value to you, and I couldn't keep it.

"I dressed that way because Brody told me I was to do something which stood out. It was by chance we liked the same comic. But it shouldn't surprise me. Sometimes, I feel like you're my other half."

"Brody has been the puppet master this entire time," I say with bite. "His time has come."

Babydoll is quiet, and I wonder if she's having second thoughts. "How are you going to get him alone without raising suspicion?"

I haven't thought that far ahead as this plan wasn't on the cards until a few minutes ago.

She reads my silence for what it is. "I know a way."

I arch a brow, indicating I'm listening.

"You won't be able to get him alone unless—"

"Unless what?"

She licks her lips. "Unless you take him out in public. He'll assume it's safety in numbers. It'll be unexpected, and the only time he'll have his guard down. The busier the place, the better."

This is madness…but she's right.

"And I know the perfect place. He is hosting a fundraiser this weekend. It's very private and invite only. It's his way to appear like a law-abiding citizen to the masses, but the people who will be attending are just as corrupt as he is. A public execution will get more people on your side.

"You're going to kill him, and you're going to challenge Sean by doing so. No one will fuck with you because they'll fear you. You air the Doyles' dirty laundry and let everyone know there is a new king now. The rightful Kelly king."

It takes a lot to render me speechless, but Babydoll's evil genius makes me all warm and gushy inside.

This plan is brilliant, and it will work.

Babydoll is right. Killing Brody in public will instill the fear of God into people, and it will also challenge Sean. Brody was the one thing standing in the way. With him gone, it comes down to us. It will show Sean that I'm not afraid of him. I'm ready and waiting.

"I won't raise any suspicion being there because I'm invited. Brody wants the world to think we're one big happy family. I think he feels the closer I am to him, the less risk there is for me to betray him. Or maybe he believes I fell for his bullshit sob story back at the pub. He is clearly fucking delusional. Or desperate. I don't know.

"Normally, I would tell him to go fuck himself. But not this time. I'll get you in and help any way I can."

None of this would be possible without her. I thought I was alone, but I'm not.

She's my equal in every sense of the word. And I vow here, now, that I will do everything to make her happy for the rest of her life.

"Yes, let's do this," I say, drawing her closer and nudging her nose with mine.

"It's black and white themed," she states, gasping as I softly bite her bottom lip. "I like that you've put your piercings back in. It reminds me of when we first met."

"But we're not those people anymore, are we?"

I kiss her neck, relishing in her breathless sighs. "We'll always be us," she whispers. "Babydoll and Punky. And nothing can change that."

"Will ya help me pick out a suit?" I ask before sliding down her body and coming to rest between her thighs.

She peers down at me, eyes wide, but her surprise turns to desire when I slip two of my fingers into her mouth before sinking them into her pussy.

"Aye!" she cries out in ecstasy. Whether she is replying to my question or the fact that I'm playing with her pussy, I don't know. It doesn't matter either way because all that matters is this…and killing Brody Doyle.

TWELVE

PUNKY

Cian and Rory are parked a few streets away. They insisted they come because this started with us three, and it'll end the same way.

Hannah and Babydoll's sister, Eva, are on Ethan watch. It's been four days since he's gone cold turkey, and he's withdrawing badly. I didn't want to leave him, but Hannah assured me she'd be okay. I've left her handcuffs and a Taser in case she needs them.

I would prefer to be there, but I don't know when another opportunity like tonight will present itself again.

Hannah is armed to the teeth, and she knows how to shoot and not miss—she is a Kelly, after all. But I'm not taking any chances, which is why Ronan and his men are guarding the property. If anything happens to them, they'll pay with their lives and the lives of their loved ones.

Relying on others is still a hard pill to swallow, but I've learned that I can't do this on my own. Every person in my life has helped me in some way, and I need to accept that, for some reason, these people love and respect me.

Squashing down the questions I'll never find answers to, I walk down the alleyway where the food deliveries are brought and transported down the hallway and into the kitchen of the cathedral-turned-venue for hire.

The fundraiser is in the crypt—seems very appropriate for what's about to go down.

I see the delivery truck is right on time, just how Babydoll said it would be. I watch and wait as the deliverymen carry in crates of food and wine. When there is no one guarding the truck, I quickly make a beeline for it and reach for a wooden crate of wine bottles out of the back.

I'm in white overalls, the same uniform as the deliverymen, so no one questions me as I walk through the back door and into the venue, which will serve as my killing field.

The place is a flurry of people; everyone's in a hurry to get things organized for tonight's grand affair. I take in my surroundings, looking for exits in case I need to make a hasty departure. I walk past the kitchen, crate in hand, as it's my excuse in case I get caught.

Babydoll said to meet her in the staff bathroom, which is

the third door on the left. I continue walking like I belong here, and when I see the bathroom, I push open the door, sighing in relief when I see Babydoll standing in the middle of the room.

"Oh, thank God," she says, rushing over to me.

I place the crate by the door so I can hug her.

She holds me tightly, her nerves clear as she trembles in my arms. "It's goin' to be okay, Baby."

"I know. I'm just worried something will go wrong."

"Don't be thinkin' that. Nothin' will go wrong," I assure her because I will not fail.

Tonight, I *will* kill the man who murdered my ma, and by doing so, I'll challenge my dad to come out of hiding. Once I commit this sin, everyone who associates themselves with me will be in danger. Those I love will be used as pawns.

I wish it were different, but it's not. They all know the risks, yet, here they are, sticking their neck out for me.

Holding Babydoll out at arm's length, I level her with a soft gaze. "It'll be all right."

She sighs, not appearing convinced.

"Ya look lovely," I say, wanting to compliment her because she looks beautiful.

She's wearing a jeweled white ball gown. It dips low, but it's tasteful with a mesh collar. Her hair is twisted into an elegant bun, and her face has a light coat of makeup. Her lips are a succulent pink, and it takes all my willpower not to press my mouth to hers and mess up her masterpiece.

"Thank you," she says with a small smile. "I have your tux."

She retrieves a suit bag hanging from a toilet door and hands it to me.

I slip out of my overalls and change into the suit, feeling empowered, knowing this outfit will end the life of the man who's haunted my dreams since I was five years old.

Babydoll steps forward and extends her hand, gesturing for the bow tie. "Here, let me help you."

With expertise, she begins knotting my tie, but it seems she needs to keep busy in fear her mind will wander otherwise. I understand this is a lot for her, but I know asking her to sit this one out isn't an option. So all I can do is assure her that things will be all right.

She has tears in her eyes once she finishes. I grip her trembling fingers in mine. "I was thinkin', once this is over with, maybe we could go on a...date?"

My question catches her off guard, and I suddenly feel stupid for asking.

"A date?" she says, her lips twitching. "I think we're past dating."

"I know, but we didn't do things proper," I explain. "Ya deserve...stuff."

"Stuff?" she questions, doing a poor job of covering her smirk.

"Aye, like flowers and chocolates and whatever else happens on a date." This is foreign territory for me, so I actually have no idea if this is a thing or not.

She bursts into laughter, unable to control herself.

"Ack, forget I said anythin," I say, shaking my head at my stupidity.

I'm about to turn away, but Babydoll quickly grabs my arm. "I'm sorry for laughing. I would love to go on a date with you, Puck Kelly."

"Ya would?"

"Of course, I would, silly. I've only waited ten years for you to ask me to go steady with you." She grins, biting her bottom lip to stop another outburst.

"All right, that's enough," I playfully say, drawing her into my arms and pressing us chest to chest. Even in heels, she's still a head shorter than me.

Her playfulness soon simmers and blossoms into something else. "You look really good in a suit. Too bad we'll have to throw it away once tonight is over with."

She means because it'll be covered in her father's blood.

"I'll wear one on our date," I promise, wishing to ease her fears.

"Promise?"

"Cross my heart," I reply before pressing my lips to hers.

She moans, arching into me as she wraps her arms around my neck. We kiss softly, but the hunger is always beneath the surface, always demanding more. But more will have to wait.

Brushing my thumb across her cheek, I break our kiss,

smiling when she pulls out her lip in disappointment.

"I want more," she whispers, her eyes animated. "I always want more."

I do too. I want nothing more than to lose myself in her for days, but not yet.

She reads my thoughts and walks to the mirror to reapply some lipstick and fix her hair. She looks perfect, but she needs to do something with her hands.

I slip into my jacket, buttoning it and joining Babydoll in front of the mirror.

We peer at one another's reflections, our looks saying more than words ever could. So much awaits us because there isn't a plan, per se. I don't know how or when I'm going to strike. I just know, when the time is right, I'm going to rip Brody's head from his shoulders.

And I mean that literally.

"Ready?" I ask, giving her one final chance to back out.

But Babydoll isn't a quitter. Her loyalty and love for me over the years have proven this.

"Yes," she replies with a sharp nod. "It's now or never."

She doesn't understand the significance of that phrase as that song changed my life forever. It seems fitting this ends with it.

"Be careful," she says, turning to me.

"I will. You too."

"I'll be all right," she affirms, and when she averts her gaze,

I know she's not telling me everything.

"Cami?" I question, not wanting any surprises when we go in there.

"I may have called in a favor with Ron Brady," she confesses coyly. "Before you get angry with me, he was the one who jumped at the chance to help. He and fifteen of Connor's friends want to do this. We're going to need all the allies we can get.

"We're speculating that doing this won't be met with retaliation," she explains quickly. "But what if we're wrong? If we are met with gunfire, at least we have an army to help us fight. I know we have Cian and Rory, but I won't allow that bastard, my *father*, to win, even in death."

Once, we were strong, and no one would dare challenge us. We had the loyalty of all, but now, we're fumbling our way through the dark. I don't know who is friend or foe, but what I do know is that if Babydoll trusts Ron Brady, then so do I.

"You're mad," she states, sighing in defeat. "I thought—"

I don't allow her to finish.

I grip the back of her neck and draw us both together, brow to brow. "Thank you."

She opens, but soon closes her mouth, obviously not expecting that reply. "I just want this done," she whispers against my lips.

I almost go weak at the knees at the feel of her wet mouth pressed to mine.

There is an urgency to our kiss because so much will change

once the night is through. I wish I could predict how tonight ends, but I can only hope we're all alive come morning. But just in case, I need her to know that I love her. That I've always loved her, even when I wasn't supposed to.

"I lo—"

But she presses her finger over my lips, silencing me. I don't understand why.

"Not now," she whispers against my lips. "Tell me when we're not fighting for our lives so I know you wanted to say it, not because you were afraid you couldn't."

With a sigh, I nudge my nose with hers, moving from side to side. "I'll see ya soon."

A quiver leaves her as she nods.

There will never be a good time, so we reluctantly break apart. She gives me my gold invite before opening the door and closing it softly behind her.

It's time.

She will text me once it's safe as she said she has everything under control. Until then, I'm to wait quietly.

I text Rory and Cian the updates as we're no longer alone. Thanks to Babydoll, we have allies on our side, willing to fight with us. The plans have veered off course, but this plan was never foolproof. I was always hoping a better option would come about.

And it has.

Tonight, Brody Doyle will take his last breath.

I check in with Hannah, who says that Ethan is asleep. I worry he'll try to sweet-talk her into cutting him some slack because if she does, Ethan will be lost to us for good. He'll do anything to find his next fix and will tell her anything she wants to hear.

She promises me she won't fall for his lies, but I know how convincing a junkie can be.

Anger courses through me when I think of the reason my baby brother is hooked. Sean no doubt pushed the drugs onto Ethan so he could control him. An addict will do anything to score, and this is how Sean has been able to control Ethan for so long.

He's a drug-dependent zombie who is lost and alone in this world. The only thing which gives him joy is getting high. He won't give that up without a fight. I know that. So I need to replace that high with something else.

Love.

Ethan needs to know how sorry I am for leaving him all alone. I never meant to abandon him, and I'll spend the rest of my life proving to him that he is loved. I can only hope he finds it in his heart to forgive me.

My phone lights up, and when I read the message from Babydoll, the devil within rattles at the bars on his cage.

Let's do this. Meet me by the ice sculpture.

With a deep breath, I take one last look at my reflection in the mirror and nod. This is the first time in a long time I've seen a man I recognize. There is passion and fire behind my eyes because this is the first step to taking back my life.

I send Rory and Cian a text, letting them know it's showtime.

Opening the door, I exit the bathroom and walk down the hallway like I belong. No one pays any attention to me as they're all too busy ensuring the night goes off without a hitch.

Thankfully, the crypt is small, so it's easy to find. The moment I walk down the stone stairs and see it up ahead, a bubble of excitement rises because I couldn't have set a better scene myself. It's Gothic and haunting, and I can imagine this crypt was used for more sinister events back in the day.

The security guard at the door is too busy chatting to some busty blonde to pay any attention to me as I flash him my invite. He nods that I'm to enter without even bothering to frisk me first. This is a blessing and a curse because I wonder who else is armed.

Babydoll has my gun and knife in her bag as the guards won't search her, but it seems they're not searching anyone, which is strange.

Taking in my surroundings, I'm thankful the lighting is dim, as it allows me to keep to the shadows. I walk through the room, passing a harpist playing a soft piece on her large white harp. The room is lit up with candles, setting a romantic mood for some, but to me, it is the perfect place to spill blood.

Tall tables covered with white tablecloths are set up around the room as it's not a formal dinner. Guests stand around, sipping French champagne and laughing like they're here to have a good time. But we're all privy to the fact that this fundraiser is a load of shite.

Every person in this room is as corrupt as the other, and soon, they'll learn what happens when you side with the wrong team. From the looks of their fancy jewels and expensive dresses and suits, they are the rich who are considered upstanding citizens to the unsuspecting.

Behind closed doors, though, these arseholes are depraved, cruel sadists who exploit anyone for their own personal gain. I think about the gangs Brody is offering protection against. Taking in the crowd, I'd bet anything the gangs are made up of these men and women.

The more fear they instill in people, the more power they have. Their time has come to an end.

I see an ice statue of a cherub up ahead. Babydoll stands behind it, casually sipping champagne. In the room of hundreds, she stands out. She is my beacon of light in a weathering storm.

I make my way over to her, not drawing any attention to myself as I keep to the shadows with my chin downcast. When I reach her, she doesn't flinch. She doesn't acknowledge my presence because to onlookers, we're merely strangers, waiting for our host to address the room.

I reach for a glass of champagne and drink it coolly while

examining the room from behind the rim. I can't see any familiar faces, but that doesn't mean they're not here.

The music suddenly quiets, and the room erupts into loud applause when Brody Doyle appears. His friends slap him on the back while his smugness has me guessing he has no idea I'm here. Liam stands to the left of the small stage, watching the room closely.

I'm thankful Brody has chosen candlelight to set the theme because Babydoll and I remain hidden at the back of the room.

Brody taps the microphone once, ensuring it's on. "Friends," he starts, giving the room a false sense of security. "Thank you for coming tonight. It means a lot to my family and me."

He takes a deep breath, which is all for show, as he ensures it echoes across the speakers.

"We're here tonight because my daughter, Erin, was taken away from me. She was innocent. She never hurt a soul. But that didn't stop those terrorists. The police are still searching for her killers, but it'll never bring back my Erin."

Sniffles around the room reveal some people have fallen for Brody's bullshit, but I know better. He's bitter because Sean outsmarted him. I don't know what he hopes to achieve with this fundraiser, but I doubt he's hosting this out of the goodness of his heart.

Both Sean's and Brody's allies are split down the middle, meaning one can't overthrow the other. They are both as spineless and untrustworthy as the other, which is why my plan to eliminate both won't fail.

"Tonight is in honor of my late daughter, who was taken away far too soon. All money raised will be donated to the Seek Help Foundation here in Dublin who help unfortunate children so they don't end up on the streets, their future fated to be one of crime and gang-related activities. So please dig deep."

I scoff softly because this sob story is fucking pathetic.

His claims of caring for anyone other than himself are laughable. This fundraiser is no doubt a ruse for him to seek out future employees. The misfits, the kids who won't be missed, are most valuable to men like Brody.

"Can I call my daughter, Camilla, up here to help with the auction?"

I don't allow my emotion to show because I didn't know about this. Babydoll said to trust her, so this is me trusting her. But going in blind turns my stomach. If anything were to happen to her up there…

I swallow past the thought because I need to focus.

The crowd watches her as she passes them gracefully. She holds her head high, owning the room like the queen she is. When she gets on stage, Brody pulls her in for a hug. She kisses his cheek, not letting on what's about to transpire.

I keep my eye on Liam because something about him appears off. I can't place my finger on it, but he seems… distracted. An ominous weight settles in my gut, but I shrug it off as my paranoid mind just adding to the ever-growing shite pile.

"Thank you for coming," Babydoll says into the microphone, addressing the room. "It means a lot to…my family."

Her pause reveals the disgust she feels at associating herself with the Doyle name. But she'll never be one of those fuckers.

"The first thing we have up for auction is a personal training session with Lachlan O'Malley."

When the crowd ooh and aah, I assume Lachlan is some expert in his field as I've never heard of him.

"Let's start the bidding at fifty euros," Babydoll says, peering around the room.

A lady at the front of the room raises her hand, which sets off a bidding war. This goes on for minutes, and when the final bid is settled at over a thousand euros, I realize these people have money to burn. I wonder what else is on the cards.

The bidding continues on various items for what feels like hours. I keep to the shadows, watching the major players who spend hard as they may prove to be useful to me later on.

"Okay, we've saved the best for last," Babydoll says, and when she focuses her attention my way, I know this is it. "The final auction for this evening is one which we hope will have you digging deep."

Brody smirks, his Good Samaritan act almost forcing me to vomit in disgust.

"So, ladies and gentlemen, without further ado, the final prize is…a date with my father."

Brody's head snaps to the left, hinting this was never discussed with him, which means this is my time to strike.

He doesn't make a scene, though, and smiles cordially.

The crowd also appears surprised as nervous looks are exchanged between the partygoers. But when Babydoll starts the bidding at one hundred euros the nerves are replaced with greed.

The woman sitting a few feet away raises her hand. "Five hundred euros" she shouts, her excitement palpable.

This gives me an idea.

As Babydoll keeps track of the bids, I subtly move through the shadows, concealing my motives as I slowly walk through the room. The bidding is at three thousand euros which reveals how desperate these lickarses are.

I scan the room for who I need, and I see that person in the shape of a woman wearing some ridiculous contraption on her head. The brim of her elaborate hat gives her a clearing of about five feet around her as no one can stand close by in fear of losing an eye.

But this acts as the perfect camouflage.

As the bidding continues, I ensure not to alert anyone as I walk past them, keeping my eyes peeled on Babydoll and Brody. No one notices me lurking as they're all too excited at the fact that the auction has now reached six thousand euros.

But I'm about to give them something to be excited about.

When I'm within reach of the woman, I make eye contact

with Babydoll. She has no idea what I have planned, but nods artfully, divulging that she trusts me.

"Do I have seven thousand euros?" she asks, scanning the room.

Brody stands proudly, hands in his pockets, oblivious to what's about to unfold.

"Going once, going twice…"

It's now my turn to show Brody Doyle just how valuable he is to me.

With the subtlest of movements, I reach out and tug at the long peacock feather hanging from the lady's hat. Instinctively, she raises her arm to stop her hat from falling off; just how I knew she would. But everyone around her gasps, as they all assume she's just bid seven thousand euros for a date with the devil.

"Sold!" Babydoll exclaims quickly as she clearly saw me.

The woman smiles uncomfortably as there is no way she can take it back.

I stand off to the side, biding my time, and when Babydoll calls the woman to claim her "prize," my time has come—finally.

The harpist commences a soft tune as the auction is done. The crowd whispers behind their hands, no doubt gossiping about who won what and how much was paid. I follow close behind the lady, using her as a shield to glide through the room without detection.

Babydoll is aware of my movements and takes care of the

thing which stands between Brody and me—Liam.

She taps him on the shoulder, gesturing toward the hallway. I don't know what she whispered into his ear, but it has him making a quick beeline for the exit. The stage is set…

Brody advances forward with a smile, but that soon fades and is replaced with utter fear—he knows, he knows his time has come.

Stepping out from behind the lady, I smirk in victory. "Boo."

Before he has a chance to reach for his gun, the room is suddenly eclipsed into darkness. The only source of light is the flicker of flames which illuminate this place into a morbid paradise. I push the lady aside and storm forward, gripping Brody by the throat and walking him backward until his back hits the brick wall.

He tries to fight me, but I knee him in the balls and then elbow him in the stomach to wind him further. As he's bent in half, gasping for air, I disarm him, placing his gun at the small of my back. I take off my suit jacket and roll up the sleeves of my white shirt.

"She betrayed me," he wheezes, eyes on fire when he realizes Babydoll was never interested in playing happy families; when he realizes their little heart-to-heart chat meant nothing to her because she chose me. She will always choose me. "That fucking slut."

With a growl, I press my forearm over his throat. "I'd be watchin' what ya say now."

When he tries to push off the wall, I press down harder over his larynx. He soon realizes I'm done playing.

"Ya don't have the bollocks to do it, son," he challenges, eyeing me viciously. "Yer goin' to end my life with so many witnesses, are ya? I don't think so."

Babydoll was right.

She said Brody would have his guard down, believing he had safety in numbers. But it's the numbers that will help me get my message across.

Brody's attention soon focuses over my shoulder, and I know it's Babydoll without looking. A sharp, familiar object is placed into my open palm, a silent invitation to do what I must.

When I remove my forearm, Brody instantly tries to fight me, but I soon put him in line when I break his nose with my elbow. He hollers, but that doesn't subdue him. So, when he attempts to kick me in the stomach, I grab his leg and slice across his Achilles tendon.

He collapses with a pained howl because standing on two feet is a thing of the past.

Gripping him by the hair, I drag him to the front of the stage, then stop and breathe. I take a moment to really appreciate my surroundings, because inflicting screams on those who are usually the abusers gives me great pleasure.

The lights suddenly flicker back on, showcasing the glorious sight I've created.

Men and women stop mid-flee, blinking quickly as they

adjust to the change in lighting. When they see the exit is manned by Ron Brady with a machine gun in hand, they gasp. That gasp turns to screams when their eyes are riveted my way.

"I'm awful sorry I messed up yer black and white theme," I say with a smirk when I see the trail of red I left while dragging Brody to his impending death.

"Liam!" Brody screams, squirming madly, but he's not going anywhere.

"Get on yer knees," I order firmly.

When he doesn't comply, I yank on his hair, forcing him to obey as best he can with a split Achilles.

I have no idea what happened to the incompetent security working the door because there is no one here to save Brody. Ron Brady mans the exit, grinning broadly, a warning to anyone who dares to take him on.

I decide to introduce myself in case anyone decides to be a hero. "If I could trouble ya for a minute of yer time, I'd much appreciate it."

The fact that I'm holding a bleeding Brody hostage assures their utmost attention.

"Thank you," I say when all eyes are on me. "My name is Puck Kelly. My father was Connor Kelly."

The silence can be cut with a knife.

There is no need to explain who Connor was. They all know. They also know shit is about to go down.

"Northern Ireland is my home. As it was to my family

generations ago. But ya see, Brody here, well, he wants to use my home for his own personal greed. In case ya didn't know, which I'm sure most of ya do, Brody is a liar, a cheat, and a murderer."

No one dares speak.

"Brody, along with his brother, Aidan, raped and killed my ma. I saw everythin'. I was locked in the wardrobe, helpless to help her. I was five years old. But I'm not helpless anymore. I wasn't helpless when I slit Aidan Doyle's throat. Nor was I when I burned Hugh Doyle alive."

The crowd gasp, their curiosity soon turning to fear.

"So, I'm here tonight to avenge what is rightfully mine. Brody took my ma's life, and now, in front of you good people, I'm goin' to take his."

A lady to the left of the stage dry retches, holding back her vomit behind her hand.

"You can't do this," a middle-aged man says, stepping forward, phone in hand. "I'm calling the Garda."

With a chuckle, I call his bluff. "Go on then. I'm sure they'll be interested to know yer all as guilty, in one way or another, as Brody."

His bravado soon dies as he didn't think I was privy to his dirty little secrets.

Babydoll mentioned that the people here are as vile and corrupt as the Doyles, so I know none of them would risk their freedom to save Brody. They will be forced to watch an affluent man take his last breath and know that I, Puck Kelly, am responsible for this war I'm about to start.

I don't know where Liam is, but he won't stop hunting me until I'm dead. So, I need to beat him to it. *I* will be the last man standing because I've done my time.

When I tighten my grip on Brody's hair, he begins to flail, knowing his time on this earth is running out. "Take it all," he pleads. "I don't want Belfast. Y'll never see me again."

"We're past negotiatin'," I snarl, yanking his head back. "This is a long time comin'."

"You think ye can beat Sean on yer own?" he shouts, eyes wide as he peers up at me. "You need me!"

"Naw, I don't," I counter with a smirk. "I have all the help I need."

On cue, Babydoll stands beside me. "Hi, Daddy." She smugly waves.

Her betrayal infuriates him. "Ya fucking whore! Yer just like yer mother! Ye'll never be my daughter. I should have let him have his way with ya."

She hisses, taking a small step back. "You knew?"

"Aye, I knew yer brother, Hugh, wanted to fuck ya. I knew he was straddlin' the line. But I didn't think ye'd have an issue with it, seeing as ya had no problems spreadin' yer legs for Puck."

Her eyes fill with tears because, although I know about Hugh being infatuated with her, I didn't realize the full extent of it. To find out Brody was aware of the sick things he did to her has me pressing my blade to his throat.

"Y'll never speak to her like that again."

The crowd gasps—some in horror, others in excitement.

Brody raises his trembling hands in surrender, but that's not an option. It never was. "My death will be avenged!" he exclaims. "Yer startin' a war, Puck Kelly."

Yanking his head back farther and exposing his throat, I grin. "Oh, I'm countin' on it."

"Please, naw," he begs, interlacing his hands. "I've got money. Don't kill me."

"Yer pathetic," I spit. "Pleadin' for yer life like a little pussy when ya had no mercy for my ma, for the hundreds of people y've killed. Or for yer daughter who ya used like a pawn."

Babydoll moves closer to me. I want her to know this is *our* vengeance. This is a war we *will* win because of her.

"Ya can have it all." Brody implores me to see reason. But this is the only reason I see.

"I don't want anythin' from ya…" I pause, before adding, "Except for yer head."

Brody closes his eyes and begins to pray.

"I wish I had days, weeks to torture ya, but honestly, forever wouldn't be long enough time to do unto ye for what ya deserve." His death will never be long, bloody, or violent enough, but it'll send a message to Sean. So, it'll do…for now.

He continues praying. Maybe he thinks his God will offer

him salvation.

"Forgive those who trespass against us; and lead us not into temptation."

But here, now, his God doesn't exist. The only person who does is me—the devil he created.

His neck is arched back at a painful angle, and when he opens his eyes, I smirk. Vengeance is finally mine.

"But deliver us from evil," I finish for him, and when I see hope reflected in his eyes, hope that was taken away from Mum when he played a part in her death, I slash my knife in one fluid movement across his throat.

His warm blood coats my arms and shirt. I inhale deeply, a sense of calm overcoming me as he gurgles, choking on his own blood. He's still alive when I make good on my promise and detach his head from his shoulders.

His body flops forward, landing with a squelch on the stage as I hold his severed head in my hand. Peering down at it, I smile. Nothing has looked more perfect.

There is the calm before the storm as the masses watch in disbelief, unsure if what they just witnessed actually occurred. But when I drop his head by his twitching torso, blood splattering the faces and clothes of people standing close by, the calm erupts into bedlam.

Screams pierce the night air as the rich and powerful realize that won't save them this time. Their social standing means nothing to me.

"Let this be a warning to youse all…don't fuck with me. If yer not with me, yer against me. And if ye know where Sean Kelly is…tell him it's only a matter of time. Ats us nai."

It's a flurry of panic as the guests desperately try to leave. I nod at Ron Brady, and he steps aside to let them go. For now.

I take a moment to appreciate the mayhem and compare it to what I once saw—a black, white, and red imagery reflecting the death of my childhood.

Liam Doyle suddenly appears in the archway, frantically shoving people aside to get to me. His time is coming, but that time is not now.

"Babydoll, go!" I order over the hysterical screams. "I'll find ya."

She appears to be in shock, staring at the dismembered body of her father with wide eyes.

Ron is at her side, dragging her away toward the door behind the stage as she continues to stoically stare at Brody's corpse. She doesn't fight, which is unlike her.

"Ron, take her someplace safe."

He nods firmly.

I will deal with the consequences later, no matter what they are, because when Liam is a few feet away, I calmly walk to where Brody's head lays. I memorize the image before I spit on it. Liam's incensed cries cut through the carnage as he comes charging for me, but he stops dead in his tracks when I kick his father's severed head like a football.

On instinct, he catches it, which is what I knew he would do.

He peers down at the head cradled in his hands. A surreal moment, no doubt. His revenge will wait because now, he has to collect the pieces of his father.

A look of promise is exchanged between us. The next time we meet, only one of us will be left standing. With Brody's blood coating my fingers, I strike two lines down the center of my forehead in honor of my ma.

Two down, one to go.

With that as my motivation, I quickly exit through the same door as Ron and gather my sense of direction. Following the signs, I find my way out back to where Rory has parked the car. He and Cian were here for backup, but I'm glad they weren't needed because we're about to fight a bigger war.

Opening the back door, I dive inside. "Drive."

The car tears off down the road while I lay on the back seat, my heart racing uncontrollably. Now that I'm out of there, the brutality of what I did hits me, and when I look at my bloody hands, turning them over and over, a maniacal laugh spills from me.

I did it.

I have taken back a small piece of my soul.

"Where's Cami?" Rory asks, looking at me in the rearview mirror.

"She's with Ron Brady."

"Cian, send him a text and ask where they're headed, will ya?"

Cian does as Rory says.

Once he's done, he turns over his shoulder to look at me. "What did ya do?"

He can guess, seeing as I'm covered in another man's blood. But he wants to hear it from me.

"I did what I promised," I say, inhaling at the memory of my blade effortlessly cutting through muscle and flesh. "I took Brody Doyle's head."

There is no need to elaborate further because the fact that I'm still standing and he isn't is a sure sign we've won the war— for now.

Rory drives to the address Ron text to Cian. We're all silent, pensive to what transpired and what's headed our way.

I can still feel Brody's warm blood coating my hands as I detached his head from his shoulders. I can still taste his fear as he took his last breath. I didn't know how I'd feel when I finally avenged my mum, and now that it's done, I realize I still feel numb.

Sean is the one that I want. Brody and Aidan were the starters, and now, I'm ready for the main course.

"What the fuck?"

Rory's curse has me sitting up, and when I see a car parked on the side of the road with its hazard lights on and Ron Brady standing by it, my heart begins to race for an entirely different reason.

I'm out of the car before Rory puts it into park.

"Where is she?" I ask, the tone of my voice hinting to Ron that I'm not fucking around.

When he sees me, he quickly raises his hands in surrender. "She was out of the car before I could stop her."

"*Where* is she?" I repeat dangerously slow, not interested in his excuses.

He gestures to his head to the aul' abandoned manor. "She ran into there."

Just as I'm about to go in search of her, Rory rushes past me. "I'll go."

He doesn't give me the option to argue, but I wouldn't because even though they're no longer engaged, he still sees himself as her closest confidant. It kills me not to go after her, but maybe he is the better choice anyway.

Cian stands by me, reading my thoughts, but doesn't say a word.

"What happened?"

Ron removes his cap and rubs his sweaty brow. "We were on the way to the address I text ya. One minute, she was sittin' quietly, and then the next, she's jumpin' out the car. If I was drivin' any faster, she would have been killed."

Looking at the manor, it takes all my willpower not to chase after her.

"She's in shock," I say, angry with myself for allowing her to see what I did.

"She's tough, Puck. Don't underestimate her."

Ron is right, but there is no shame in needing a breather after witnessing your father's head being removed from his body by the man you love.

"Thank you, Ron. What ya did back there, it's changed everythin'. We've sent a message, and that message is…ya don't want to fuck with Connor Kelly's son."

I don't fail to see the irony in that statement as once upon a time, I would have rather cut out my own tongue than admit I was Connor's son, but now, I wear that title with pride. I wish he were alive so I could tell him that.

But I'll have to make it up to him in another way, and that's rebuilding the kingdom he worked so hard to protect.

"We're glad yer back, son," Ron says, his sincerity ringing true. "Northern Ireland missed ya."

"Aye, I missed her too."

Cian nudges me with his elbow and when I see Rory walking toward us alone, I brace for the worst. "She doesn't want me… She wants you."

I open but soon close my mouth because there is nothing I can say that will erase the pain Rory feels at that fact. For him to phrase it the way he did, I make the assumption that he knows she wants me in more ways than one.

With a sigh, I walk past him, bracing for him to knock me on my arse. I won't fight back. I deserve it. But he doesn't strike me. He simply lowers his chin, unable to watch me console the woman he loves.

Like an utter bastard, I quickly go in search of Babydoll, forgetting about everything because the only thing that matters is finding her.

Sections of the roof are missing, allowing the moonlight to be my beacon as I search the dilapidated manor for Cami. I use caution when I climb the staircase as the floor is unstable. This place is barely standing. I need to find her and get her to safety.

I turn the corner, and a long hallway awaits me.

This place would have been the envy of many back in the day, but now, it's just a sad reminder of what once was.

Strips of gold-flowered wallpaper curl from the walls, and the soggy carpet squelches with each step I take. I poke my head around each of the doorjambs—which no longer have any doors attached—as I approach the many rooms, but Babydoll is nowhere to be found.

I reach the last room on the left, and when I look into it, I sigh in relief. Babydoll is standing out on the balcony. With an unhurried pace, I walk into the bedroom, not wanting to frighten her as the balcony looks far from stable.

She knows I'm here as my footsteps announce my arrival, but she won't turn around.

"Baby," I quietly say. "Are ya all right?"

I know it's a stupid question, considering the circumstances, but I need her to tell me what's wrong.

She remains perfectly still, the moonlight catching the jewels on her dress. I've never seen her so…quiet. It worries me.

The balcony floor has holes, and when I step onto the concrete, the sound of crumbling pieces bounces off the ground below us. I stand beside her, ensuring to leave some space between us because I don't want to crowd her.

She continues staring off into the distance, her hands gripping the railing.

"I'm sorry ya had to see what ya did." I wasn't thinking about anyone when I slit Brody's throat. All I cared about was the vengeance coursing through my veins.

But I've clearly scarred Babydoll as she won't even look at me.

"I should have thought of ye, and how it would affect ya. I should have killed him quicker and not taken pleasure in seein' him suffer."

I enjoyed torturing him, which allowed Babydoll to see my true colors. Is she disgusted by what she saw? I don't know what she's thinking, and it's driving me crazy. If she can't forgive me, then all of this will have been for nothing.

"Cami…talk to me," I beg, uncaring she can hear the desperation in my plea.

The night is cool, and a shiver rocks her quivering frame. I go to take off my jacket, but realize two things—one, I left my jacket at the crypt, and two, I'm slathered in her father's blood.

I go to turn, embarrassed to be here, pleading for mercy

when I didn't show that to her dad, but she gently grips my elbow to stop me. I look at her, confused to what's going on.

The tears in her eyes shine under the moonlight as she whispers, "Thank you."

"Thank you?" I question, taken aback. "What are ya thankin' me for?"

"No one has ever put me first, and that's all you've done. Time and time again. What happened with Hugh—" She takes a deep breath before continuing. "He humiliated me and did things I…I'm ashamed I didn't do more."

A tear trickles down her cheek.

I want to wipe it away, but I don't know if she'll withdraw from me.

"I couldn't breathe," she explains. "I needed to get out of that car. I'm embarrassed you know what he did. I wouldn't blame you if you didn't want me—"

"Stop that," I gently interrupt. "None of this is yer fault. You were doin' what ya had to, to survive."

"I'm pathetic. Nothing but a victim when I should have done more." She slams her fist onto the railing, biting her lip in anger.

But I won't stand back and allow her to blame herself.

With a hesitant touch, I place my hand over her fist, stopping her from hurting herself further. "I don't see a victim," I state. "I see a survivor. That's all y've done, Baby. Y've just tried to survive."

More tears fill her eyes as we stand together, broken and wounded under this star-filled sky.

She focuses her attention on our hands and then looks at my shirt. She only just realizes I'm covered in Brody's blood. I'm at her mercy because whatever she wants, I will obey her without a fight.

She turns to face me, and I do the same to her. She examines me slowly, no doubt reliving every step of tonight. I feel dirty in every sense of the word, so when Babydoll attempts to touch my cheek, I turn away.

"I don't want to pollute ya with my filth," I confess, chin downcast.

She reaches out and lifts my chin to meet her eyes once again. The air is suddenly on fire because finally…I know what she wants.

She stands on her toes and presses her mouth to mine, kissing me with a sense of urgency and desperation that takes my breath away. I kiss her back with passion because I never thought she'd want to kiss me again.

She winds her fingers through my snarled hair, tugging hard as she bites my bottom lip and then thrusts her tongue into my mouth.

"Fuck me," she pants, frantically fumbling with the buttons on my shirt.

"Baby," I say, attempting to stop her from undressing me. "I'm covered in yer…father's blood. Let me get cleaned up. Let's go back home and—"

"No," she interrupts, slapping my hand away. "Now."

Before I have a chance to plead she see reason, my buttons scatter all over the ground as she rips my shirt down the middle. My mouth parts in shock as her aggression is a surprise.

She doesn't give me any time to recover as she reaches for the buckle of my belt, making it clear she wants this, and she wants this now.

But not like this.

"Cami, stop," I say, firmly gripping her wrist to stop her from unfastening my trousers.

"You don't want to fuck me? Is that it?"

"Ya know that's not it," I reply, shaking my head. "Yer hurtin'. What ya saw tonight, if ya need some time to—"

"What I need is a good fuck," she aggressively spits. "And if you're not going to give it to me, then I'll find someone who will."

She's angry, confused, and probably sad, and I understand that. So I don't take her comment to heart.

"Would ya quit actin' like this? Talk to me. I want to know what yer thinkin'."

"Why?" she shouts, angry with me.

Good.

"'Cause ya saw me decapitate yer dad," I reply calmly. "No matter that he was a fucking arsehole, he was still yer father. That's got to affect ya."

"Will killing Sean affect *you*?" she challenges, arching a defiant brow.

"That's different. Sean is nothin' like Brody. He continues to fuck with me while Brody actually wanted to make amends with you, no matter how delusional that was. I think, no matter what he did, yer hurtin' that he's dead, and that's normal."

"Fuck you," she snaps, shaking her head. "You don't know what you're talking about. I'm not hurting. I hate him!"

"There's nothin' to be ashamed of," I assure her. "He was yer dad."

"He used me!" she cries, arms out wide. "How dare you say I care. He's a fucking monster. What does that say about me then? How could I love a monster? If what you say is true, then what does that say about me when I was the one who orchestrated his death?"

When I don't reply, she advances forward and shoves me in the chest.

"Answer me! You seem to have all the answers, so go on then. How could I possibly love the man who ruined my fucking life?"

I don't retaliate. I allow her to take her emotions out on me because that's the only way she'll heal. For us to work, she'll need to forgive me because if she doesn't, we won't survive this. And she needs to forgive herself.

"Ya don't choose who ya love, Cami," I honestly confess. "Love chooses you. And yer powerless to stop that. Just how I was powerless to stop from fallin' in love…with you."

She blinks once, her anger simmering as she digests what I just shared.

It's time she knows how I feel about her. Not because I'm afraid I'll not have the chance again, but rather, because I want to.

"I love you so fucking much, I can scarcely breathe at times. And that scares me. I've never loved anyone before because my entire life, I was surrounded by hate. But that changed…the day I met you."

The fire behind her eyes fades, and her walls begin to crumble.

"I was the one who took Brody's life, not you, but ya need to forgive yerself because the hate ya feel, it'll eat ya up inside, and sooner or later, y'll wish ya were dead too.

"It's okay to feel bad that he's dead. I'd be worried if ya didn't. Yer vulnerability makes ye strong. It makes ya human—my human. But his death, it's on me. And I need ya to forgive me for that."

"Forgive you?" she says in a whisper.

"Aye. If ya want forever, then ya need to be okay with the fact that the man ye love was the man who killed yer father. You need to forgive me. I mean truly forgive me, and then you'll need to forgive yerself for lovin' me."

Her chest rises and falls slowly as she processes what I just said.

"If ya need time, I understand. I—"

She steps forward, reaching for my hand and pressing it over her heart. "I don't need time. I just need you. I'll always need you. No matter what you say, no matter what you do, I'll always want you. I forgive you. And I love you too."

And just like that, the world becomes whole once more.

"I'm sorry for lashing out," she softly says. "I just…it was a lot seeing that. I thought I'd be okay with it, and I am. I just…"

"I understand," I gently interject, cupping her cheek. "There's no need to explain. Death is never an easy thing."

"And you saw your mother murdered when you were five years old. I can't imagine what that would have been like, but after tonight, I get it. I understand why you need vengeance. Not just for your mom but for yourself as well."

To hear those words appeases me of some guilt. It makes me feel like maybe I'm not such a monster, after all.

Babydoll reaches for my hands and examines them closely. "These hands," she whispers, "they've killed."

"They have. And they'll kill again."

"But they've also healed," she reasons. "They've also shown kindness. And love."

I'm her prisoner as she lifts up her ballooned skirt with my hand still in hers and places my hand over the outside of her underwear. I hiss when I feel the thin silk is damp with her arousal. She coaxes me to rub her slowly.

"I didn't mean it," she says, locking eyes with me as I begin rubbing circles over her pussy. "I would never be with anyone else. I don't want anyone else."

Her comment has me thinking about Rory. I should feel a sliver of guilt for being here, with Cami this way, but I don't.

"I don't want anyone else either. Yer my forever, Camilla. I love you."

A contented cry leaves her as she stands on her toes and presses her lips to mine. Our walls have been obliterated, and I've never been more terrified in my life.

Love is a battlefield, and we're fighting unarmed.

Babydoll arches into my touch, begging for more, and more I give when I slip my hand into her underwear and sink two fingers into her pussy. She whimpers into my mouth, circling my tongue with hers.

I begin playing with her, her body always so ready for me. It's a turn-on to know she wants me as much as I want her.

When she gets my belt and zipper undone, she slips her hand into my trousers, humming when she feels my erection. As I delve in deeper, faster, Babydoll takes my shaft into her hand and begins to stroke me up and down.

I almost come because it feels so fucking good.

I forget we're in an abandoned manor, covered in blood, with our friends waiting outside for us. I forget everything but this. Nothing else matters but her.

Removing my fingers from her pussy, I tear off her underwear with a sharp tug, kick off my trousers, and lift her up quickly before she can protest. She knows what I want as she adjusts herself over my aching cock and slowly rubs herself over me as I slam her back against the wall.

Looking into her eyes, I grip under her thighs as she wraps her hands around the back of my neck. The moment she holds on tight, I sink into her perfect cunt. We both shudder, paralyzed from being connected this way again after so long.

I bounce her on my cock, holding her weight as she uses the wall for support. This angle allows us to see our connection clearly, and each time I pull out and slam back into her, we groan at the sight. I fuck her hard and fast, her back thumping into the wall with each brutal stroke.

She whimpers, her muscles tightening around me as I fuck her without apology. This is savage and uncontrolled because we have ten years of pent-up tension to expel. When Babydoll's gaze drops to our union, I almost lose my shit and come right then and there.

"I played with myself so many times thinking of you. It was the only time I could come," she confesses, licking her lips as I pull out and rub her pussy with the tip of my cock before sliding back in.

"Come now, Baby," I pant, holding her thighs so hard, I'm certain I'll leave bruises.

"Not yet," she moans, pumping her hips and meeting me stroke for stroke. "I want more."

Before I can ask what more she wants, she presses her lips

and commences bouncing on my cock wildly. Pieces of the wall begin to crumble, and the balcony floor starts to shake.

Still rooted deep within her, I spin her around and walk into the bedroom. I don't want to put her onto the filthy floor, so I use the far wall as support. I slam her back against it and continue fucking her fiercely. She milks my body, gripping me tight, and when she arches her back, rocking against me frantically, we fall through the flimsy wall and into the next room, which happens to be the bathroom.

We don't stop, though. I hold her, fucking her as she fucks me.

Our lovemaking is clearly hazardous, and I can't stop my smirk at the fact.

She moves up and down, side to side, driving me crazy as her pussy hugs me tight. We're standing in the middle of the room, with Babydoll bouncing on my cock and me holding her weight, and nothing has been more perfect.

We're face-to-face, watching the other intently, and I don't remember ever feeling this connected to anyone before.

Even compared to before with Babydoll, this is something more.

Her breasts are trapped beneath her dress, which is a shame. "I hope yer not too attached to this dress," I pant with a grin.

Before she can ask why, I grip the mesh in my fist, tear it coarsely, and free her beautiful breasts. When they bounce free, I lower my mouth to her left nipple and suckle her hungrily.

She moans, arching her back and granting me full access to her glorious breasts. I can't stop. I want to taste every inch of her.

"I want to be on top," she breathlessly says, yanking on my hair and coaxing me to press my mouth to hers.

We kiss like starved creatures as she lowers her feet to the floor. I pull out, only for her to shove me onto my back where she bunches up her skirt and straddles me. I lean up on my elbows, watching in awe as she slowly lowers herself onto my cock.

When I'm sheathed all the way, I growl and lower myself onto the floor before I pass out in ecstasy as she commences fucking me.

She places her hands on my chest, rocking against me passionately. Her hair has come loose, and it cascades down her bowed back as she moves backward and forward. I take a moment to appreciate this moment because, wild and free, Babydoll is a vision.

She is unguarded, taking her pleasure from me because she knows where she stands. She knows this feeling is forever.

I grip her arse, encouraging her to take everything from me because I want to please her. I want to take care of my girl. She squeezes me tightly, moaning and writhing madly. I know she's close.

"Fuck!" she cries out, leaning forward and sealing her mouth over mine. I don't know where her breaths end and mine start as we consume the other whole.

She continues riding me, and when she rocks faster, I almost come because it feels so fucking good.

Gripping her throat in one hand, I use the other to rub over her clit.

"I love you," she mewls, lifting her hips and slamming onto my cock. "Say it. Tell me you love me."

"I love you, Baby. I always have."

She whimpers, squeezing her eyes shut as she tosses her head back and convulses around me. She comes loudly, not muting her cries of pleasure as she milks every last tremor from me.

When her cries quell, I give her a second to recover before I spring up and take her with me.

Her eyes pop open, and I chuckle. "Ya didn't think we were done, did ye?"

Spinning her around, I coax her to grip the sink as I lift her dress and run my hand over her beautiful arse. I can't help myself as I smack her rounded cheek.

She springs forward with the force before coming back for more. But that can wait.

Spreading her wide, I enter her pussy slowly, savoring every fucking second. She moans, gripping the sink and arching her back to deepen the angle. I take my time, watching the way my cock slips in and out of her.

She bounces back, taking all of me deeply, and I growl, the

feeling beyond words.

Gripping her hips, I increase the tempo, reading her needy mewls as her wanting more. Her body is fervently thrust backward and forward, backward and forward that when she springs back, the sink she's gripping suddenly detaches from the wall and drops to the floor with a thud.

I catch her from falling, wrapping my arms around her waist and bracing her against the wall. She presses her hands to it while I continue fucking her from behind. Babydoll leans forward to ground herself while I grip her hips and drive into her—hard.

She slams her fist against the wall, shattering the plaster. At this rate, we're going to destroy the house before I come.

"More," she demands, flipping her hair and looking over her shoulder at me.

Seeing her flushed cheeks and swollen lips has me picking up the speed. She arches her back, which allows me to hit her deep.

"Fuck! Oh God, you feel so good."

The house begins to shake around us because I'm far from gentle as I cup her throat and arch her head back so I can kiss the living fuck out of her. I continue pumping my hips, fucking her hard and fast as I chase my release.

She bites over my lip piercing before running her tongue over the sting. She's hungry for me, and I am for her, and when she convulses, coming with a sated groan, I follow suit and am about to pull out.

But she stops me by reaching around and locking her hand to my hip, forcing me to stay connected with her. "Come inside me."

I'm too far gone to argue, so with two fierce pumps, I come long and hard. "Fuck!" I growl, the world eclipsed in light as I forget everything but this feeling of utter ecstasy.

When I'm done, I sag against her back, my breathing accelerated, my heart almost soaring from my chest. We stay this way for minutes, both attempting to catch our breaths because that was something else.

Kissing her shoulder, I gently pull out, instantly missing the connection. Babydoll whimpers, revealing she misses the feel of me too.

"Fucking hell," I pant, looking around at the damage we created. "We destroyed the place."

A laugh leaves Babydoll as she too looks around the room and the demolished wall we fell through. She turns to face me, her tousled hair and flushed cheeks just getting me hard once again.

Stepping forward, I run my thumb across her plump bottom lip. It's swollen from when I almost ate her alive. "I didn't hurt ya?"

She shakes her head timidly. "No, not at all."

We're basking in the moment of utter perfection, eyes locked as a single look can say so many things. We're so lost in one another that when Rory appears, it's too late to conceal what we just did.

"If you two are done, check yer phones."

Babydoll gasps, only realizing we're no longer alone.

She quickly attempts to piece the mesh together to cover her breasts, but uses her arm instead to cover her nudity.

"Rory!" she cries, but he shakes his head firmly, not interested in hearing what she has to say.

My trousers are in the other room, so I discreetly cover my cock, not wanting to rub Rory's nose in what we just did. Seeing my torn shirt hanging off me is a sure sign that Babydoll and I didn't just have sex; we fucked like wild animals and loved every second of it.

Rory stands in the doorway, fists bunched by his sides. I won't stop him if he wants to fight me. I deserve it. He doesn't say a word, though. He just turns his back and leaves us alone, forcing us to deal with the consequences of our actions.

"Oh, fucking hell, mate," Cian says as he runs into the room. He too is now privy to what we did. "Can ya put some trousers on?"

"They're in the other room," I say, and when Cian sees the broken wall, he sighs.

Babydoll turns her back, covering herself. Her shoulders jolting hint that she's crying tears of guilt and shame.

"Ya need to sort this out with Rory, but now, we have to go to yer gaff."

The urgency in his tone has me forgetting everything. "What's happened?"

When he shakes his head, I remember what Rory said.

Kicking the wall to break through it, I find my trousers and retrieve my phone. There are an abundant number of texts and missed calls. I decide to listen to the voicemail instead. When I do, my entire world crumbles, and I doubt it'll ever be whole again.

"Punky, it's me. They're go-gone. He…took them. Pl-please help me. I'm hurt…really bad." And the line goes dead. The caller is Hannah, and there's no guessing who *he* is.

And just like that, our perfection is blown to utter shite.

THIRTEEN

Cami

I sit, staring out the window, Rory's jacket concealing what I did.

I don't deserve his kindness, but I accepted his jacket when he offered it to me, for my sake as well as his. I didn't want to rub in the fact that I had sex with his best friend, and I liked it—a lot.

Rory came to me, offering his comfort, and in return, I asked for Punky instead.

Vomit rises, but I swallow it down. I brought this onto myself, and now, my punishment is my sister being taken. I don't know the details, but neither does Punky. All we're going off is the panicked voicemail Hannah left.

Punky sits across from me in the back of Rory's car. I want

nothing more than to comfort him because, once again, Sean has outsmarted us. But I can't.

His foot continuously bouncing and his fists bunched by his sides all hint he's about to explode.

I don't understand how Sean knew Hannah and Eva were alone with Ethan. No one knew where Punky was tonight. Punky said Ronan and his men, men Punky said we could trust, were keeping watch over his house, but Sean was still able to get to them.

Whenever we underestimate Sean, he goes and does something like this, punishing us for our carelessness. If anything happens to Eva because of me…

With the subtlest of movements, Punky slides his hand across the back seat and touches my little finger with his. This is the only way he can console me without fucking things up more than we already have.

I don't look at him, but instead, stroke my little finger against his, a silent thank you for offering me comfort when I don't deserve it.

When Rory turns into Punky's driveway, we break apart because everything is about to change.

Punky doesn't wait for the car to stop. He opens the door and launches out of it, breaking into a sprint to his home. Rory turns off the car, but he doesn't get out. Cian looks over his shoulder at me, begging I clear the air because we don't need any more drama to add to the shit pile.

He exits the car and chases after Punky while I stay in the car with Rory. I don't know what to say because, honestly, there is nothing I can say to excuse what I did.

Do I regret having sex with Punky?

No. It was the first time in ten years I've felt alive.

What I regret is hurting Rory the way I did. I wish he didn't see what he did, as I can only imagine what a kick in the teeth that was for him. I don't want him to think I ended things because of Punky. He was a reason, but in the end, I did it for me.

And for Rory.

I don't love him, and pretending that I do is the cruelest thing I could ever do. He doesn't deserve that, and I know he hates me right now, but I hope one day, he'll understand.

"Is that why ya ended things? 'Cause of him?"

With a sigh, I shake my head even though Rory won't look at me. "No, not entirely."

"So in part then?"

I don't want to lie to him. "Yes, in part. But I did this for you."

"Oh, bullshit!" he exclaims, slamming his hand against the steering wheel. "Don't give me that bollocks. Ya did this 'cause ya never stopped lovin' him. Even when ya thought he was yer brother."

I don't reply because what would be the point?

He's right.

"I know you hate me."

"I don't hate ye," he counters, his voice cold. "I pity ya, Cami. Y'll never be happy with him because trouble will always follow Puck. Yer sister is now God knows where 'cause of him, and it won't stop there."

"Don't you dare say that! Eva is my responsibility. If anyone is to blame, it's me. I failed her. I thought she'd be okay."

"Well, ya thought wrong. Can't ye see that he's bad for ya?"

Tears I've tried so hard to keep at bay trickle down my cheeks because he's right. I know being with Punky isn't going to be easy, but I don't have a choice. If I could stop loving him, I would have ten years ago.

But I can't.

He is as much a part of me as I am myself. The love I feel for him is indescribable because there aren't any words to express how much he means to me. The only time I feel whole is when I'm with him. I don't care about the uncertainties which face us. As long as we're together, we can tackle anything.

"Y've got nothin' to say?" He finally looks at me in the rearview mirror, and I see pure hate reflected in his eyes.

"What do you want me to say, Rory? That I'm sorry? Well, I'm not. I can't help who I love, and I won't apologize for putting myself first for once. I didn't want you to find out this way, but I—"

"Get out," he snarls, not allowing me to finish. "Y've made yer choice."

Not once has he ever spoken to me this way. But I suppose you can only break someone's heart so many times before they snap.

With a sigh, I open the door and get out of the car, but jump back when Rory takes off so quickly, gravel kicks up in his haste. He speeds down the driveway, almost taking out an oncoming car as he pulls out onto the road.

I'm utterly defeated when I walk toward Punky's house, but the scaffolding around the castle is a wonderful sight. Witnessing it deteriorate with time was a hard pill to swallow. It was like it didn't want to stand without Punky either.

When I arrive at Punky's house, I brace myself for the worst, but when I see Hannah sitting on the couch, beaten and bloody, I realize I haven't braced myself for jack shit.

Punky sits beside her, legs splayed and head cradled in his hands. When he hears me enter, he lifts his chin. He doesn't need to say it—this is bad.

"I'm sorry," Hannah sobs when she sees me. "I tried to stop them."

"Shh," I say, walking to the couch and dropping to my knees in front of her. "It's okay. I know you did."

"She's with Ethan," Hannah says, looking at me through one eye as the other is closed over.

Taking her hands in mine, I try my best to smile. "She'll be fine."

My voice is alien as I know nothing will be fine ever again.

"Let me help clean you up." I stand and offer her my hand.

Hannah nods and slowly rises, flinching when she stands. But the fighter in her won't allow her to concede defeat. We take our time, hobbling toward the bathroom. Cian is on the phone while Punky merely stares into thin air.

He needs time to process this. We all do. But seeing him this way just cements the shitshow headed our way.

I close the bathroom door, giving us some privacy.

Hannah tries to take off her T-shirt but cringes in pain.

"Here, let me."

She nods.

Carefully, I remove her bloody clothes, holding back my vomit when I see the full extent of her injuries. Her small, fragile body is beaten black and blue.

"Hannah, you need to go to the hospital."

"Naw, I can't. They'll call Mum."

And this is why she hasn't called the police.

She knows contacting the authorities will bring about questions we can't answer. Sean knew this as well.

"I just want a bath," she says, wrapping her arms around herself.

I do as she asks and run her a hot bath. Once I've helped her into the water, I dip the sponge into the bath and gently wash her face. She whimpers as her cuts are deep.

"What happened? If you're not comfortable talking about it, I understand."

She takes her time, peering into the bloody water as if it'll give her the answers. "We heard gunshots, and before I had a chance to grab the gun Punky left for me, three men in balaclavas broke down the door. Ethan tried to protect us, but he's still so weak.

"They knocked him out so he couldn't fight. Eva and I, we fought them, I swear it."

"I know that you did," I say, not wanting her to feel guilty for surviving.

"They beat us both. I thought that would be enough. But then Uncle Sean called off his dogs. He didn't get his hands dirty. Typical, him allowin' others to do his dirty work. He said that I was to tell Punky to back down, or he would make them pay.

"I didn't know what he meant until they took Eva and Ethan. Uncle Sean said as long as we played by his rules, no harm would come to them. And then he…then he told me to say hello to Punky from him, before knockin' me out cold."

I swallow down my disgust and take a minute to digest what Hannah just shared.

"I'm sorry, Cami. I fucked up, so I did. I never meant for anyone to get hurt. I just wanted to help Ethan." She covers her face, sobbing into her palms.

"Hey, there's nothing for you to be sorry for." I console her, rubbing her back because this isn't her fault. "We'll find them. I know my sister. She won't give up, and neither will Ethan."

"What i-if Ethan falls for Uncle Sean's b-bullshit again. I just go-got him ba-back."

"Shh, don't think that way." I try my best to comfort her, but she's scarred. Not just on the outside but on the inside as well.

She leans into my touch, sobbing hysterically. I don't speak. I let her get it all out because she can't keep this bottled up.

After a while, her cries become sporadic sniffles, then she grows quiet, almost in a hypnotic trance.

She's exhausted and emotionally spent, so once she's clean, I dry her off, then reach for Punky's black T-shirt hanging off the back of the door. I slip it over her head and search the drawers for some first aid supplies. I disinfect the wounds on her face and arms, but she needs a lot more than that.

She needs to see a doctor.

I open the door and lead her into Punky's bedroom. Pulling back the blankets on the bed, I gently encourage her to lie down. She settles in low, and when I tuck her in, my heart weeps.

She looks so young and innocent. But that didn't make a difference to her own flesh and blood.

"Get some rest, Hannah. I'll just be outside this door if you need me."

Her eyes droop closed as exhaustion wins out.

Brushing her hair from her brow, I place a gentle kiss on her forehead, promising those who did this to her will pay. She's passed out before I'm out the door.

I enter the living room, but no one is here.

I soon uncover where Punky and Cian are when I hear the unmissable sound of someone begging for their life as they're getting the shit kicked out of them.

Rushing out the door, I stop dead in my tracks when I see a man on his knees, beaten and bloody, pleading Punky doesn't kill him.

"I'm sorry," he weeps, interlacing his hands in mercy as Punky stands above him, fists clenched. "We were ambushed. I promise ya. I'm not workin' with Sean."

Punky snarls before kneeing him under the chin.

The man falls onto his back with a thud, attempting to escape, but he's not going anywhere. Punky grabs him by the feet and drags him forward.

"Fool me once, Ronan," he spits. "But fool me twice. How did he know I wasn't here?"

In response, he stomps on Ronan's knee, and from the pained wail which leaves Ronan, I dare say Punky just broke bone.

"I don't know. I swear it!" he exclaims. "If I was workin' with him, why am I shot? Bleedin' to death in yer fucking garden! Why would I come crawlin' back here to tell ya the truth if I betrayed ye?"

Cian turns away, unable to witness his friend show no mercy because we both know that no matter what Ronan says, he's dead.

"I tried to stop them, but Sean knew ya wouldn't be here.

Someone tipped him off. Whoever ya think are yer friends, yer wrong. Ya can't trust anyone."

"Aye, I know that now. I shouldn't have trusted you."

"Punky, naw, please, no." Ronan sobs as Punky places a gun to his temple.

But his pleas don't affect Punky in the slightest. A look of utter emptiness is stamped on Punky's face, and I know that numbness will just continue to grow if he takes this man's life.

"Punky, don't," I say softly. "You've got no proof. Don't be like him. Be the man Connor taught you to be."

Punky inhales sharply, turning his cheek and squeezing his eyes shut. "Go inside, Cami."

"No, I will not," I gently argue, taking cautious steps toward him. "You don't have to do this. Deep down, you know this is wrong."

"I don't know anythin'," he spits, his pain palpable.

Cian nods, encouraging me to help Punky see the light because right now, he is lost to the darkness.

"You know that I love you," I say, taking my time as I approach him. "You know that this isn't your fault."

"Bullshit!" he shouts, turning around to face me. "Yer sister and Ethan are gone because of me. Hannah was beaten within an inch of her life because of me! My need for vengeance once again got people hurt. Connor was right—emotions make ya weak.

"Ya should run now when y've got the chance," he says, eyes

filled with tears. "People I love tend to die as yer collateral."

"I'm not going anywhere," I affirm, gripping the gun and placing it over my heart. "Where you go, I go, and if you're headed into hell, then take me with you because living without you will be far worse than any hell on earth."

"Camilla, don't say things I don't deserve. Yer sister is in danger because of me."

"Yes, she is, but never forget that she's my sister. My blood runs through her veins, and you can bet she will fight with everything that she's got. He won't kill her because he needs her. Like you said, the people you love are collateral.

"He will use her and Ethan as pawns to get what he wants. As long as he needs them, they're safe. We just need to come up with a plan."

Punky's grip on the gun wavers, and I gently lower it, removing it from his hands.

Tossing it aside, I step forward and cup his cheek tenderly. He leans into my touch, broken and defeated in ways I've never seen before.

"I'm sorry I got youse involved in this. If anythin' happens to Eva…"

I don't let him finish that sentence because I don't want to hear it. Eva will be okay. She has to be.

With a sigh, Punky accepts defeat, but that doesn't make him a failure. No, he is victorious in every sense of the word.

"Take him to the hospital," he says to Cian, eyes still locked with mine.

"Thank you, Puck," Ronan cries, coming to a shaky stand. "I heard them say they were headed to the factory. I don't know where that is, though."

Punky nods but doesn't seem too enthused by the news as he knows he's at Sean's mercy.

Cian helps Ronan as he can't stand on his own, and they make their way toward Punky's truck. Only when they're gone does Punky breathe again.

He pulls out of the embrace and peers into the night sky. "Ronan is right. Sean was tipped off. He knew the kids would be all alone and vulnerable here. He let me kill Brody because I just eliminated the competition for him.

"I did his dirty work, thinkin' I was in control, but I was wrong. Loyalties may be divided, but Sean has power in the right places. He's been watchin' and waitin', and it's only a matter of time now."

A shiver rocks my body at his ominous words. "What do we do now?"

"Now, we wait for him to make his demands. He knows I'll agree to whatever he proposes. I won't allow more lives to be destroyed because of me."

We're stuck between a rock and a hard place because we're gambling with Ethan's and Eva's lives. Sean took them instead of Hannah because he knew taking my sister would just be extra insurance for him.

"Even if his proposal involves your death?" I question quietly, unable to conceal my fear.

With a sigh, Punky nods. "Aye, I'll accept it."

I wrap my arms around myself, his words having me trembling in fear. "Well, I don't accept it. There's got to be another way."

Punky merely smiles weakly in response.

Before I have a chance to demand he fight, headlights light up the driveway. He instantly shields me with his body as he places me behind his back.

"Is it the police?" I ask, unsure who would be here at such an early hour. I doubt the enemy would announce their arrival this way.

Punky stares into the distance, and when he sees who it is, he curses under his breath. "No, worse."

Worse than the police?

I understand what he means when the car comes to a screeching halt, and Fiona comes charging out of the driver's side, not bothering to switch off the engine.

"Where is she?" she screams hysterically. This will not end well.

"Fiona—"

She doesn't give Punky time to explain before she slaps him across the cheek. "You bastard! Ye good for nothin' arsehole! What did you do to my daughter?"

She pounds her fists against his chest, cursing and calling

him every name under the sun. He doesn't fight back. He accepts her abuse because I know he believes he deserves it.

"She's inside sleepin'," he says blankly. "Ethan is gone."

"No!" she screams over and over again. "This is your fault! All of this is yer fault. Everythin' ya touch turns to shite! I hate ya! I fuckin' hate ye!"

She slaps him again, and like before, he doesn't retaliate. He merely stands still, a broken statue, dead inside.

"Ya took Connor away from me, and now yer takin' my wains. Ye won't be happy until they're all dead."

She goes to slap him again, but I seize her wrist midair. I've had enough. "You've made your point, Fiona."

Ripping from my hold, she snarls, primed on hitting me.

"Go ahead. I dare you," I challenge her because, unlike Punky, I'll hit back.

She reads my threat for what it is and steps back. "You're next," she sneers. "Mark my words. That boy is cursed."

"Oh, shut up," I snap, not interested in her bullshit. "It's a little too late to play concerned mother now. Have you ever wondered why Hannah has no worry for her safety when it comes to Puck? Because he was there for her when you weren't.

"He went to prison to protect them, and all you cared about was finding another man to fill Connor's shoes because you're so afraid of being alone. You're pathetic."

"He's got you fooled too then," she says, shaking her head in pity.

But she can shove her pity right up her arrogant ass. "I'm not fooled. I see Puck for who he is. I always have. Too bad you never did. You married your dead best friend's husband before she was dead and buried. The least you could have done was look after her son.

"But you're so fucking selfish, and now, the karma train is coming."

She blinks once, horrified at my words.

"Well, choo fucking choo."

Her mouth gapes open as she doesn't know what to say. I've never spoken to her this way before. Even when Hannah would come to me with stories of her negligent mother growing up, I always kept the peace.

But no more.

"Hannah is sleeping, and she will not be disturbed. You can come back tomorrow."

"How dare you," Fiona says, her face twisting into a scowl. "She's my daughter."

"When it suits you," I reply. "She wasn't your daughter when you took off with what's-his-name for three weeks and left her and Ethan alone. They were ten, in case you've forgotten. Amber and I were the ones who were their mothers then."

Fiona's fight soon dies because she knows this example is one of many. "I'll be back tomorrow."

She goes to turn, but Punky stops her as he says, "I don't know who told ya Hannah was here, but yer in danger now. Be careful."

She snickers, shaking her head as she gets into her car and speeds off. We both watch her dramatic exit, unmoved by her theatrics.

"Sean no doubt was the one who told her," Punky says. "He's movin' in because it's just him and me now."

The defeat in his voice kills me.

"Then we need to be ready."

He looks at me and nods. "Everyone is the enemy."

And he's right.

Killing my father changed everything, but just not in the way we anticipated.

"How's Rory?"

I don't bother replying because he can guess how he is.

"If ya ever change yer mind, I'll understand."

"I won't," I assure him as I reach for his hand.

We stand quietly, both hoping the peace will help reveal the answers we so desperately seek. So far, however, we're greeted with nothing but silence.

FOURTEEN

PUNKY

Dr. Shannon saw Hannah early this morning and gave her some strong medication to help deal with the pain. He assured me nothing is broken. She got lucky, he said, but there is no such thing when a young girl gets beaten within an inch of her life.

I haven't slept. I can't. I'm sick of waiting…waiting for everything.

I'm hoping that by pummeling this punching bag, the answers I need will miraculously appear. No such luck sadly. But I won't give up. Ethan and Eva are relying on me.

"Hey." Babydoll appears in the doorway of the barn, dressed in one of my T-shirts.

She crashed on the couch last night, exhausted and

emotionally drained.

She's handling this well, but I know deep down, she's beside herself with worry. Her sister has been kidnapped by a psychopath, and there isn't a fucking thing I can do about it.

"Hi," I reply, focusing on the bag as I wallop it a few times.

She comes a little closer but keeps her distance as she knows I don't want to be smothered. "Hannah is looking a little better."

"Aye." I can't look at her because I know what she's doing. She wants to assure me that everything will be all right. But we don't know that.

Every step we've taken has been a risk, but this is different. Ethan's and Eva's lives are on the line if I make the wrong move.

"Punky, please don't do this."

"Do what?"

"Don't shut me out. I want to be here."

"Ya shouldn't want that," I snap, punching the bag so hard, the cord snaps from the rafter, and the bag drops to the ground with a thud.

Babydoll sighs, folding her arms across her chest. "Well, too bad because I do. I'm not going anywhere. So can you stop sulking and listen to my idea?"

I don't have a choice in the matter so I gesture that I'm all ears.

"We need allies, ones we can trust. Ron Brady and his friends proved they could be trusted last night. What about Brody's men? Do you have a list of names?"

I nod. "Yes. I met them. Well, most of them. I don't think they can be trusted, though."

"They'll be looking for a leader," she says. "Brody paid their bills, and in the end, they'll go where there is stability. They don't care about our family feuds."

"Ya don't think Liam will be the one they turn to?"

"Not after word spreads about what you did. We just need to make sure Sean doesn't get to them first. With enough people on our side, we can still beat him. We can still stick to the original plan."

"Everythin' has changed now. With Ethan and Eva gone, it doesn't matter how many men and women we have on our side, Sean will always have the upper hand.

"He will undo all the progress we made with Ethan and just get him hooked on that shite again. If that happens, then he'll be lost to us for good."

I'm not trying to be negative, merely realistic because no matter how big an army we have, Sean will always have an advantage point. Until I can find *his* collateral, then we'll always be playing with a losing hand.

"I know, but it can't hurt to see who's on our side, right?" she says, half pleading. "We can't just sit around doing nothing."

She needs to do something because something is better than nothing. And then, I'm suddenly struck with an idea. Probably the most foolish one I've ever had.

I think I've found Sean's collateral.

"Yes, yer right." I remember the conversation I had with Logan Doherty the night I introduced myself to Brody's men.

He was supposed to run the list I asked for over to me days ago. It slipped my mind, seeing as I had other shite to deal with.

Babydoll recognizes the look on my face and smiles.

Reaching for my phone off the wooden rail, I quickly dial Logan's number.

"Hello?" he answers, unsure who the caller is.

"What's the craic, Logan?"

"Puck?" His voice raises an octave.

"Aye, it's me. I'm awful sorry if y've tried to reach me. I've been busy."

"Yes, I heard," he says, hinting the news has spread. "I have the list. Do ya want me to run it over to ye?"

"No, I want ya to organize a meetin' with those names on that list."

"All of them?" he questions, his concern clear.

"Aye. Will that be a problem?"

"Naw, no problem. It might take me some time."

"How about tomorrow?"

Logan exhales, realizing this isn't optional. "All right. I'll see ya tomorrow."

"Grand. Ya remember where yer loyalties used to lay?" I don't wait for him to reply. "The meetin' will be held there."

I hang up, hoping this works. This might be the smartest or the rashest idea I've ever had. We will see how loyal these men truly are. They made their choice when they sided with the Doyles. But a second chance is coming for them.

Babydoll looks at me, waiting for me to explain.

"Logan Doherty used to work for us, but he got lost along the way. He's got one chance to make amends for his error. He's organizing a meetin' at Connor's old factory."

"The same factory Sean is at?" she asks, putting two and two together.

"I don't know if he's there. But he wanted Ronan to overhear him for a reason. We're safer going there with numbers behind us. Well, I hope so. We'll find out soon enough."

"What if they all turn? What if Sean got to them first?"

"I can only hope their loyalty to Connor will lead them in the right direction. If not, we'll come prepared."

"Prepared for what?"

"For war," I reply firmly. "I'm countin' on Sean being there. No more waitin'. We bring him, then we bring all of them to us. I'm certain one of those arseholes will tell Sean what I'm plannin', and he won't miss an opportunity like that."

Babydoll inhales deeply, understanding the seriousness of what I have planned. "So you want the men we do trust, like Ron, to wait hidden, and we ambush Sean?"

I shrug because I'm going into this blind. "Maybe. I don't know. It didn't work for me ten years ago, but I'm done waitin' for him to show himself. We entice him and offer him somethin' he can't refuse."

"And what's that?" she asks, her slender throat dipping as she swallows deeply. She knows what, but she needs me to say it.

"Me."

I needed to find Sean's collateral, and I have.

I offer myself to Sean if all else fails in exchange for Ethan and Eva. I don't want it to come to that, but I'll be prepared if it does.

Sean needs me alive to help him gain face. He can't do it alone. Ten years of fighting for dominance proves this. If we play happy families, then the men who were once loyal will return to serving the Kelly name. And the men loyal to the Doyles? They can have them.

I want no part in Ireland.

It troubles me that Liam hasn't struck yet. I thought he'd have attacked last night, but this proves he doesn't have the numbers on his side. These men don't want a part in a personal war. They don't care that our families have been feuding for years.

They just want to do their job, get paid, and not get caught.

I have a feeling Sean won't settle for just part governance. He'll want it all. But we will tackle this one step at a time.

Babydoll lowers her gaze, chewing on her bottom lip.

"Hey." I lift her chin with my finger. "This is the worst-case scenario. We don't know that he'll be there."

"We both know that he will be," she says, reading between

the lines. "This is you challenging him again. But this time, he'll show."

"If that happens, then we'll be ready for him."

Every step we've taken has led to this. No more guessing who's on our side because tomorrow, everyone's true colors will show. It was an impossible task to determine who would be loyal because loyalties shift with power.

But this will force them to choose.

"What if it's not only Sean you're fighting?"

I stroke the apple of her cheek with my thumb. "I expect Liam will be there too. Three men fightin' for power. Only one man can win."

What I'm proposing will be an all-out brawl. There will be many casualties, but this is needed to start over. We can't live in the past, only the future. The men who survive will be loyal because there will only be one leader standing come tomorrow nightfall.

"Don'tcha be worryin' 'bout me. I'll be all right," I assure her, but she's not convinced.

"I'm coming," she says with conviction, just how I knew she would.

"We can talk about it later," I reply, pressing my mouth over hers to stop the argument we're bound to have over this.

She melts into me, whimpering as I kiss her softly. I love how receptive she is to my touch. Most recoil when I'm near, but not Cami. She always wants more.

Standing on her toes, she wraps her arms around my neck, deepening the angle. Even though the world is falling to bits around us, at least we've got this. I don't know how I lived without her for so long. But I suppose I was half living.

"I love you," she says against my lips, running her tongue across the piercing in my bottom lip.

I'll never tire of her saying it. "Say it again."

"I love you. I love you. I love you."

With a growl, I steal her breath and kiss the ever-living fuck out of her. I am insatiable when it comes to her. But as much as I'd like nothing more than to lose myself in her for hours, I can't. For that to be our future, though, I need to get ready.

"Not yet," she whispers, sensing my retreat.

I can't say no to her.

Lifting her up, she wraps her legs around me, kissing me frantically. I slam her back to the wall, pinning her with my body as I devour her whole. She tugs at my hair, moaning when we break apart, only for me to kiss down her neck.

Sliding my hand up her thigh, I touch over her underwear, hissing when I feel she's already wet. I can't leave her wanting, so I sink two fingers inside her. Her body shudders, a tiny whimper escaping her as she rocks her hips.

I'm not gentle, but she doesn't want me to be as she places her hand over mine, encouraging me to go faster, harder. I give her what she wants, stretching her wide and savoring the feel of her coming apart in my hand.

She pumps against me, eyes locked because the connection isn't just physical; it's emotional as well.

A single look can express so much, and the desperation in Babydoll's gaze reveals she's frightened. We're diving into the unknown with a lot of what-ifs. The odds aren't in our favor. But they never have been.

"Promise you won't leave me?"

"I'll try my best," I reply, not wanting to lie to her because if I have the choice to save Ethan, Eva, and her, I'll take it.

"I don't want to do this without you."

I know *this* means living because I feel the same way.

"I'll always be with ya. Death isn't the end. Our bodies may perish, but the memories will last forever. No matter what happens, remember that. Remember that you gave me a reason worth living for."

She nods, holding back her tears because that's the best I can offer her right now.

"I love you, Camilla. I always have. And I always will."

Using her name, which is a rarity, has the desired effect because she comes with a sated groan when I circle her swollen clit. I slam my mouth over hers, wishing to share in her orgasm because it's the purest of things.

Watching her be vulnerable and free is a turn-on within itself. We are finally whole. Together. And I'll do everything in my power to ensure we stay that way.

Once the last tremor rocks her body, I remove my fingers

from her, only to slip them into my mouth. Her eyes widen, and her cheeks redden further. But she's too delicious to waste.

She lowers her feet to the ground, bashfully brushing her wild hair from her face. I love that after everything we've done, she's still so timid.

"Are you hungry? I can make some breakfast. Hannah needs to eat as well."

Nodding, I kiss her forehead. "Thank you. I'll be there in a minute. I need to make some calls."

She smiles, but it's strained.

Once she's gone, I reach for my phone and dial Cian.

"I know yer angry with me for what I did to Rory, but I need yer help."

He sighs, hinting he's listening.

I tell him my plan and that although it'll probably end in a lot of bloodshed, it's the only way we can end this once and for all. Hearing it aloud confirms this is possibly the worst idea I've ever had. This is an open invitation to all my enemies.

But I'm ready.

"Well, what d'you think?"

"I think yer goin' to need a fucking arsenal to pull this off. And double the number of men to help."

"Aye, yer right. I was thinkin' of payin' a visit to Ron. Surely he knows where I can get what I need."

Cian is quiet, clearly processing what I'm proposing.

"Ya do realize Liam and Sean won't pass this opportunity

by. It's open season on ye if ya do this."

"I know that, but I'm done waitin'. I'm hopin' Sean's arrogance will have him slippin' up somehow. He has collateral over me, and this is the only thing I have on him."

Cian doesn't need me to draw him a diagram. He understands. "Yer goin' to offer yerself to him, are ya not? In exchange for Ethan and Eva."

"I hope it doesn't come to that. But I won't be blackmailed again. That's why he took them. That's what he wants. He either wants me to surrender or work with him 'cause he can't do this on his own. I'll do what I have to, and I hope y'll be by my side when I do."

"Course I will," Cian says with gusto. "We're in this together. But don't be actin' the martyr. We fight first. Promise me that."

"I promise ya," I reply, and I mean it.

The last thing I intend to do is surrender. I will fight until the very end. But if defeated, I'll have one final ace up my sleeve. A proposition Sean won't be able to refuse. I just need to uncover what his motives are. And I can only do that with a face-to-face meeting.

"All right then. Pick me up, and we'll go see Ron. What about Rory?"

And that is one problem I don't think I'll ever solve.

"I think I'm the last person he wants to see right now. It's better if he keeps his distance."

"I hate this. I wish things were different."

"Me too, but I hope to make things right. I've fucked up a lot in my life, Cian, but Cami isn't a mistake. If I could do this all over again, I would always choose her."

I need him to know that this isn't some phase that will pass.

"Aye, I know that. Love is a tricky thing."

Things were a lot simpler when our fathers were in control. The older I get, the clearer that becomes. I was so hard on Connor, but looking back on what he did, on what he achieved, I realize I'm only half the man that he was.

But tomorrow changes that. History is about to be made.

"This is a suicide mission," Ron says, blowing out a puff of smoke. "Sean will be there, ready and waitin' for ye. As will Liam Brody."

"I'm countin' on it," I reply with a grin.

We're in the alleyway behind Ron's butcher store, talking business in hushed voices because everyone is the enemy until we can prove otherwise.

This is risky, and if Ron decides to opt out, I'll understand. I really hope he doesn't, though, because he is the link to the past that I need. He proved his loyalty last night. He can be trusted. So can the men he vouches for.

"Y've my support, Puck. And the men who served Connor.

We want change, and we want yer uncle gone. He's done nothin' to help us. Our loyalties will always lie with you."

Inhaling, I can't hide my relief at hearing those words. "Thank you, Ron. I'll not forget it. D'you think ya can get the word out about tomorrow? We need men who are willing to fight for what's right. Men we can trust."

"Aye, leave it to me. I suppose ya need guns? And other weapons?"

I nod. "I hate to ask this of ya—"

"Don't be concernin' yerself with that," he interrupts. "Just bring back the Belfast we all know and miss."

"I promise ya, I'll do my best."

All of this is possible because of Cami. If she didn't keep in touch with good men like Ron, we wouldn't be able to pull this off.

I won't fail them.

"I'll make a few calls and let ya know who's with us. I think it'll be a good idea to have men surroundin' the factory on the lookout."

"Yes, definitely. But I need to find out about Ethan and Eva before we use violence."

Ron nods, but I know he can't guarantee that'll happen.

The truth is, we are going into this blind, where every possible scenario is probable. We need to be prepared for all circumstances and not be blindsided.

"I think a lot of Brody's men are goin' to retaliate. Liam will lead that pack. Sean will have his. And you will have yer army behind ye. It'll be who shoots first in the end. Are ya sure this is what ya want to do?"

"I'm not sure of anythin'," I reply honestly. "But what I am sure of is that I won't cower in fear. Connor taught me better than that. I will do this to honor him and everything he worked so hard to protect."

"Happy days!" Ron says, tossing his feg onto the ground. "I will get everythin' sorted and phone ya."

We bid him farewell and cautiously make our way to the truck. We can't be too careful because no doubt, Sean and Liam have their allies watching us.

Cian's phone rings, and when I see his reaction to who's calling, I guess it's Amber. I haven't seen her since the engagement party, but I suppose like Rory, she'd have preferred I stayed where I was. Since returning, all I've done is drag Cian into my mess.

Even though it's his choice, I can understand why she's not my biggest fan.

"I can't tomorrow night," he says to her. "Why? Er, 'cause I'm busy doin' some things."

Cian is the world's worst liar, which isn't a bad thing. I just feel terrible that he's in this position because of me.

I can hear her yelling at him through the phone before he yanks it away from his ear to see she's hung up on him.

"Fuck," he curses under his breath before putting his mobile away.

"I'm sorry, mate. If Amber is goin' to be ragin', then don't worry about tomorrow."

"She'll be fine once everythin' sorts itself out."

"And until then?"

Cian sighs and slouches back in the seat. "Remember when life was easy?"

Laughing, I signal to change lanes. "When was that exactly?"

"Sure, this is it."

"We've always been fightin' for our lives in one way or another. But now, there's no one to blame but ourselves."

Cian nods, mulling over my statement. "Will ya speak with Rory before tomorrow?"

I know why he's asking this.

If tomorrow turns to shite and we lose, then he wants to make sure I enter the afterlife with a clean conscience. And for Rory's sake as well.

"I'll try," I reply. "But I don't think he'll want to speak to me. Sometimes, I think youse would have been better off if I'd died alongside Connor."

"Don'tcha be sayin' that shite," he rebukes, shaking his head.

"It's true. I'm not sayin' it 'cause I want sympathy. But so many people have been hurt because of me."

"Yer worried about tomorrow, are ya not?"

"Aye," I confess. "Not for me, but for everyone else stickin' their neck out for me. Cami wants to come, and I know I can't stop her. But the thought of her being there makes me sick to my stomach."

"Maybe ya can," Cian says with caution as I turn to look at him.

"How so?"

"Everyone who is connected to us is in potential danger. They'll be safer together. Cami, Rory, Hannah, Amber, Darcy, fuck, even Fiona, they're all at risk of ending up where Ethan and Eva are. But together, they have a chance. Someone has to defend the kingdom we're fighting so hard to protect.

"Rory and Cami are the strongest and street smart. They can protect our friends and also, yer home. If we sit down with them and explain that, they'll listen. Well, I think."

Tapping my fingers against the steering wheel, I ponder on what he just said. "It *might* work, but for this to succeed, I'd need Rory on board, and after last night, I doubt he's in a mood to do anything to help me."

"But he'd do anythin' to protect Cami," he counters quickly because he's right.

Rory may hate us both, but if push came to shove, he'd do the right thing. He'd do it because he loves Babydoll.

"Fuck. I hate this. Asking either of them is an arrogant request. Cami has every right to be there. And Rory has every right to tell me to go fuck myself."

"He won't, and Cami will see reason. Eventually," he adds, making a pained face as he knows she's going to lose her shite.

She will understand when I explain it, but I hate that I have to ask this of her. But Hannah is at risk, and if anything happens to her, I'll never forgive myself for it. And neither will Babydoll.

Confronting Rory is far less scary than asking Babydoll, so I dial his number. I'm surprised when he answers.

"What the fuck do ya want?"

"Hi, Rory. Look, ya have every right to hate me. *I* hate me for what I've done. But I need ya. Cami and Hannah need ye."

I don't care that I'm begging. I will get on my knees if it means protecting the people I love.

"Fuck you," he replies, and just as I'm about to hang up, something unbelievable happens. "I'm at home. See ya soon."

The line goes dead, and I look at Cian, confused.

He merely shrugs, knowing all along that our friendship will always win.

I feel beyond awkward knocking on the door of the flat Rory and Babydoll once shared together. But when Rory opens the door, that awkwardness turns to guilt and shame.

He can't even look at me without wanting to punch me in the face, and I can't blame him. I wanted to do the same thing when I found out they were engaged. But we need to get over our differences because we have one thing in common—we both love Cami.

He steps aside, indicating we can enter.

Cian clears his throat, always stuck in the middle. "Hey, Rory. I like what y've, um, done with the place."

He is clearly being sarcastic because the place looks like it's been robbed. There are the basics like a couch and a coffee table, but any decorative pieces are gone. I'm guessing that's because he couldn't stand to see things in his house, reminding him of Babydoll.

Rory grunts in response, not offering for us to sit. He stands by the door, arms folded, hinting if I have anything to say, then to do so now.

"Rory, I won't insult ya by sayin' I'm sorry."

He scoffs, shaking his head, while Cian moves away from us, not interested in being involved in World War III.

"Aye, I'm sorry yer hurtin', but I'm not sorry for actin' on somethin' both Cami and I wanted."

"That's grand for youse. I couldn't be happier," he quips, nostrils flared. "But I don't think that's the reason yer here."

"Yer right," I reply, appreciating that he wants to get straight to the point. "Tomorrow, I'm callin' a meetin' with Brody's men. I predict Sean and Liam will be there. We've organized men who were loyal to our fathers to be there for us because I assume it'll be a bloodbath.

"I don't know what to expect because Sean has proven to be unpredictable. So, we're not takin' any chances and preparing for every scenario. I suspect some men will fight, but most will probably run, not interested in being caught up in our war.

"But this is personal to us. Blood feuds last forever, but I'm going to end it tomorrow…and I need yer help."

Rory snickers, curling his lip. "Y've some bollocks on ye, comin' here and askin' for my help."

"I know that," I agree, "but if I weren't desperate, I wouldn't be here."

"I used to love this flat," he says, ignoring my statement. "It was a home Cami and I built together. But now, all I can think 'bout is how yer gaff is where she calls home. How your bed is where she sleeps. Ya couldn't leave her alone, could ya?

"Ye can have anyone, but why her? Darcy Duffy, for fuck's sake, is knockin' at yer door, yet ya had to steal the woman I love when ya could have had anyone!"

"It doesn't work like that," I reply, standing my ground when Rory walks forward. "I didn't want to hurt ye, Rory. But I love her. I've always loved her, and she loves me. I know yer the better match. I can't get my head around it, but she wants to be with me. And I will do everythin' in my power to protect her."

Rory isn't interested in sentiments, however, and with a roar, he strikes me in the jaw.

My head snaps back with a sharp crack, but I slowly turn to face him once again. I don't retaliate. This has been a long time coming.

"For fuck's sake," Cian groans, stepping back.

"I'm not goin' to fight ya, Rory."

"Too bad then, 'cause I plan on fightin' you." He punches me again, this time in the nose.

Blood instantly pours from my nose as Rory has always had a killer right hook. He launches at me, sending me toppling onto the floor. He commences punching my face, cursing the day I was born. I don't fight back because I deserve this.

This is Rory's therapy, and if this will help him heal, help him forgive me for betraying him, then I will endure each strike until he can look at me again.

"Enough!" Cian cries, attempting to pull Rory off me. But Rory shoves him so hard, Cian slams against the wall.

"Always jumpin' to his defense," he sneers, slamming his fist to my jaw. "Nothing has changed. Since we were kids, ya were always makin' excuses for him."

"Dry yer eyes, will ya," I retort, not interested in Rory's sob story. Cian has nothing to do with this.

My comment only adds fuel to the fire, and with a snarl, he splits my lip open.

"Fight me!" he demands, hovering over me, my blood dripping from his fists.

"Naw, I won't fight ya." I spit out blood, daring him to do his best.

"Fuck!" he screams, punching me one final time before crawling off me. He joins Cian against the wall, panting and clenching his bloody fists.

Sitting up, I fruitlessly wipe my bloody lip with the back of my hand because it's going to take a lot more than that to stop the bleeding. "Ye may hate me, but we want the same thing—to protect Cami. I can't do that when I'm fightin', but you can."

He nods, indicating he's listening.

"I need someone I can trust to stay with Cami, Amber, Hannah, Darcy, and the long list of others who are in danger. I want that person to be you. I can't protect them, but I know you can. I have no right askin' ya this, but please help me.

"Stay with them and keep them safe."

"And what makes ya think Cami is going to stay put? She'll want to go with ya."

"We present her with both options and let her decide," I say, hating how this hits so close to home. "I don't want to lie to her, and I don't want to take away her free will. If she decides to come, then so be it. That'll be her choice, but I hope she sees reason.

"You two are the only people who can do this. I don't want anyone else getting hurt."

"It's a little late for that," he snaps, but his anger has subsided.

"I know that, but I'll never stop tryin' to make things right." I mean that in every possible way.

Rory flexes his swollen hand, flinching. "Y've still got a hard head, I see."

"Sure, this is it."

Just like Babydoll, this is Rory's choice. If he tells me

to go fuck myself, then at least I tried. But I know he won't. Regardless of his feelings for me, he would never let those who are innocent suffer.

His love for Cami has him nodding. "Ats us nai."

Cian sighs, thankful no more blood will be spilled—for now.

However, being pummeled to a pulp was the easy part because Rory's punches will seem like a piece of piss compared to what I'm about to face—asking Babydoll to sit this one out.

I suddenly wish he'd knocked me out cold.

FIFTEEN

Cami

Hannah is asleep because the pain medication Dr. Shannon prescribed has knocked her out. It's good she sleeps because she needs to recover—in more ways than one.

Her young eyes have seen so much. I hate that she can't live the life of a typical teenager, but I suppose Hannah has never been "normal," and that's a good thing. She's far wiser and stronger than I was at her age.

Fiona hasn't shown up. I'm surprised because after her theatrics last night, I thought she'd be here with the police, demanding mine and Puck's head. Deep down, she knows that we can protect Hannah when she can't.

It's the first selfless thing she's done.

When I hear the gravel crunch, the sure sign a car is approaching, I carefully part the curtain an inch and look out the living room window. I sigh when I see Punky's truck, but that turns to a gasp when he hobbles from the passenger side, beaten and bloody.

I jump up from the sofa, but stop dead in my tracks when Rory gets out of the truck as well.

What the fuck is going on?

Cian opens the door while I stand in the middle of the living room, not concealing my confusion and concern. Punky stumbles in after him, looking at me sheepishly when we lock eyes. The fact that there isn't a scratch on Rory has me inhaling sharply.

"Are you all right?"

Punky nods, not wanting to make a fuss, but I'm angry. How dare Rory do this? I don't need an explanation. I can read between the lines.

He limps into the bathroom to clean himself up and probably change because his white T-shirt is covered in blood. Rory doesn't say a word.

"You fucking hit him?" I demand he has the balls to tell me what happened.

"Aye, I did." He shows no remorse for his actions, which merely infuriates me further.

"You had no right to do that. If you're going to get physical with him, then do so with me too." I charge forward, daring him to hit me. "I'm just as much to blame as he is."

"No," he admonishes, taking a step back, horrified. "I will not. I won't strike ya."

"Why not?" I press, getting in his face as he continues backing away. "'Cause I'm a girl?"

"Cami, enough now!"

But I won't stop. "No, I think we've just begun! Go on, do to me what you did to Punky. It's only fair. Or maybe you won't because you know I'll fight back!"

Rory turns his cheek, my words wounding him.

"Cat got your tongue, tough guy?"

Punky's heavy footsteps announce his arrival, and I'm thankful he doesn't tell me to back off because this is my fight as well. If Rory wants to lash out, then let it be to both Punky and me because that's only fair. But I know Rory won't hurt me. He may hate me, but his love for me is still strong.

Only when Punky gently places his hand on my lower back does my anger simmer.

I turn to look at him, his beaten face upsetting me. He could have fought back, but I know he didn't because he believes he deserves it. Punky is so fucking noble, and that's one of the many things I love about him.

"There's something I need to ask ye," he says, and his tone has my stomach dropping.

"Okay."

He takes his time, which just adds to my nerves.

"I know ya want to come with me tomorrow. I respect that. But…I want ya to stay here."

I arch a brow, indicating he has three seconds to explain before I tell him what I think of his request.

"Hannah, Amber, my grandparents, and a long list of others are in danger. They can be used as collateral. Just how Ethan and Eva are. I'm askin' that you and—" he swallows deeply, revealing how hard his request is. "That you and Rory stay here and protect them. Protect the legacy we're fighting to save.

"So, I'm giving ya the choice because this is just as much yer fight as it is mine. If ya want to come tomorrow, then I won't stop ya. But I'm askin' ya to stay here and defend the people who need protectin'.

"You and Rory are smart and can fight if it comes to that. I'll have men here guardin' ya, but that didn't seem to make a difference for Ethan, Eva, and Hannah."

My breathing is measured because I'm livid he would ask this of me. He says it's my choice, but he knows my hands are tied. I won't allow anything to happen to Hannah or Amber, but this isn't fair. I don't want to sit here, waiting, while he fights.

"How can you ask this of me? It's not fair. Not to mention, it's fucking sexist. I'm expected to stay here, hoping that I'll see you again. Is that it?"

"Baby, no, this has nothin' to do with ya being a girl. Y've got bigger bollocks than Cian and me combined, and that's why I need ya here. Hannah can't protect herself. If yer all together, then we'll have a fighting shot at winnin' this."

"And this has nothing to do with the fact that you'd prefer I stay here where it's likely to be less dangerous?"

"Of course, I'd prefer ya to stay here," he confesses without pause. "Yer my everythin', and if I have a chance at keepin' ya safe, then I make no apologies for that."

Goddamn him.

"This is your choice, Cami. It always has been," Rory says without bite as he knows I'll tear him to shreds if he insinuates I'm being unreasonable. "If ya want to go with Punky, then do it. I'll stay here because what Punky says makes sense.

"Sean has managed to outsmart us time and time again. I won't give him another opportunity to do so. But that's my choice. Just how whatever you decide to do is yers."

I'm put on the spot because everything they're saying makes sense, but the thought of being here, worrying about Punky and whether he'll come back to me, makes me want to be sick.

On cue, vomit rises. "Excuse me."

I run to the bathroom with my hand over my mouth, making it just in time as I throw up into the toilet. I've barely eaten, but my body won't quit, and soon, I'm retching, hoping to expel the emptiness within.

Wiping my mouth with some toilet paper, I flush the toilet and turn on the faucet on the sink. Cupping some water, I splash it onto my cheeks because I feel like I'm burning up. It doesn't help, so I gulp down handfuls of water.

"Baby?"

Groaning, I close my eyes and grip the counter. "You're not done with your guerrilla tactics yet?"

"It's not like that," Punky says. "I'm sorry if ya felt attacked."

"I don't feel attacked," I declare, opening my eyes and looking at his reflection in the mirror. "I'm insulted. I thought we were equals."

"We are," he insists, running his fingers through his hair. "That's why I need ya here. I know ya can protect Hannah. And I know ye can protect yerself."

"If that's true, then why not ask Cian to stay here with Rory, and I'll fight alongside you?"

He averts his gaze, which is all the answer I need.

"Exactly my point," I say, shaking my head in defeat. "I can't shake this feeling in my gut that something bad will happen if we split up."

"Ya think I want ya here with Rory? I hate that he can protect ya while I can't!" he bellows, arms out wide. "I hate that any of youse are in this position in the first place."

I turn around and lock eyes with him. "You said I have a choice. Well, my choice is I'm coming with you. Rory can stay here because I agree, someone needs to be here to protect our friends. But he can handle that himself."

Punky opens his mouth but soon closes it, exhaling in defeat.

I dare him to fight me on this because I know he wishes I

would choose what's behind door number two, but he doesn't. He won't be a hypocrite. I also know he won't do anything devious like tie me to the bed so I can't leave.

He will support my choice because he loves me.

"Okay. If that's what ya want."

"It is," I counter, folding my arms across my chest.

We've come to an agreement, but we may as well be oceans apart. This is something we will never agree on.

Even though I've made my choice, I can't help but feel selfish for it. Like I've made it to prove a point. I suddenly can't breathe. "I need some air."

Punky doesn't stop me as I push past him and race out the front door. I continue running, feeling freer the farther I go.

Tears leak from my eyes because I know I'm being unreasonable, but the thought of Punky facing Sean alone tears me apart inside. I want to be there to protect him, just as he wants to protect me. If this is the end, I want to be there with him.

I know the odds aren't in our favor, and I'm scared. I'm scared if Punky goes alone, I'll never see him again.

A guttural sob robs me of air, and I fall to my knees in the middle of the grassy field and cry the tears I've tried so hard to keep at bay. I cry for my sister, who doesn't want a part in this war. I cry for Hannah and Ethan, whose lives have been destroyed. I cry for Rory, for hurting him when I never wanted to.

I cry for every innocent man and woman who has suffered because of this feud.

But most of all, I cry for Punky and me because all we wanted was to live a simple life, but that was taken away from us by monsters who still haunt our dreams.

"I'm sorry," I whimper to no one in particular because everyone involved in this has had their life destroyed in some way or form.

Hugging my middle, I tip my face to the heavens and beg for a sign that things will be okay. I plead that come tomorrow, Punky will be alive.

I don't get the divine intervention I was hoping for as the world continues to turn, regardless of my troubles. But I suppose that's what being alive entails—no matter your hardships, you have to keep going. The world won't stop just because you want to—you just have to learn to keep up.

Fatigue overcomes me, and I succumb to the darkness… just for a little while.

I wake with a start, not recognizing the shrill noise until I see my cell ringing a few feet away.

It's dark out. I've slept for longer than I thought. The blanket draped over me reveals that Punky has checked on me to make sure I'm okay. He didn't wake me, however, as it seems we both needed some time alone.

Sitting up, I reach for my cell and answer it without looking at who the caller is.

"Cami. It's me."

"Eva?" I say, choking on three simple letters. "Is that really you?"

"Y-yes, it's me. I'm okay," she quickly assures me while I attempt to find my voice. "We're both okay."

"Ethan is with you?" I frantically ask.

"Yes, he's been looking after me."

The sentiment in her tone exposes that Ethan is still on our side, which means Sean plans on using him in other ways.

"Where are you?"

"I don't know. It's dark. I'm so sorry. I fucked everything up."

She's being elusive because I realize Sean is listening. There is a reason for this call, and I intend on finding out what that is.

"It's okay, Eva. We're coming for you. Don't let them break you."

Her jerky sniffles break my heart, but I have to be strong. "All r-right," she cries. "Ethan asked if you can pass a message on?"

"Of course."

"Can you tell Hannah that he's sorry? For everything."

I'm barely holding on. "I will."

"And can you tell Puck that he loves him. That he never stopped."

"I promise," I whisper, clenching the phone in my hand. "I know Sean is there listening. Put him on."

"Bye, Cami. I l-love you."

Although my heart is breaking in two, the scathing anger coursing through me takes a front seat when I hear Sean's voice.

"Hello, love. It's been a long time."

"Yes, it has," I reply sharply. "And I don't understand why you decided to resurface after so long. You had ample time to do your business. Ten years, to be precise."

"Ach, well my son knows how to send a message," he states. "I didn't want it to come to this."

"Oh, bullshit," I snap, not interested in playing his games. "You're responsible for all of this. You've lied, and you've used everyone, especially Punky. How could you do that to him? He's your son."

"And I'm his father," he counters calmly like this is somehow Punky's doing. "And that doesn't seem to make a difference to him as he continuously tries to destroy me. He isn't innocent in all of this. None of ye are."

"You're wrong. The difference between you and Punky is that he's fighting for honor, while you're only interested in greed. Ethan, Eva, and Hannah are just kids! They want no part in your war, yet you've dragged them into your mess. You and Punky are *nothing* alike."

"Yer quick to defend him, but do ya really know him?"

I have no idea what he means, but I pass it off as Sean trying to mess with my head. "I know enough," I reply, wanting this conversation to be done with. "I'm presuming you're calling for a reason. What do you want?"

His arrogant chuckle has me hating him all the more. "I wanted ya to see that I haven't hurt yer wee sister or Ethan."

"And?" I coax because there is more.

"And for it to remain that way, I want ye to pass a message on to Punky—tell him to surrender. He won't win. I'm givin' him one chance and one chance only."

This is a sure sign that Sean is scared. He knows he can't win against Punky and the army behind him.

"I'll pass the message on, but we both know that won't happen." I want to say so much more, but I don't want to speak out of turn.

"That's one thing we have in common…our stubbornness. Oh, and our taste in women."

His sleazy comment catches me off guard because, what the fuck is that supposed to mean? I don't let it show, though, because men like Sean thrive on power.

"I'll be sure to let Punky know you called."

I know Ethan and Eva are safe for now. Sean needs them, and he won't hurt them as long as they serve a purpose to him.

"Thank you. I'll be seein' ya really soon, doll. You and yer sister"—he smacks his lips together—"are so much alike. No wonder my son fought so hard for ya."

His comment is a low blow as he's trying to rile me on up purpose. It works. "Fuck you."

"I can see why he loves ya." He laughs, and I kick myself for falling for his ploy.

I hang up as I'll lose my cool if forced to speak to him any longer.

Eva and Ethan are all right, I remind myself. But I can't stop my hands from shaking as I pocket my phone and go in search of Punky.

The reality of what just happened hits me, and adrenaline courses through me. My brisk walk soon becomes a frantic run as I sprint to Punky's house. With my heart in my throat, I burst through his front door, and when I see him in front of a canvas, sketching deep in thought, I say to him what I should have hours ago.

"Okay, I'll stay," I pant, begging he forgives me for my stubbornness as he turns over his shoulder to look at me. "I'm sorry for…being difficult."

He places the charcoal pencil on the ledge of the easel. "Don't ever apologize for being you. What happened?"

He can read me like a book.

"Sean called. He wanted me to pass a message on—surrender or else."

Punky tongues his cheek, processing what I just shared. "I hope ya told him to go fuck himself."

"In a roundabout way. I have another message. It's from Eva."

He nods, his nerves evident as his Adam's apple dips when he swallows deeply. "Ethan wants Hannah to know he's sorry. And he wants you to know that…he loves you. He never stopped."

Punky is deadly quiet, his poker face in play. I know what this means to him. To know that Ethan forgives him and still loves him will mend a small piece of Punky's broken heart.

"They're all right?"

"For now," I reply, "which is why tomorrow, I want you to kill that motherfucker and bring them back home."

A long, comforted sigh leaves him. "I promise ya, I will."

He launches for me, meeting me halfway as I do the same thing to him. I slam my mouth to his, kissing him frantically because we've wasted so much time.

"I'm scared," I whisper, wrapping my arms around him.

"I am too," he confesses against my lips. "I don't want ya doin' anythin' yer not comfortable with."

I know what he means.

I didn't think I'd freak out the way I did seeing Punky take Brody's life. I was the one who suggested it, after all. But actually seeing Punky take that knife and end my father's life was something I've never experienced before.

"Is that why you wear the face paint?" I ask. "Because it helps you to wear a mask?"

Punky nods. "In some ways, yes, yer right."

"Will you, will you help me with mine?"

I don't know what tomorrow holds, but what I do know is that I need to be prepared to fight. I need to be prepared to kill. Maybe if I detach myself, I can do so without the darkness eclipsing the light.

He kisses the tip of my nose before breaking apart.

I watch as he retrieves the face paint from the coffee table. "Are ye sure?"

I nod.

The way he observes me has me wetting my lips, as I'm suddenly worried I've bitten off more than I can chew.

He lifts me and walks toward the kitchen, placing me on the breakfast bar. We're now equal in height. He gently brushes the hair from my face, peering longingly into my eyes. He doesn't want me to kill, but he won't leave me defenseless, which is why he unscrews the lid on the white paint.

Circling his fingers and coating them with white paint, he gently applies it to my face. I close my eyes, getting lost in his precise strokes. I recall the first time I saw him wearing his war paint. It took my breath away.

There was something almost tranquil about it, like that face allowed Punky to be himself. I know he sees himself split right down the middle, wearing both those faces on any given day.

I hear another container opening and feel the bristles of a brush delicately paint around my eyes and nose. I don't move a muscle as this is somewhat hypnotic, trusting someone so deeply. But Punky isn't just someone—he's everything and so much more.

I know he's done when he lays a soft kiss on my temple.

Without haste, I open my eyes and take in the world with new eyes. Punky stands before me, and the look reflected on his face sets a fire within.

"Your turn," I whisper, wanting him to know that I love all the faces he wears.

With a nod, he repeats the same action he did to me. But he doesn't need a mirror. He knows every stroke by heart, and I suppose that's because he's worn this face since he was five years old.

I'm caught in a spell, watching him transform into the man who is as much a part of him as his natural self is. Once he's done, he stands before me, offering himself to me—the good and the bad.

"I want ye to have somethin'." He removes the silver chain around his neck and places it into my upturned palm.

When I see what it is, I shake my head. "I can't. That was your mom's."

"And now, it's yours," he says, folding my fingers over the brooch which hangs off the chain.

This brooch means so much to him. That's why I stole it a lifetime ago. I just never anticipated it would end up back in my hands, but this time, it's been given, not stolen.

"Thank you," I say, placing it on the counter for safekeeping.

A bunch of red roses sit on the counter, roses Punky planted to honor the garden his mother once grew. So, it seems fitting when I pluck one from the vase and give it to him.

"A rose for a rose." I offer it to him.

He accepts, and when he draws it up to his nose, it's a perfect oxymoron. The red contrasts the black and white slathered on his face. He looks purely evil.

But when he reaches for his phone so I'm able to see my reflection, I realize we're a pair—a perfect pair of survivors who will do what they must.

"Ya look beautiful."

"So do you," I reply, fisting his T-shirt and dragging him toward my mouth.

I kiss him wildly, unable to get enough of him. I never will. I bite over his lip ring, obsessed with it. I'm obsessed with him.

Tearing off his T-shirt, I lean back on my hands and take a moment to appreciate Punky in his war paint, no shirt, and ripped black jeans. His body looks like it's been carved from granite, and I give in to temptation, leaning forward and running my tongue over each hardened pectoral muscle.

He moans, bowing his back to grant me greater access, which I take with pleasure.

Caressing over his taut abs, I unbuckle his belt and slip my hand inside his jeans. He's already hard, and knowing he's this turned on just by a simple touch makes me feel like a goddess.

Making my intentions clear, I jump down from the counter where I then drop to my knees. Punky peers down, rubbing his thumb over my bottom lip. Lowering his zipper, I waste no time taking down his boxers and jeans as well.

When his cock springs free, I whimper, remembering how many times we've straddled that line between pleasure and pain. I want that again, and I want more.

In one languid stroke, I lick him from head to hilt, but it's not enough. I take him into my mouth, inch by glorious inch, and don't stop until he hits the back of my throat. Gagging, I pull back a fraction, then do it again.

"Fucking hell," he curses, wrapping my loose hair around his fist.

He gently guides me as I commence bobbing up and down, not shying away from taking him deep. He's big, so I relax my throat, enjoying the feel of pleasuring him because I know this gets him off. Tears leak from my eyes as he encourages me to move faster, and I do.

The noises spilling from me are matched with his guttural growls as he pumps his hips. I place my hands on his upper thighs, loving the feel of him all over me.

"Fuck, Babydoll," he groans in that sensual accent that hits me between my legs. "I'm gonna come."

My mother taught me not to talk with my mouth full, so in response, I take him in faster, deeper.

"Naw," he roars, yanking me up from under my arms.

Before I can protest, he sweeps the counter clear and slams my ass onto it. He reaches under my dress, and with a sharp tug, my underwear disintegrates in his hand.

"When I come," he pants, licking his fingers and sinking them into me. "It's going to be in this grand pussy."

My eyes roll to the back of my head, but when he removes his fingers and thrusts into me, I see stars. I wrap my legs around his waist and arch backward as Punky begins fucking me. He's far from gentle, but I don't want him to be.

I want him to eat me alive.

The slamming of our flesh crashes with our sated moans because it feels so good. He hits me deep, thanks to the angle, and when he begins playing with my clit, I know it won't be long until I come. Our eyes are locked, and even though this act can't be considered making love, the emotion I see reflected on his face is nothing but pure love.

I want to give myself to him—in every way.

"Bedroom," I pant, wanting to be somewhere else. When I ask, he gives me what I want. I assume Hannah has gone to Fiona's.

The vase comes crashing to the floor with the force of Punky's strokes, but he complies, lifting me off the counter. He doesn't stop fucking me, however. I bounce on his length as he carries me to the bedroom. He tosses me onto the bed, where he climbs on top of me, re-entering me without missing a stroke.

We're slick and hot, and it's everything I could want, which is why I say, "I want you to lose control."

He slows down, looking for any clues to what exactly I mean.

This face paint flames my bravado as I clear up any confusion. "I want to see what this face can really do."

He groans, dropping his chin to look at where we're connected. "Are ye sure?"

"Yes," I reply without pause because I know Punky has a kink, and I want to explore it.

He kisses me deeply, not ceasing his strokes. I wait with anticipation, wanting him to let go. He pulls out and flips me onto all fours, where he drags his finger along the middle of my back. When he comes to my ass, he cups my cheek and brings down his hand—hard, just how I knew he would.

He's spanked me a couple of times in the past, and I surprisingly enjoyed it, which has me subtly wriggling my ass.

"Don't be wavin' that parful arse my way unless yer prepared for the consequences," he warns, running his hand over me.

"I'm prepared," I reply softly.

"Is that so?" His sinister tone sends a shiver down my spine.

When he spanks me again, harder this time, I jolt forward, gripping the blankets to stop from falling onto my front. I bounce back, however, as I asked for this.

Reaching over my shoulder, he grips my chin and arches my neck back. I gasp as the feral look emphasized by that face paint promises this is the point of no return.

"Has anyone touched ya here?" He cups my lower back and dips his thumb into the pleat of my ass.

I jolt instinctively, giving him the answer he seeks. But I open my legs, ready for whatever comes my way.

"Ach, we have plenty of time for that."

Disappointment overwhelms me, but that soon turns to a surprised moan when Punky coaxes me onto my stomach and to spread my legs as he comes to rest between them. I have no idea what he's doing until he encourages me to arch my back and raise my hips so my ass is high in the air.

As I turn over my shoulder to look at him, my eyes widen when he buries his face between my ass cheeks. I try to scamper away, but he holds me in place and commences swirling his tongue around my puckered entrance.

I don't know how to feel. Something so taboo shouldn't feel this good, but it does.

He uses his tongue and mouth to stimulate me in ways that turn my cheeks a bright red. But as I get over the stigma associated with this act, I relax and let go.

His light stubble adds to the sensation, and before long, I'm moving into his touches, lost to this feeling of utter freedom because there are no boundaries with Punky. He makes something I never thought I'd enjoy feel fucking incredible.

Before long, I'm bending to his touches and savoring the sensation of being loved by my man; in every way.

He kisses my ass cheek before slapping it lightly. "Feel

good?"

"Yes," I reply timidly, gripping the blankets beneath me.

I don't know what happens now because I did ask him to lose control with me, but so far, he's been quite controlled.

He plants a kiss to the small of my back and wraps his arms around my waist, coaxing me to rise onto my knees. He presses his chest to my back, skin to skin. Nothing separates us, and I've never felt more vulnerable in my life.

He commences touching over my chest, my stomach, and then sinks two fingers inside my sex. Moaning, I spread my legs wider, granting him entry because I want him everywhere. I can feel his cock against me, and on instinct, I rub my ass against him.

He groans, and even though I'm scared, I encourage him to do what I asked—lose control.

"Are ye sure?" he pants against my ear before sucking it into his warm mouth.

"I want to experience all my firsts with you." And I mean it. "I thought I knew what love was…but then I met you."

A contented sigh leaves him.

His fingers work in and out of me as he reaches for the tub of Vaseline on the nightstand with his other hand. Dr. Shannon suggested Hannah put this on her wounds to help them heal faster, but now, we've found another use for it.

Punky pops off the lid, and I hear him scoop his fingers inside the container. He then gently applies some of the cool gel to my backside. I freeze, but he kisses my shoulder, a silent reassurance to help me relax. I anticipate a sharp sting but don't feel anything as Punky continues kissing my skin while working my sex into a frenzy down below.

"Whatever happens tomorrow, know that I love ye more than I've ever loved anyone."

Even though I wish he wouldn't speak this way, I know he needs to get this off his chest. We don't know what tomorrow brings, but we can march into it with no regrets.

"We'll be okay," I say for both our sakes.

"I hope so, but we don't know that. But what I do know is that I'm a better man for lovin' you."

I feel a soft prod against my back entrance, and when I freeze, Punky continues whispering sweet nothings into my ear.

"And no matter what happens"—he enters me an inch—"I want you to know that."

When my muscles accept this foreign intrusion, Punky sinks into me a little farther. I suddenly feel so full.

"I want ye to know that my heart belongs to you. You own me—mind."

He continues entering me while I mewl at this unexpected pleasure.

"Body."

I feel like I'm being split in two…and I like it.

"And soul."

When Punky stops, placing his forehead on my shoulder, I

wonder if he's done. But when I turn over my shoulder, I see he's not even halfway there.

"Do ya want me to stop?"

"No," I whisper, wanting this more than I need air to breathe.

He grips my chin between his thumb and finger and presses his lips to mine. I whimper into his mouth as he continues to enter me slowly from behind and plays with my clit. He is everywhere, all over me, and just when I think this can't get any better, he's buried inside me to the hilt.

A shudder passes through me as he stills, allowing me time to adjust. I never thought I could feel so complete, but I've never felt more connected to another human being than I do right now, which is why I reach around and place a hand on Punky's lower back.

With our lips still locked, I gently encourage him to move, and move he does.

He gently thrusts his hips, stretching me wide, before he pulls out halfway and then slides back in. The Vaseline allows him to move inside me a little more comfortably, and when we move in unison, finding our rhythm, he whispers, "Can I go faster?"

I nod.

He sinks into me deeply before pulling all the way out. I instantly miss the connection, but he soon slides back in, smoother this time, making me moan at the sensation. He removes his fingers from my sex and places his hands on my hips.

He drives into me harder and faster, and the burn I feel is toeing the line between pleasure and pain. But I focus on the pleasure because knowing Punky is losing himself this way, knowing he is finally letting go has me bouncing back and taking everything he gives.

The burn soon fades, and I am lost to every passionate moment, every breathless moan which spills from him as he devours every inch of me. This act is filled with nothing but love and respect, and I promise myself here, now, I'll do everything in my power to protect Punky.

The mirror in front of me allows me to see how the world sees us. We fit, in every sense of the word. We are both slathered in war paint, our bodies bending in need. If the sight of Punky, wearing his skull face and fucking me brutally, isn't the hottest thing I have ever seen, then I don't know what is.

"Oh, fuck," he grunts, dropping his forehead to my back as he pumps his hips.

I reach down and begin playing with my clit because the build-up is almost unbearable. He is everywhere, yet I can't get enough. He rotates his hips in a way that has me feeling so incredibly full.

"Ye feel fucking incredible," he says in that smooth accent that gets me so damn hot. "I love you. No matter what happens, y'll always be the one for me. I know we can't live forever, but

I want to leave behind something that will—my love for you."

His words touch me in ways that have tears springing to life. "I love you too. I always have. Come back to me. Promise me?"

He suckles the side of my neck, fucking me hard. "I'll always be with ye."

It's not the answer I want, but it's enough. "And I with you."

"And for that, I'm the luckiest man alive."

He places his hand over mine, circling my clit in just the right way and as he thrusts deep, I come with a loud, sated moan.

"Fucking beautiful," Punky grunts before I feel him join me in this pure bliss.

Our bodies are sweaty and warm, and I bask in the afterglow because I feel so content being united this way. Punky kisses my shoulder before pulling out. The moment he does, my body grows lax, and I fall onto my stomach, placing the pillow under my head.

I hear him moving about, but I don't know where he's gone until I feel a warmth at my backside. Turning over my shoulder, I smile when I see Punky gently cleaning me.

"I hope I wasn't too rough with ya." He uses another washcloth to wipe my face clean. Most of his face paint has smudged off, but he still looks like a beautiful mess.

"No," I reply, suddenly exhausted. "I did ask for you to lose control. You were quite tame."

He smirks, wiping his face clean, before tossing the washcloth into the laundry hamper and joins me on the bed. He drags me into his arms so we're nose to nose.

A lifetime ago, I would have felt self-conscious being nestled this way. I would have been afraid Punky could see straight through me and see my flaws. But not now. This confirms how far we've come. The thought that it might be ripped away tomorrow has tears welling.

"No tears," he whispers, wiping a tear away with his thumb. "I couldn't bear it."

I know he's asking me to be strong tomorrow because he can't do what he must without a clear head.

Quickly pulling it together, I smile, but it's strained. "No tears. I promise."

He nods, gently pressing a kiss to my brow.

Moments later, his soft breathing indicates he is asleep. Pressing my ear to his chest, I listen to the steady rhythm of his heart. The sound comforts me, and if possible, I snuggle closer to him, never wanting to let go.

But come tomorrow, I won't have a choice. To save the world as we know it, I have to sacrifice *my* world.

Even though I promised Punky no tears, a single one trickles down my cheek and I hope it's the last one I'll shed for a long time.

I hope.

SIXTEEN

PUNKY

"**A**re you sure this is what you want?"

"I'm sure."

"All right then. It's all done. Good luck, Puck," Darcy says as she signs on the dotted line near my signature.

I didn't go into details, but she knows today will change everything. That is why I called her and organized a will.

If anything goes wrong, I want to be prepared.

She's told her dad to be on alert, but he can look after himself. Patrick Duffy has an army of men who will protect him. Darcy should be with him, but she insisted she would be of more use here. I understand what she means—she'll fight and help protect everything dear to me.

"Thank you, Darcy. For everythin." I want her to know that

I appreciate everything she's done for me.

"You can take me out for tea to say thanks," she says, wanting to lighten the mood. She still has feelings for me but has accepted that we won't be anything but friends.

"Sure thing." I don't know if I'll ever be able to make good on that promise, but I hope that I do.

I'm relieved I got that sorted so I can focus on the task at hand. And when there is a knock on my front door, it seems that time is now.

Opening it, I smile on instinct when I see Babydoll. However, she looks to be anything but happy. She gives me a warm embrace, snuggling close.

She left this morning to grab a few things and pick up Hannah and Fiona, who stand behind her. If looks could kill, I'd be a smothering pile of ashes because Fiona makes clear she's here because she has no other choice.

"Hi, Baby," I whisper into her ear.

She merely holds on tighter in response.

I understand how difficult this is for her. It is for me too. But, together, they are safe. I can go into this fight with a clear head, which is what I need to defeat Sean.

She lets me go and enters, nodding a greeting when she sees Darcy.

I've asked Darcy not to tell anyone about the will. It'll just worry them.

Cian arrives a few minutes later with Amber and my

grandparents. I haven't spoken to them since I got out of jail. The last time I saw my grandparents, I had burned down the house which started this quest for revenge.

I made it clear I had no interest in them being a part of my life, and that hasn't changed. But I won't leave them vulnerable. Anyone tied to me is at risk, and I won't give Sean the satisfaction of gathering more pawns to blackmail me with.

Amber stays close to Cian, making clear she wishes Cian was the one staying here, not Rory.

She looks how I remember, and seeing her after all this time has a flood of memories coming back. She was good to the twins and me. She deserves more than a casual wave.

"Hi, Amber. It's good seein' ye." She nods, and when I extend my hand, she begrudgingly accepts.

"Hi, Puck. It's good seeing you too. I wish it was under different circumstances, but trouble always seems to follow you. That hasn't changed."

"Amber," Cian gently scolds, shaking his head.

But she's right. "It's all right, Cian."

He sighs, and they enter my home without another word.

My grandparents sheepishly enter. Keegan is too proud to acknowledge me, but my grandma, Imogen, gives me a loose hug. "We've missed ya, chile."

I don't bother replying because even though I am still angry with them for what they did to my mum, I can't deny being with them helps me feel closer to my ma.

She realizes this is the best she's going to get, and she and Keegan quickly stand off to the side.

"How ye feelin'?" I ask Hannah, gently touching her cheek.

Fiona instantly steps forward, a silent warning I'll lose a finger if I don't remove my hand from her daughter.

Hannah ignores her mum. "I'm better. I'm worried about ye, though."

Fiona scoffs, rolling her eyes. "It's 'cause of him we're in this mess."

No one bothers to take the bait, though, because we have bigger fish to fry.

"Be careful, Puck," Hannah says, her lower lip trembling. "I can't lose ye again."

When tears begin to fall, I draw her into my arms and kiss the top of her head. "Ya can't get rid of me that easily."

"Good, 'cause I don't want to."

Amber walks over, gently consoling Hannah. She can't help but come to her aid as a part of her, I'm sure, still sees her as the little girl she raised. Fiona was too busy spending Connor's money to care for her kids. So her caring mother act has come too little, too late.

When I hear Rory's tires crunch over the gravel, I inhale evenly because it's time.

When Cian and I walk outside to greet him, we see a convoy of cars driving toward us. Logan Doherty and his men are here to help Rory if needed. I only hope I've done the right thing in trusting him. The other names on that list are waiting for me at the factory. This is what happens when you forget where loyalty lies.

May the best man win.

Rory has a large bag over his shoulder, no doubt filled with weapons. He nods at Cian but grunts my way. He's still pissed off at me, and that's okay. As long as he protects Cami, he can hate me for as long as he likes.

"Everyone inside?"

"Aye," Cian replies. "Yer all set?"

Rory nods. "As ready as I can be. Are ye sure Logan and his men can be trusted?"

"I'm not sure of anythin'," I reply honestly. "But what other choice do we have? Hide like a bunch of pussies, waitin' for Sean and Liam to strike? Or bring the fight to us? If Logan steps out of line, ya know what to do."

Rory's nostrils flare. "He wouldn't dare after everythin' he's done."

We're all hoping that's the case, but we can't be sure.

Cian and Rory go inside, and Cian knows what to do—arm everyone.

I wait for Logan to approach me. "Bout ye? Ye ready?"

"Aye, I am. Did ya do what I asked?"

"Yes. I've let everyone know yer callin' a meetin' at the factory. Some are awful mad at what ya did to Brody. I suspect they've told Liam where y'll be. Even though all of them know about the meetin', most of them won't be there. I assume they'll be with Liam.

"The ones that do come, they were once loyal to Connor. I believe if it comes down to that, they will fight with ya. That's why they'll come. To listen to what ye have to say."

"Grand, that's what I was hopin' for."

Logan doesn't hide his surprise but doesn't ask questions. "Ya can count on us, Puck. We won't let anythin' happen to yer family. Connor was good to us. We haven't forgotten that."

I hope he's telling me the truth.

I give him directions to where his men are to wait. The grounds are open, so we need eyes everywhere. I wish I had more time to set traps, but I don't. This is the best I can do.

He shakes my hand. "Good luck to ye. May God be on yer side."

"God has nothin' to do with this. But thank you."

The men behind Logan are all familiar faces. Some left the business when Connor died, and others worked for Brody and maybe Sean. I hate that I don't have the time to interrogate them, but I have to trust Logan because he knows if he fucks me over, his family will pay for his sins.

With nothing left to say, I turn back to the house, and when I see Babydoll waiting in the doorway for me, I gesture she's to meet me around the back. We walk in silence, both pensive because, how do you say goodbye to the person you love?

We come to a stop in front of the rose garden.

She wraps her arms around her middle, a tiny whimper escaping her.

"Rory given ya a gun?"

She nods, staring vacantly at the roses.

"Cami, please look at me."

She takes her time but eventually does what I ask.

"It's going to be okay."

"You don't know that."

"I know, but I'm going to try my hardest to make sure that it is," I reply honestly. "If this were a film, or some romance novel, the hero would have a flawless plan where he wins and lives happily ever after. But it's not. And I'm no hero."

"Yes, you are," she argues, toying with the necklace around her neck. It's under her T-shirt, but I can see it's the chain I gave her. It gives me comfort knowing she wears it. "You're going into the unknown, but what you *do* know is that Liam and Sean will be waiting for you."

"I can't wait any longer. I wish this were different. But ten years ago, I learned that even the best-laid plans fail."

"Please don't die," she whispers, expressing her fears aloud.

"I'll try not to." And I mean it because, if all else fails, I have a plan B. But no one can know of it because they'll all stop me. But if it comes to it, I won't falter. This way, everyone wins.

She sniffs back her tears, keeping to her promise. "Good, because you still owe me a date."

I smirk, reaching for her and holding her close.

"Don't hesitate," I say. "If anyone is at risk, ya shoot."

"I will."

I wish I didn't have to leave, but I do, and I wonder if this is what your heart being torn into two feels like. "I love you, but love is just a word we give to somethin' so primeval. What I feel for ye can't be put into words."

She throws her arms around me, hugging me tightly.

I memorize her scent. The way she feels in my arms. I memorize what it's like being loved by her because it's what will help me fight.

"Stay safe."

"You too." Her voice cracks as she lets me go.

I can't stand to see her in pain.

Slamming my mouth over hers, I rob her of air as I want this to be the last memory we have. I want it to be of our love and not sadness or fear.

She kisses me back, gripping my hair and pressing me close. She doesn't want me to go, but she knows she must.

On an exhale, I let her go and nuzzle my nose against hers. "See ya soon."

"Yup, see ya." She can barely speak, but that's okay.

We walk back to the house, where she lets go of my hand and quickly enters without looking back. I understand why.

Rory stands outside, waiting for me. "Here." He offers me a phone. "It's a secure line, and I'll be able to track yer every move. And y'll be able to track mine."

Rory's knowledge of this sort of stuff is priceless. No matter our differences, he has come through in the end.

"Take care of her," I say, pushing aside the awkwardness.

"I will," he replies. "I'm doin' this *for* her."

He wants to make clear he isn't here for me, and that's all right.

Cian appears with a bag slung over his shoulder. "Should we head?"

I nod, taking one last look at the house filled with the people who are relying on me not to fail.

We say our goodbyes, and I'm thankful Rory didn't make it a soppy farewell. Regardless of what we face, he still wants me to know he won't forgive me.

We get into Cian's truck and drive toward the unknown.

A rock song is playing over the radio, but Cian turns it off, much preferring the silence, it seems. He's nervous.

"I want ya to know that yer my best mate. Thank you for always havin' my back." I want him to know I appreciate everything he's doing for me. Everything he has done.

"Gettin' soft in yer old age, are ye?" he replies with a smirk, breaking the ice.

"Don'tcha be tellin' anyone."

He laughs loudly.

We arrive at the factory, both taking a look at our surroundings. Cars are parked, which hint the men are already inside. The question is, what men?

Calling the peelers would be the sensible thing to do, but what side of the law do they sit? Constable Shane Moore would no doubt love to see me back behind bars. I have to treat him like the enemy.

Once Cian parks his truck, we put on our bulletproof vests. It'll probably be in vain, but anything we can do to protect ourselves will help us get the upper hand in one way or another. Cian reaches for the bag of goodies, and we make our way toward the factory.

Just like the castle, this place is crumbling. But it's deserted, and the peelers won't be sniffing around because trespassing would just be another day in the office for them. Ron Brady and his men, *Connor's* men, surround the perimeter, just as we discussed.

Some are on display, while others are hidden in and around the surrounding abandoned buildings.

It's expected I would have men guarding the outer limits. To not have anyone would raise red flags. I want this to appear as "normal" as possible.

I nod to Ron, who holds a rifle. He knows what to do.

When we enter the factory, I whistle because this place looks worse on the inside than it does on the outside. There are about forty men inside, a mixture of Brody's men who were probably sent by Liam to ambush me—but mostly, the men here are ones who once worked for us. They're milling around in groups, and when they see me, their chatter silences.

Their familiar faces transport me back in time.

I greet them, hoping they're here in peace. But we will see where their loyalties are when push comes to shove. This is the only way this will work—I need to start from scratch to know whose side they're on. Who they're willing to die for.

"Is that everyone?" I ask Rogan Shea, one of Connor's closest friends. Ron told me he opened his own strawberry farm after I was sent to prison.

It seems that the farming life wasn't for him, though. He's on our side, one of Ron's men, and he's here to relay information to Ron if things take a turn.

"Aye, Puck. *Most* of us left the life once ye were gone." I don't fail to note the sarcasm in his voice as he sees the men, even though here now, who worked for Brody as traitors.

I agree with him, but I also understand that they had a family to feed. They gravitated toward the stability and a paycheck. Connor's death destroyed so many as a true king fell from his throne. But that doesn't excuse the fact that they made the wrong choice.

"Grand, I won't waste yer time then," I commence as Cian stands beside me. "Yer here 'cause, as ya know, I killed Brody, and I plan on doin' the same to my uncle. He betrayed all of us. He was the one responsible for Connor's death.

"I know youse don't respect him 'cause if ya did, y'd be with him right now. But alliances are torn. And I won't work that way. I need yer loyalty. If ya give it to me, then I promise I'll look after youse. Just how Connor did.

"I am his son, and Northern Ireland belongs not only to me but to us! The fact that a Doyle was allowed to take control was because of Sean. He sided with Brody but was merely using him for his own selfish gain.

"They were both using each other. Kingdoms can't have two kings, which is why I'm challenging anyone who thinks they can take me on."

"Fucking Catholics," Rogan spits, shaking his head in disgust.

"There is more to this than religion. That's a thing of the past. Now, this is about honor. This is about revenge. Youse know me. Ya know I will fight for what I believe in. I will fight for our home!"

The men erupt into applause, clapping wildly at my words.

"I want ya to pledge yer loyalty here, now, and I promise youse, I'll make Belfast what it once was. But if yer in two minds, this is yer chance to leave. No hard feelin's. But I'm givin' ya one chance and one chance only.

"The reason Northern Ireland is such a mess is 'cause there is no authority. Paramilitary groups fight against one another because there is no one leader. Everyone is fighting for power. When Connor ruled, the Kelly name was respected.

"Everyone knew their place. Everyone *had* a place. I want that back. It's going to take an army to do that, but I can, and I will. My uncle wants me dead, and that's because he isn't my uncle, after all."

The room falls silent.

"Connor will always be my father, but biologically, I am Sean's son. And he knew that when he sent me to prison. Greed is the only thing he cares about, and I think most of ye know that. That's why yer here and not fightin' with him.

"Brody was one of the men who killed my ma. As was his brother, Aidan. In return, I killed them both. One man is left standing, and that man is Sean. He was the one who killed my mum. Slit her throat when he knew I watched him, hidden away.

"He isn't a leader. He's a fucking coward. He's remained hidden for ten years, tryin' to persuade people to come join him. But youse see right through his shite. Youse know he isn't fit to fill Connor's shoes. I am sick of this fucking cunt…and I want him dead."

One of the men, whose name I don't know, nervously looks over his shoulder toward the door. Cian notices it too.

It seems publicly shaming my father is the antidote we need.

"I am huntin' him, and mark my words, father or not, I'm going to cut off his balls and feed them to him. And as for Liam Doyle, I plan on doing to him what I did to his brother, father, and uncle. I am going to end the Doyle bloodline for what they did to my ma."

The man subtly reaches for his gun, and Cian and I let him.

"We're with ya, Puck. All of us are. Y've our word," says Rogan, bowing in servitude.

All the other men follow suit, except the fucker who clearly doesn't share the same sentiment. This is why I wanted ex-Kelly men. I knew they'd see reason—eventually. If they survive this, I will give them a lifeline as long as they pledge loyalty to the Kelly name.

"Grand, 'cause yer first test is now. Are youse armed?"

The men look around confused, but nod.

"Good, 'cause we've company."

Before they can question me, a large boom explodes around us. The sound is from the stray bullet which missed my head by miles and lodged into the wall behind me.

Everyone draws their guns, armed and ready to fight.

The arsehole who aimed and missed runs for cover, but he collapses onto his stomach when I shoot out his kneecap. Howling in pain, he rolls over and fires, missing again. For his error, I shoot his hand. His gun slides across the ground.

I don't have time to question whose side he plays on because gunfire erupts outside. It's started…

"Liam and Sean are outside, as I knew they would be. Bein' here like this is like leaving a trail of blood for hungry sharks."

"Ya could have warned us!" screams Matthew, ex-Kelly and newfound Doyle devotee, as he ducks low.

"Would ye have come if I did?"

He mulls over my question as it's a fair one to ask. I could have told them, but now, those left standing will never switch sides. This is a fight to the death. A fight for warriors—warriors I want on my side. There will be casualties, but that's always the risk in war.

Most of these men are traitors in one way or another. This is their chance for redemption, and if they survive, they will cherish every sunrise from this day forward.

Men come flooding in from the door and holes in the wall, which were made over time. It's an ambush, and that's okay because Sean won't kill me. But that doesn't mean I won't kill him and all the men who fight with him.

Cian and I spring into action, operating as a tag team as we work back-to-back to take the enemy down. Our men protect us, shooting anything that moves. But we're outnumbered, which can only mean one thing.

"Liam is workin' with Sean!" I shout so Cian can hear me over the gunfire.

I factored in this possibility, but honestly, I'm shocked he would work with the man who killed his sister. I suppose he sees Sean as the lesser of two evils. His hatred for me has forced his hand—just how mine did to work with Brody.

But if they overthrow me, which they won't, no doubt Liam will do to Sean what Brody did to him.

And vice versa.

They need the other to defeat me.

I laugh happily at the fact because they won't win.

"Ya think they're both here?" Cian asks as we continue covering the other.

"Aye, no doubt. Liam is here for revenge. And Sean is here 'cause he wants everyone to do the dirty work for him."

I don't want to jinx it, but this might mean Babydoll will be okay. Most of the men will be here, protecting their leader. I didn't know what we faced going into this, but now, I can see clearly. This is a good old-fashioned gunfight where only the strong will remain standing.

The factory explodes in both sight and sound. The smoke from the gunfire makes it almost impossible to see, but together, Cian and I are unstoppable. And so are the men who fight for their lives.

We jump over fallen bodies, shooting anyone who is the enemy. It's bedlam, and I thrive in the anarchy because I feel fucking alive. Each man I kill brings me closer to getting back Ethan and Eva. And killing the two men who dare think they can fight me and win.

"It's Liam!" Cian shouts, gesturing to him running through the door.

I still can't believe how stupid he is, thinking an ambush would work. I suppose he underestimated the power the Kelly name holds. Sean is nowhere to be seen as he's a smart predator. He's waiting for the perfect moment to strike.

With a roar, Liam comes charging for us, but the bulk under his shirt reveals he's wearing a bulletproof vest as well.

That won't be a problem, however.

Targeting his thigh, I aim and shoot, and watch in joy as he hollers and drops to the ground. That doesn't deter him, however, and he continues crawling toward us, shooting.

Cian snickers and shoots him in the shoulder. He never misses.

Liam's men realize their leader has fallen and stop when I shout, "Drop yer guns. Otherwise, y'll be obeying a corpse."

"Do what he says!" screams Liam, finally coming to a stop.

The men look at one another, looking for cues from their associates. What a bunch of disloyal pussies as they do as he says with reluctance.

My men cease gunfire—for now.

Cian and I walk toward a squirming Liam, never dropping our guard. But they all know, one wrong move, and they'll join the pile of bloody bodies.

Peering down at Liam, I'm almost disappointed at how easy this was. "Where is he?"

"Fuck you," he spits, rolling away from me.

Tsking him, I stomp on his knee to explain this is going only one way—my way. "Spare me the theatrics 'cause I know ya didn't pull this off alone. Why would ye protect him after what he did to yer sister?"

Liam's eyes are filled with pure hate as he snarls, "I'd rather that than see you succeed. My da was a fucking idiot for trustin' ya. I told him not to but he didn't listen, and look where he is now. Fucking dead, killed like a nobody.

"I'm so fucking angry with him. He has destroyed everythin', and his stubbornness has led to the death of my family! Deaths you delivered. So I will work with anyone, even the devil himself, if it results in yer death."

He waits for a reaction, and he gets one in the shape of a bored yawn. "Yer all a bunch of pussies," I spit, disgusted. "Grow a pair and dry yer eyes. What did ya think would happen? We're not friends, we're enemies, and that's because yer dad was a greedy cunt who trusted the wrong man.

"It's not my fault he was a weak fuck. If he were any leader, his men wouldn't stray. He'd have their loyalty and respect. But he didn't."

Liam clenches his jaw, clearly not appreciating me having no respect for the dead.

"Connor wasn't perfect. His men weren't loyal either," he snarls, squirming as I press harder down on his knee.

"Yer right, but his kingdom never fell until he was murdered. Yer dad was barely holdin' on. It takes a real leader to rule…and to win. Yer da and *mine*…they're both failures because this is all mine."

The horror on Liam's face reveals he wasn't privy to the fact that Sean is indeed my dad. He had no idea this was very personal to Sean and me.

"So I ask ya again, where is he?"

Before he can answer, a car's screeching tires and then a

loud bang hint someone has been hit. Cian quickly runs for the door while I stay with Liam.

"Ya don't actually think he'd spare yer life, do ya? Yer nothin' to him. A pawn to get what he wants."

Liam smirks, and the sight sends a chill right through me. I don't know why he's smiling when he knows he's minutes away from joining his family.

With my gun still trained on him, I quickly dig into my pocket for my phone and send a text to Rory.

Everything okay?

While I wait for his reply, I check his location how he showed me and sigh in relief when it indicates he's still at my gaff.

All good here.

I pass it off as me just being paranoid, and when Cian and Ron enter through the door with a hostage, that paranoia settles because the enemy is here—finally.

I can barely believe my eyes, but I savor this moment as I know it's one I will revisit for the rest of my life. Monsters are real…and they come in the shape of my father, who stands before me.

My brain can't process that he is really here, and my heart softens for a fraction of a second, remembering the good times.

But those memories are soon destroyed when everything he's done for his own greed comes careering to me like a freight train.

This man who gave me life, took it from me in the same breath.

Cian and Ron are on either side of him, holding on tightly so he can't escape. But he wouldn't. He's too bleedin' proud for that. And that's confirmed when he has the audacity to smile as we lock eyes.

"How y've grown, son. Look at ya. A big man now."

He's baiting me, and it's worked.

"Let him go," I order Cian and Ron, who hesitate for a moment before doing as I've asked. They step aside, knowing this is going to get ugly.

I take my time examining the man who has taken everything from me. Now that I'm older, I see the similarities between us. Same eye color, same facial features, and the same sarcastic grin when we know we're going to win.

That's soon to change when I punch him square in the face. A pained *oof* leaves him as his head snaps back with a crack.

The bloodlust rouses the demons, demanding more, but they'll have to wait because we have a lot to catch up on.

"Don't call me son."

He nods, wiping his bloodied lip with a smile. "Still got that temper, so you have. I'm to blame for that."

Inhaling sharply, I count to three to calm myself down. "Where are Ethan and Eva? I know ya came here 'cause ye want somethin' from me. So let's stop with the bullshit."

But Sean has other ideas. "Ye look just like yer ma. I always wanted to tell ya that but could not. Keepin' the truth from ye almost killed me."

"I'll happily put ye out of yer misery then."

He laughs in response, and why wouldn't he? He's in control. Until Ethan and Eva are safe, he knows he has the upper hand.

"I loved her, and she loved me," he continues, while I clench my fists, barely holding on.

"Is that why ye killed her? 'Cause ya loved her so much? That why ya slit her throat, knowin' I was watchin'? 'Cause of yer love for her?"

He isn't moved by my recollection of that night. "What would ya have me do?" he questions calmly. "She was going to ruin everythin' for me. For *us*."

"There is no *us*, thanks to you. Ye made sure of it when ya killed my entire family."

"I *am* yer family, Puck," he corrects with a smug smile. "Don'tcha be forgettin' that. We're the same, you and I. We want the same thing…even though you can't see that."

Smacking my lips together, I reply, "What I want is for ye to be dead, but I know that can't happen until ya get what ya want. So stop wasting my time."

Sean nods, appearing to respect me for my honesty. "Aye, yer right. I'm not going to insult ya by apologizin' for what I did. I can't change the past, but I can the future…join me, son. I want ya by my side.

"I can't do this on my own. I've tried. But these men still cling to Connor's ruling and see you as their true leader. We could rule all of Ireland and Northern Ireland together. Father and son…just how it was supposed to be."

I take a moment to process what he just said because, what in the ever-living fuck? Does he really expect me to fall for this shite?

"Ya said ye didn't want to insult me," I state, folding my arms across my chest. "And then ya go and say such nonsense. We will *never* rule side by side, and ya know that."

A jubilant chuckle spills from Sean. "It was worth a shot. That's why I was forced to do what I did."

"No one forced ya to get yer nephew hooked on whatever shite he's takin'. That's all on you. The people surrounding ye are not there by choice. They're either junkies or yer blackmailing them somehow."

"Yer ma made the choice, though, cub. She came to me. And that's the God's honest truth."

As I clench my jaw, Sean's journal entry comes crashing into me.

She betrayed me after she told me she loved me. After she promised she'd never leave me. That I was the one she wanted, not him.

She was going to leave him. She told me so.

"I don't know what she was thinkin', but what I do know is that I don't blame her for fallin' for yer bullshit. I did. I believed ya actually gave a fuck about me."

"I did. I do," he counters, and I hate that I can't sense a lie in him. "I protected ye, did I not? When Connor was beating ye black and blue, I stepped in to help ya. Ye saw me more as a father than Connor. Ya can't deny that."

I want to argue, to tell him to shut his fucking mouth, but he's right. He always had my back, and at times, I wished he was my dad, not Connor. Now that I know the truth, however, I realize Connor raised me as best he could.

He wasn't shown love or affection as a wain because my grandfather was too busy chasing tail, and my grandmother was oblivious to it as her first—and only—love was any liquor she could drown herself in.

Connor and Sean were doomed from the very beginning until my ma came along. She showed them both kindness and love and paid the ultimate price for it.

I hate that this piece of shite is the only link to my past, a past I so desperately want to know more about. My whole life wasn't just trying to find out who Cara Kelly was, but it was also about finding out who *I* am.

I've always felt like I don't belong, and that's because I don't know anything about who I was until I was old enough to make those decisions for myself. I don't know if I was always this stubborn or if I preferred winter to summer.

I don't know anything because my past is a thing Connor wanted me to forget.

But now, my past, present, and future stand in front of me, offering me breadcrumbs because he knows me too well.

I thought I would come into this forgetting our past, but looking at him now, all I'm reminded of is how Sean was the person who helped shape me into the man I am today. He was the one who took care of me when Connor was too busy to care.

And I hate how he has that over me because I don't know why he would do that when he had ample opportunity to kill me.

"Ya may hate me with every breath ya take…but I know that ya hate yerself more for not being able to kill me."

His words stoke this already intense fire, and I reach for my gun, proving him wrong.

He sarcastically raises his hands in surrender, not at all threatened. "Go on then, shoot me. But y'll never see Ethan or Eva again."

Gripping the gun, I rein in the urge to prove him wrong

because he's right. Ethan and Eva are the reason he's still breathing. "Name yer price."

"Punky," Cian warns, but I am done playing.

With his hands still raised, Sean sets the rules. "You. I give ye Ethan and Eva, and in return, you give me your word that yer loyal to me."

And there it is.

I always knew it would come to this.

"It seems like a rather easy choice. Yer life for theirs. What's more important?"

"Punky, no." Cian shakes his head, but I always had a plan B. I just needed to figure out what Sean's demands were.

With a grin on my face, I surrender to the devil. "Finally, y've stopped talking shite and given me what I wanted. Ya have my word, Sean. My life for theirs."

Sean smiles while Cian and Ron gasp in horror.

"Don't be the hero. Y'll be his prisoner for the rest of yer life!" Cian roars, storming forward. "Kill the fucking cunt and give him what he deserves."

"Cian, stop," I calmly demand, but when he continues to advance, I do something I've never done before—I turn my gun on my best friend.

He stops dead in his tracks, eyes wide. "What's this? Yer gonna shoot me? Yer gonna let this ballbag ruin yer life—again? If ye agree to this, y've just given up one prison cell for another."

I know that, but there is no way that's happening again. I

wish I could tell Cian, but I can't. He would stop me. They all would.

"Take him to them," I command Sean, who nods.

"Frederick, take Liam and have him show youse where they are," Sean orders a man who is still standing.

Cian shakes his head, demanding I see reason, but until Ethan and Eva are safe, Sean is the one calling the shots.

"I'm not goin' anywhere," Cian stubbornly states, and when Frederick has the balls to try to change Cian's mind, he gets an elbow to the face. "Touch me again, and it won't just be yer nose I break."

I appreciate his tenacity, but the truth is, he is the only one I trust to retrieve Ethan and Eva. I need him to tell me they're okay so I can end this…once and for all.

"Please, Cian," I say, hoping for once, he does as I ask as I lower my gun. "Just go with them. I don't trust anyone else."

"Puck," Cian pleads, begging I don't ask this of him as he knows what it means. "I'm not leavin' ye alone with this psychopath!"

"I'll be all right. I promise ye. Sean needs me alive."

"And that's what worries me," Cian counters with a sigh.

We do this, and it'll be history repeating itself. I surrender my freedom to help another arsehole rule. But this time, it's different. I'll make sure of it.

Walking slowly toward Cian, I see the desperation in his eyes. He wants me to fight, and I will…just not until everyone involved is safe. I won't allow another person to be hurt because of me.

Cupping the back of his neck, I draw us brow to brow. "I need ye to make sure they're all right. Call me when ya get them."

"Don't do this. Y've already sacrificed so much. Don't let another bastard use ye for his gain."

His voice trembles, revealing his pain, but we always knew it would end this way.

"I don't plan on it," I whisper, wanting him to know I will never be a prisoner ever again.

His eyes widen because he's finally worked out what I plan to do. "Punky, no—"

He doesn't get a chance to finish his sentence because I pull back and headbutt him. He drops to the ground, out cold.

Looking at my best friend, I sigh. He'll come to in a few minutes as his head is as hard as mine. "Sorry, mate, but this was the only way ye'd go. If any harm comes to him—"

Sean nods. "I promise ye. Not a hair on his head. Frederick, take them."

Frederick is a big man and lifts an unconscious Cian with ease. A piece of my heart walks out the door with Cian because I didn't get to say goodbye.

Another man helps Liam to his feet, who narrows his eyes. "This isn't over. It's just the beginning."

Again, his cryptic statement sends a shiver down my spine,

but I don't let it get to me because I have to focus.

Once they're gone, I look at Ron and the remaining men. "Leave us. This isn't yer fight."

"Puck—"

"I said away now," I interrupt Ron, who appears stunned I would request he leave. But he's done enough. I won't let another man lose their life for a war that isn't theirs.

Ron doesn't argue when he senses this isn't negotiable, and he and the men limp out of the door, thankful they leave with their lives, unlike their fallen colleagues whose blood stains the ground red.

The moment they're out the door, I smile because it's just Sean and me—just how it should be.

I need to keep him entertained until I hear from Cian, because when I do…I'm going to fucking murder this arsehole. There is no way I'm going to be someone's errand boy again. So as I see it, he or I, or *both*, will die today.

"I don't know why yer so desperate for me to join. Didn't Babydoll and I fuck everythin' up for ye last time?"

"It didn't go to plan, but it worked in my favor in the end. Who's still standin'?" he questions victoriously.

It's time that changes.

"With Connor's dying breath, he told me not to trust ye. He knew ye were nothin' but a dog. Weak and pathetic."

Sean attempts to conceal his anger, but the clenching of his jaw betrays him.

"That's why ye were left outta his will. He changed it and left everythin' to his bastard chile. He'd rather I have it than see it destroyed in the hands of you.

"Ye had to fake yer own death to overcome him." I laugh, eyeing him confidently. "Looks like ye better sleep with yer bulletproof vest from here on…*Dad.*"

Sean snarls, stepping forward, but soon restrains himself, realizing I'm baiting him. I need him riled up, blinded with rage because that's what will force him to make an error; and I plan on exploiting that.

"Ya don't think I see the significance of ya sendin' three masked men to kidnap Ethan and Eva? Yer so fucking predictable, it's actually kinda pathetic."

"If I'm so predictable, cub, take off yer bulletproof vest then."

"No problem." Without hesitation, I take off my T-shirt and remove the bulletproof vest. It drops by my feet with a thud.

Once I slip my T-shirt back on, I arch a cocky brow.

"I didn't take ya for the Dear Diary type. Dear Diary," I mock, clutching my chest. "Everyone hates me…boo-fucking-hoo."

Sean is silent, but his temper is rising.

"This is what ye wanted, was it not? For us to be together, like father and son. Yer wish has been granted."

"You were always a smart-arse," Sean says. "But yer tongue is sharp now. Is that what ye learned in prison?"

Inhaling sharply, I'm the one to now rein in my temper because this cunt was out enjoying his freedom while I was locked away for a crime I didn't commit.

"Yer ma also had a temper. It's why it wasn't a bother for her to end up in my bed. She was angry with Connor for workin' all the time, and to get back at him, well—" He spreads his arms out wide, hinting her revenge was fucking his brother.

"But after a while, it wasn't for payback. She liked it. She liked being my whore."

"You shut yer fucking mouth," I snap, unable to hold back.

"What's wrong? Does the truth hurt? Does it hurt knowin' yer ma was nothin' but a slut?"

On instinct, I strike him in the jaw, cursing the moment I hit him because I've let him win. I need to be smarter than that.

Sean cups his face with a smirk. "I hate to tell ya this, but yer ma wanted to get rid of ya. She knew Connor would find out that ye weren't his."

"You lie," I snarl between clenched teeth.

"It's the truth," he argues. "I was the one who convinced her to keep ye. I knew ye'd be useful to me. No matter yer ma's faults, I loved her."

I slam my fist into his face once again, unable to restrain the murderous rage festering within. He doesn't fight back. He merely laughs in response, knowing he has crawled under my skin.

"Careful, cub. Ya wouldn't want Liam to take his anger out

on sweet, innocent Eva, would ya?"

Curling my lip, I don't disguise my disgust at his suggestion.

"Ach, don't be actin' like yer better than him. The heart wants what the heart wants, and you wanted Cami, even when ya thought she was yer sister."

"Aye, but she's not. Not to mention, Eva is merely a child."

"She certainly doesn't look like a chile. But I much prefer my woman to be exactly that. A woman, and Cami—" he wets his lips, a look of pure lust overtaking him. "She's all woman. Does she taste as sweet as she looks?"

I know he's baiting me, but something about this suddenly feels…wrong. The same foreboding feeling I sensed earlier overcomes me once again.

"I dare ya to say another word 'bout her…I fucking dare ye," I warn because if he continues down this path, it'll be without his tongue.

He reads my caution for what it is. "Y've got bollocks, Punky. I heard whatcha did to Brody. I'm thinkin' that was yer way of sendin' me a message?"

I don't reply.

"Well, yer message has been received. Loud and clear. I know that yer stronger than me," he confesses, which piques my interest. "It's why I needed collateral. I was never goin' to hurt Ethan or Eva. They were always goin' to be returned."

"Is that so? Were ya so confident I would agree to yer plan?"

Sean nods. "Aye, and that's because yer noble. Ya care. Ya

can't help but try to save the day. That's what got ya into this mess in the first place. If only y'd left Cara's death alone, none of this would have happened.

"But ya had to avenge her. Ya couldn't leave it alone. And now, y've forced my hand."

"Naw, this is on you. *You* are the one who killed her because yer greed comes first and last," I retaliate, refusing to allow him to slander my mum.

"I only want what was promised to me. Connor said we'd be partners, but it was only him. I was always his second, but that changed when the men saw him in you. Just like his father, they'd say, but he wasn't yer da.

"Even as a wain, they saw what a great leader ye'd be."

"Yer jealous of yer own son," I spit. "This lifestyle was forced onto me. I don't want it. All it does is destroy. It's turned me into someone I hardly recognize anymore."

My phone chimes, and when I see a photo and text message flash on my screen, I sigh in relief. They're safe.

Cian is standing by Ethan and Eva. They all look okay.

"I'm a man of my word, son," Sean says, realizing the message was from Cian. "Are you?"

There is one last thing I have to do. I text Rory.

It's almost over. Is everyone all right?

He replies a moment later.

Everyone is where they should be.

A little cryptic, but it's Rory, he's probably paranoid our phones are tapped.

Pocketing my phone, I exhale deeply because it's time.

"Yer awful confident, are ya not?"

Sean pulls his shoulders back. "We had a deal. Ya gave me yer word."

Tsking him, I shake my head slowly. "Ya didn't actually believe I would be yer errand boy, did you? I fucking hate ya, and I would rather kill us both than help ye destroy this country."

And just like that…my plan B is revealed.

I always knew it would come to this. Sean's greed has once again blindsided him and given him the illusion he's on top. Even though he's handed over Ethan and Eva, he knows every person I love is collateral—collateral he can easily use if he needs to.

He handed over Ethan and Eva as a sign of good faith, to show me that he wants to make peace, but I'm not fooled. I know that if I don't do what he wants, there will be no second chances, and this time, he'll go for Cami.

I can't protect her all the time, which is why the only way to keep her safe is to kill Sean. But I know that's easier said than done. This arsehole has fooled me my entire life. No matter how hard I try, he's always two steps ahead.

But now, it's just him and me, and it's a fight to the death. I hope to win, but nothing is ever certain in this war.

"We have a problem then, son," he says, realizing I'm serious. "I thought ye were a man of honor, but it seems yer more like Connor than I thought. So it's come to this? We're going to fight?"

"Aye, Father, it's always come down to this."

"The men respect ye and yer goin' to throw it all away, and for what? The men don't know what a wee pussy y'are."

Sean's eyes dart from left to right as I have no doubt Cian and Ron frisked him of his weapons. He's powerless, and to a narcissist, that's a fate far worse than death.

"Throw me to the wolves, and I come back leadin' the pack. And that's why ya need me. Yer nothin' without me."

Sean's jaw clenches because the truth fucking hurts. "Let's finish this then. Like men. But I ask ya this…do ya have the bollocks to kill yer da?"

He waits for my reply, hoping his wee speech influences me. It doesn't.

"Aye, I do." Before he can dodge my attack, I strike out and punch him in the face.

He staggers backward, regaining his footing, but I don't give him time to attack. I launch for him, delivering a quick succession of punches to his face and body that he can't sidestep.

The pained grunts leaving him feed my depravity, and years of anger explode from me. All I can focus on is expelling this anger and forcing it down the throat of the man who is the cause of it. He showed my mum no mercy, and now I plan on doing the same to him.

His lame attempts to fight me off are laughable, and when he gets in a lucky shot, I jump back, laughing. "Is that the best ye got, aul' lad?"

With a roar, he charges for me, but he isn't fast enough, and I knock him to the ground.

Pinning him to the floor, I commence punching his face over and over again. My fists ache, but the pain reminds me of the anguish my mum suffered at the hands of this monster.

"She didn't deserve to die that way!" I scream, gripping his hair and slamming his skull against the concrete.

His eyes roll to the back of his head.

"Ye humiliated her. Ye allowed men to rape her. Yer nothin' but a fucking coward! Ye hide behind others because yer scared. Yer a leech, latchin' onto others' hard work. Ya want the glory but aren't prepared to work for it.

"Ye make me sick." I spit on him.

Reaching into my back pocket for my knife, I inhale sharply because the time has finally come. The men who hurt my ma are no more. She can rest now. And so can I.

Just as I press the blade to his throat, something which I didn't expect happens—Sean laughs.

It's more of a wheeze as I'm certain I've punctured a lung, but the sound is one of victory, and I need to know why.

"I'm about to slit yer throat and yer laughin'? What's so funny?"

Sean is barely recognizable as his face has been beaten to a pulp. The macabre sight has me jumping to my feet and yanking him up.

"Answer me!"

He sways on his feet, his bone-chilling laughter echoing around me. "Yer some pup, thinkin' ya could beat me."

"What the fuck does that mean?"

"It means, yer so predictable. Always wantin' to do good by everyone. When will ya learn that just 'cause yer good…that doesn't mean others are…or ever will be?"

Thinking back over everything, I try to find holes in the plan. Everything went smoothly—too smoothly perhaps?

This was too easy…something is wrong.

"I will fucking kill you!" I snarl, drawing us nose to nose.

"I thought that was the plan all along…but here I am, still standing…the same can't be said for others, however."

I headbutt him but hold him up, and he sags like a ragdoll. "Yer bluffin'. Cian has Ethan and Eva, and Rory is keepin' dick for me. Y've lost. They would have rung me if anythin' was wrong."

But my bravado is fading by the second because this smells like a setup. Sean wanted me here, allowed me to fight him for a reason.

"I killed yer ma and…yer da," he confesses while I gasp as I never saw who shot Connor. This arsehole made sure I suffered in every possible way. "Don'tcha see? Ya can't beat me, Puck. Join me, and I promise ye, everyone ye love will be saved.

"The peelers work for me. Yer alone."

This is just a ploy. Cian and Rory would have alerted me if anything was wrong. But what Sean says next brings me to my knees.

"He knew ye weren't related, but he still chased her. Did ya know that? Did ya know he read my journal before any of youse? He was the one who made sure it remained hidden until Hannah found it."

"Ye'd say anythin' to save yer arse," I snarl, but a small part of me knows he's telling the truth. This was too easy because I… trusted the wrong man.

I thrust the knife out and press the blade to his throat. One simple stroke, and I can end this. But if I do that, I know I'll regret it.

"Fuck!" I scream, the blade trembling in my hand. "Fuck!"

Sean smirks, and why wouldn't he—he's won. And I all but handed his victory over on a silver platter. "She was always the main prize."

Without thought, I punch him one final time, knocking him out cold. He collapses onto the ground, and it takes all my willpower not to kill him. But I can't.

My boots slip and slide on the spilled blood as I run out the door toward Cian's truck. My fingers fumble as I flip down the visor, and the spare key falls into my lap. I tear off into the night, frantically dialing Rory.

"He knew ye weren't related, but he still chased her."

Sean's words play over in my mind. He's lying. He's got to be. There's no way he's telling the truth. But when Rory doesn't answer my call, the reality of what's happening winds me.

I dial Cian, who answers immediately. "Thank fuck, yer alive."

"Where are ya?" I ask, the panic in my voice clear.

"Just 'bout to drop off Ethan and Eva at yer gaff. Why? Do ya want me to come there? Ron told me he's keepin' dick—even though ya told him to leave—and would phone if ya needed help. What's happened?"

"I need to speak to Rory, but he's not answerin' his phone."

The moment the words leave me, I realize he made a rookie mistake.

"I've got to go. Go to my house and phone me when ye do."

"Puck!" Cian exclaims. "What's going on?"

"I don't know! I need to hang up now."

Before he can protest, I disconnect the call and use the app, which gives me a lifeline to Rory. I'm not the praying type, but desperate times call for desperate measures, and I call on everything holy that Rory is where he said he would be—my gaff.

But he's not.

He's at his flat. Why?

I almost hit an oncoming car as I pull a U-turn and speed down the road toward Rory's.

Nothing else matters but finding him so he can explain. So he can assure me that my father is once again playing with my emotions like only he knows how.

I pull up at Rory's, not even bothering to close the door as I race toward Rory's flat. When I get to his door, I don't knock. It's locked, but that doesn't stop me as I kick down the door.

"Rory!" I shout, racing through the flat to find him. When I catch him frantically packing his bag, I realize my worst fears have come true.

He desperately reaches for a gun on the nightstand and points it at me. But it's going to take a lot more than that to stop me.

"Where is she?" I snarl, walking toward him slowly as he backs away.

"Away from you!" he replies. "Away from us both."

"So help me God, if ya don't tell me where she is, I'm going to—"

"To what?" he cuts me off, eyes narrowed. "Kill me? Go ahead. Y've already torn out my heart. Both of youse have."

"Just tell me where she is, Rory. I know ya. I know ya don't want to do this."

"Ya know nothin'!" he shouts, spittle flying from his mouth. "If ya did, ya would have just stayed in prison. We could have been happy. But her love for ye always stood in the way! I fucking loved her, but it didn't matter. *I* didn't matter the moment you were free."

"What did ya do?" I ask, my heart in my throat.

"I did everythin' ya think I did," he replies, siphoning the life from me.

"Why?" I cry, not understanding any of this. "Ya hate me that much? Ye hate *her* that much?"

"Aye," he answers without missing a beat. "Ye destroy everythin' ya touch. Ya both do."

"So ye handed her over to Sean, knowin' he would use her to get me to do whatever he wants? She's not fucking chattel ya can exploit! None of us are. Do ya have any idea what y've done?"

I look into the eyes of a stranger because this man isn't the boy I grew up with. The lad who had my back no matter what. This person has been poisoned by Sean Kelly as Sean preyed on his weakness.

"What did he offer ye in exchange for her? A part in his business?"

Rory scoffs, his red-rimmed eyes darting around the room. "I want none of it! I want to get out of this fucking country and start over. Northern Ireland is riddled with ghosts, ones I want to escape."

Lifting my chin, I stare at the ceiling as tears fill my eyes. "Y'll be one them, so I suppose I'll never be able to escape ye."

Rory sold out Babydoll for greed—Sean offered him money

in exchange for her life. Rory wanted to hurt us in the worst possible way—just how we hurt him. And now, he must pay… with his life.

The trigger squeaks as Rory's finger dithers, but I'm a man hell-bent on revenge. I deliver a roundhouse kick, knocking the gun from Rory's hands. He's caught unaware, allowing me to punch him in the face.

He staggers back, cupping his bleeding nose, but that doesn't stop him as we charge for the other. He knows how to fight and is able to connect with my ribs and stomach, but I grip him by the collar and slam his head through the plaster.

Yanking him back out, I knee him under the chin, sending him careering backward and into the hallway. He dives for me, but I kick out and break his kneecap, which has him collapsing to the carpeted floor, howling in pain.

"Why, Rory? I don't understand it. Ya knew she wasn't my sister?"

Rory crawls away from me, desperately searching for something to fend me off. "I knew. I wanted more time with her but proposed when I found out ye were gettin' out of prison. I thought it would have been enough.

"But the moment she saw ye, I knew it never would be enough. I loved her, Puck! Y've taken Darcy, Cami, everyone I've ever cared for away from me!"

"And that's my fault?" I question. "Stop actin' like a pussy and grow the fuck up!"

He continues moving away from me, but he's not going anywhere ever again. I sensed an inside man was feeding Sean the information he needed—and that man was Rory.

I don't know how long he's betrayed us, but it doesn't matter. It won't change what I have to do.

"I trusted ya!" I scream, breaking his other kneecap as I stomp on it. "Ye betrayed me! Y've torn out my fucking heart!"

"Hurts, does it not?" he wheezes in pain. "Havin' the person ye love betray ya? Now ya know how I feel."

I don't know where Babydoll is. I don't know if she's dead or alive. I don't know if she'll be used for ransom. Or did Sean have her killed, knowing I would have nothing worth fighting for, so the fight in me would wither and die, and I would eventually surrender to him?

That was Sean's plan this entire time—Ethan and Eva were just decoys. He was after Babydoll all along.

I drop to my knees, a guttural sob spilling from me as I cup my face with bloody hands.

So much blood has been spilled, I don't know whose blood is whose anymore. This country has been painted red, and it's because of me.

In my quest for revenge for my ma, I have fucked things up beyond repair, and I don't know how to fix it. I am broken, and the glue holding me together is now gone. She is gone... and so am I.

Our pain drives us to act in certain ways, and this is Rory's pain, spewed all over us. Our betrayal was enough for him to give up everything, and now, my pain is about to meet his.

However, Cian's warning sounds behind me, followed by an earsplitting *boom*, and it changes the course of where my pain flows as I duck and turn to see my worst nightmare before my eyes.

Cian lies in a bloody heap, clutching at his chest, gasping for air. I don't understand what I'm seeing as Cian has been shot, but when I turn to see Rory holding a gun, I realize fate won't be satisfied until she takes everything from me.

The gun Cian held lies near his feet, and without hesitation, I reach for it, walk over to Rory, who seems to be in shock that he shot Cian and not me, and aim it at him.

"Puck, n-no!" Cian wheezes as Rory drops the gun and raises his trembling hands in surrender.

"Puck, I fucked up, so I did. I'm s-sorry," Rory begs, tears streaming down his face. "Please don't kill me. I don't want to die."

But it's too late.

He made his choice…and now, it's time I made mine.

I shoot Rory between the eyes, the last shred of humanity I held onto evaporating, making room for the monster I knew would always be born.

Staring at my once friend, I feel absolutely nothing because I'm just as dead as he is. This is what they all wanted.

I numbly walk over to Cian and drop to my knees as I assess

his wound. Thankfully, Rory is a shite shot. "Y'll live."

The whites of his eyes reveal he too sees the face of a monster I tried so hard to keep at bay.

I take off my T-shirt and offer it to him to press over the wound. "We need to go. The peelers will be here soon. Can ya stand?"

When I offer him my hand, he smacks it away. Good, he hates me too. It will be easier this way.

"Fine, be a pussy. I'll wait for ye outside then."

I leave my two best friends, one bloody and…one dead as I take the stairs, whistling a jolly tune as people run from the building, terrified thanks to the gunshots.

Feelings make you weak, Connor said, and he's right. It's all because of feelings that I'm here once again. But no more.

I tried to beat Sean. But I failed. I tried. I tried so fucking hard.

Retrieving my phone, I shoulder open the foyer door and nick a feg off a passerby from his gaping mouth when he sees my bloody appearance.

I continue on my journey, phone pressed to my ear, and when Sean answers, I seal our fate forevermore. "Keep her lit… ats us nai."

And just like that…I've sold my soul to the devil, and I don't feel a fucking thing.

BOOK THREE COMING SOON

Subscribe to my Newsletter:

https://landing.mailerlite.com/webforms/landing/b4j1v6

Into Temptation Playlist:

https://tinyurl.com/3cp9f5jb

ACKNOWLEDGEMENTS

My author family: Elle and Vi—I love you both very much.

My husband, Daniel. Love you. Always. Forever. Thanks for putting up with my craziness.

My ever-supporting parents. You guys are the best. I am who I am because of you. I love you. RIP Papa. Gone but never forgotten. You're in my heart. Always.

My agent, Kimberly Brower from Brower Literary & Management. Thank you for your patience and thank you for being an amazing human being.

My editor, Jenny Sims. What can I say other than I LOVE YOU! Thank you for everything. You go above and beyond for me.

My Irish Queens—Shauna McDonnell and Aimee Walker, your advice was priceless. Thank you so much for allowing me to pick your brains.

My proofreaders—Aimee Walker and Rumi Khan, you are amazing!

Michelle Lancaster—you took this story and created an image which is utter perfection. Your vision and talent are absolutely mind-blowing, and I feel so blessed to have worked with you. Your photos SLAY! Actually, YOU slay!! That makeup was FANTASTIC!! I love your face! #mytribe

Lochie Carey—dude, like wtf?! You are incredible! You are

my Punky. Thank you for bringing him to life. I adore you.

Leigh—You are an amazing human being. Your support over the years has helped me through some dark times. Your friendship means everything to me and I appreciate you so much. I can't wait to see you again soon. And thank you for loving Punky as much as me. Ps. I still owe you for the gelato!

Lauren Rosa—this cover was born because of your suggestion. I thank you so much for always being there for me.

Giana—Thanks for all the love and support.

Sommer Stein, you NAILED this cover! Thank you for being so patient and making the process so fun. I'm sorry for annoying you constantly.

My publicist—Danielle Sanchez from Wildfire Marketing Solutions. Thank you for all your help.

A special shout-out to: Bombay Sapphire Gin, Ashlee O'Brien, Conor King, Christina Lauren, Lisa Edward, Dani Rene, Trilina Pucci, Cheri Grand Anderman, Louise, Nasha Lama, Sarah Sentz, Gel Ytayz, Jessica—PeaceLoveBooks.

To the endless blogs that have supported me since day one—You guys rock my world.

My bookstagrammers—Your creativity astounds me. The effort you go to is just amazing. Thank you for the posts, the teasers, the support, the messages, the love, the EVERYTHING! I see what you do, and I am so, so thankful.

My ARC TEAM—You guys are THE BEST! Thanks for all the support.

My reader group—sending you all a big kiss.

Samantha and Amelia—I love you both so very much.

To my family in Holland and Italy, and abroad. Sending you guys much love and kisses.

Papa, Zio Nello, Zio Frank, Zia Rosetta, and Zia Giuseppina—you are in our hearts. Always.

My fur babies—mamma loves you so much! Dacca, I know you're hanging with Jaggy, Dina, Ninja, and Papa.

To anyone I have missed, I'm sorry. It wasn't intentional!

Last but certainly not least, I want to thank YOU! Thank you for welcoming me into your hearts and homes. My readers are the BEST readers in this entire universe! Love you all!

ABOUT THE AUTHOR

Monica James spent her youth devouring the works of Anne Rice, William Shakespeare, and Emily Dickinson.

When she is not writing, Monica is busy running her own business, but she always finds a balance between the two. She enjoys writing honest, heartfelt, and turbulent stories, hoping to leave an imprint on her readers. She draws her inspiration from life.

She is a bestselling author in the U.S.A., Australia, Canada, France, Germany, Israel, and The U.K.

Monica James resides in Melbourne, Australia, with her wonderful family, and menagerie of animals. She is slightly obsessed with cats, chucks, and lip gloss, and secretly wishes she was a ninja on the weekends.

CONNECT WITH
MONICA JAMES

Facebook: facebook.com/authormonicajames

Twitter: twitter.com/monicajames81

Goodreads: goodreads.com/MonicaJames

Instagram: instagram.com/authormonicajames

Website: authormonicajames.com

Pinterest: pinterest.com/monicajames81

BookBub: bookbub.com/authors/monica-james

Amazon: https://amzn.to/2EWZSyS

Join my Reader Group: http://bit.ly/2nUaRyi